FOR
UNCLE DENNIS

Acknowledgements

There are many people who have helped bring together the publication of this book. It would be impossible to name them all here. The research for the book has spanned over three decades and thirty years ago, the concept of that research being converted into a novel was way beyond my imagination.

St Helens Library/Archives has been a great source of information but once again, my thanks extend to Doreen who took on the role of researcher in the quest to bring this story to life.

Abbey for her professional portrayal of Lizzie.

Brian Wilcox Photography for an amazing photo shoot.

My team of proof readers.

Tony, for his unwavering patience and support.

There may be many organisations and people out there who have also helped but are not named here. To them, my apologies and my thanks.

* * * * * *

Other Books by this author

Rubies

Spangles

Through the Eyes of a Child: A Memoir

The Three Bees (Children's)

The Creatures (Children's)

AD 1849

The deadly vapour rose from the bowels of the ditches, drifting silently and menacingly across the decaying land. Spreading its ghostly tentacles through the eerie atmosphere, it shrouded the primitive shack, infiltrating the cold, damp space inside. Darina MacSweeney imagined herself in another time, another place, as she brought her fifth child into the world. For a fraction of a second Darina held her breath. Upon hearing her baby's tiny cry, relief swathed her senses, taking her breath away into the swirling mist.

Darina's two sons had succumbed to the ravages of their poverty stricken parents and died from malnutrition, a condition forced upon the masses from the total dependence on a potato crop, which could no longer provide sustenance, due to blight. The impact was disastrous for millions and Darina's family was no exception. The Irish Potato Famine, causing mass starvation, disease and emigration would be the springboard to bring Ciaran and Darina MacSweeney and their family across the Irish Sea to what they hoped could be a better life.

* * * * *

CHAPTER ONE

Stealing had never been on Ciaran MacSweeney's agenda but the status quo was about to change. His wife had given birth to their third daughter. His grief over the deaths of his twin sons to malnutrition consumed him. His willingness to relinquish his own integrity formed his resolve. His wife and daughters were starving, he needed to act.

On a moonless night, when thick, dank smog hung in the air and the nauseous stench of the fields surrounding him permeated his nostrils, he left the cold, wooden shack. His family lay on beds of damp straw, their only warmth, each other and a stained sheet the midwife left behind. Having ensured they had enough water, his intention to take that which did not belong to him, was the only thing on his mind. He climbed over the rickety fence separating the shack from the rotting crop, his feet instantly buried in the squelchy mulch beneath him. Using the fence as a guide, to prevent him falling into the deep smelly trench, he left the confines of poverty and hoped providence would lead him to an opportunity to find sustenance. Ciaran's worst fear was of being caught, not because he might go to prison, but because if he did, he would be fed. The intolerable thought of consuming a morsel while his family lay dying in decrepit conditions, forced his weary body forward. Progressing as quickly as he could, he eased his way cautiously, towards the cart track, keeping low, until he saw the main street of town. He planned to gain entry to the back yard of the bakery, where he might find the remains of dough in the bins, or if he was lucky, stale bread. Ciaran prayed he wouldn't meet anyone. He'd seen a few drunks sprawled out on the street and stayed in the shadows of doorways. With the ragged collar of his thin coat pulled up round his face, so far, he had gone unnoticed. His breath came in short rasps, he was weak from hunger and thirst and his heart thumped against his ribcage. He came to the bakery and was horrified to see the lantern dimly illuminating what should have been a dark shop window.

'How could I have been so stupid?' he thought. 'Of course, he'll be baking for tomorrow. I can't go home with nothing. I can't.'

Ciaran prayed again. He prayed with all his might that an upbringing based on truth, paid off. He prayed the baker would respond to his plea.

'I'll tell him the truth. I'll tell him I'm sorry, I came to steal from his bakery bins because my wife and children are starving. I'll tell him my two sons died because there was no milk to feed them.'

Ciaran hoped for a kind heart.

'Oh God, please let him listen, please let him listen.'

Ciaran looked around to make sure no-one was watching and with his heart in his mouth, knocked on the window of Mr O'Shaugnessy's bakery. There was no reply. He looked around again, from left to right, up the street and down, up at the windows upstairs and knocked again. This time, old Mr O'Shaugnessy drew back the piece of ragged, torn material in the window and peered out.

"Go away," he shouted through the glass.

'I suppose the old baker's frightened of someone knocking on his window at this hour of the night,' thought Ciaran and wondered what to do next. He knocked again but there was no response. Instead of doing what his hunger begged him to do and knock even louder, he knocked gently, hoping the old man would understand he meant him no harm. Mr O'Shaugnessy came to the window again, peering out to establish who was knocking. What seemed like an eternity to Ciaran, but was only a few seconds later, he heard the key in the lock.

"What do you want lad?"

"Please may I come in sir? Please?"

Ciaran was never to fully know what softened Mr O'Shaugnessy's heart enough to let him in that night, but his prayer was answered.

Ciaran left Mr O'Shaugnessy's bakery with a journey more difficult than the one he'd left the shack for. He had to make it back with enough food to feed his starving family for two days, cleverly disguised under his ragged coat, in case there were others nearby with starving families, who would do what he'd been going to. With tears in his eyes, and munching a piece of dough bread, he swiftly ascertained there was no-one about, and taking a different route, he ran as fast as his weakened legs could carry him. Cautiously making his way back through the rotting ground, he scrambled over the fence and into the shack, where his family still lay. Finally, he let out the scream of joy, they would survive. Darina MacSweeney listened intently to his story which didn't end with the bag full of bread for their family. Mr O'Shaugnessy's assistant hadn't arrived for work; Ciaran was Mr O'Shaugnessy's new one. The girls ate their fill and drank the remaining dregs of water, baby was suckling and Ciaran lay down beside his family. He looked up and silently mouthed, "Thank you."

* * * * * *

The weeks quickly passed and the leftover scraps of bread became a welcome additional source of nourishment. Ciaran's family were gaining strength. Born tiny and frail, baby Mary was slowly developing. Ciaran was proud of his achievement; his efforts that cold dark night, whilst in a state of emaciation himself, had truly saved the lives of his family and never a day passed that he didn't raise his eyes skyward and say thank you. And then it happened.

* * * * * *

In the early hours of an April morning, before dawn beckoned the new day, Mr O'Shaugnessy's bakery burnt to the ground. It had been an intangible disaster, a travesty of justice and a mystery never to be solved. The burnt remains of Mr O'Shaugnessy were not found until two days later, due to the intensity of the flames which flared for many hours. Inhabitants of adjacent and nearby buildings fled for their lives as the molten hot flames reached towards the skies, licking everything in their path, hungry, devouring the night sky. The fire fighters had fought a valiant effort, missing their opportunity to drench the fire through lack of local communication and despite their efforts long into the next day, lost the fight, so intense was the heat.

Ciaran's detection of breathing in something bad, woke him, rendering him uneasy. An orange glow infiltrated the cracks in the makeshift door of the shack. Fear gripped his heart as he tentatively pushed it open to peer out. It was not the black sky pin-pricked with dots of light which he gazed upon, but a voluminous wall of yellow in the distance, sparks threateningly leaping from it, falling, flickering menacingly towards the ground, disappearing, followed by others. Thick, black smoke hung menacingly in acrid clouds, penetrating everything in its path, searching for weak human bodies to inhabit. A fierce, uncontrollable panic took hold and a scream emanated deep within him. A premonition of foreboding, indescribable torment and the horror of a future not yet borne, gathered in his consciousness. Ciaran used the glow from the fire, to search the floor of the shack for anything he might use as covers to protect his innocent, unsuspecting family. He closed the door and took off his clothes. His trousers and vest, he tucked into the gaps around the door and carefully placed his coat over the heads of the two sleeping girls. He gently pulled the thin threadbare lower half of Darina's cotton dress up, covering her mouth and nose and that of his newborn child. He lay beside them head down, pulled the stained cover over his own face and once again, he prayed.

* * * * * *

Ciaran was present at Mr O'Shaugnessy's burial. There had been nothing left of him, save a few black bits of bone lurking in the ashes of his burnt out bakery. Ciaran stood at the side of the grave and felt huge sorrow as they lowered the remains of his life-line into the depths of the earth, the priest's words, reminding everyone of their own sure fate.

"Ashes to ashes, dust to dust ......"

It had been at that point, Ciaran's options had occurred to him. There was no other work to find and he hadn't enough money to sustain his family. He knew, once again, unless he acted quickly, death would be the certain consequence for them all.

* * * * * *

CHAPTER TWO

The Workhouse

Horror struck to the core of Ciaran MacSweeney's soul as he slowly approached the imposing wooden door of the building, looming forebodingly in front of him. His choices had been less troublesome than he'd thought. There were only two. One, he and his family died. Two, he and his family went into the Union Workhouse. He chose the latter and as the MacSweeney family were registered and admitted, his heart wrenched as he looked back upon the happy couple who'd embarked on a lifetime together, never imagining such grief could befall them.

Ciaran looked little more than skeletal and his knees trembled. One of the visiting guardians heaved open the heavy door which made a loud groaning noise as it scraped the ice-cold stone floor. Feeling sick to his stomach, Ciaran mumbled feebly and embarrassingly.

"Hello. I was Mr O'Shaugnessy's assistant at the bakery that burnt down. I haven't found any other work and my wife and children are starving. Please can we come in?"

His sneak preview of the interior of the building which now stood before him, should have given him a premonition and encouraged him to find an alternative, but despite lying awake for three nights and weakened to the point of collapse, he knew there wasn't one. There was an additional problem. Clinging onto hope and into one another's arms had created a weakness of resolve and subsequently of the flesh, an urgent need for human contact, one which could surmount all prevailing problems, whilst creating another. Darina was pregnant.

* * * * * *

The pending segregation would have been devastating for every married couple, but the humiliation drove home when they were asked to sterilise themselves in a small tin bath in the next room. The damp atmosphere of the room yielded a lethal combination of fear and hysteria, as the painful realisation of their action took hold. Their own fear emanated within their older two children.

"No, Mammy, no, the water's freezing."

Their terrified screams as Ciaran and Darina attempted to wash them, brought the matron back into the room. Satisfied they were clean, a bundle of workhouse uniforms were thrown into the middle of the room. Stripped of all their belongings, Ciaran, Darina and their children were trapped inside a gum-stiffened grogham material, ushered into the next room and separated. Ciaran vowed he and his family would leave and the opportunity came along some months later.

Ciaran discovered he had a talent for carpentry, an asset the Master didn't hesitate to use.

He was often asked to put his skills to good use and had become one of a team of men used to repair broken pieces of furniture and various similar tasks. From one of the rooms on the top floor of the building, forbidden to inmates except those sent by the master, it was possible, on a clear day, to see the coast. Ciaran had heard talk of ships taking fare-paying passengers across the Irish Sea to the Port of Liverpool. And he wondered.

On one such occasion whilst working on a damaged windowsill, he was peering out of the window, daydreaming of a life he'd never know. An elderly gentleman from the board of governors entered the room talking animatedly to two men about his pending trip to England. Ciaran didn't turn round but continued working as quietly as he could to avoid drawing attention to himself, but strained to listen. Pensively looking out at the view of the blue sea in the distance he felt a yearning. Maybe a better life lay across the ocean in the land they called England.

'How would we ever manage to get there?' he thought dejectedly.

As the men turned to exit the room, still chattering loudly, oblivious to Ciaran's presence, he turned and watched them leave. As the last man approached the doorway, he took out a handkerchief and blowing loudly into it, stuffed it back into his pocket. Ciaran's eyes were riveted to the floor behind the man. He quickly averted his eyes and looked back out of the window in case the men returned and saw him staring at the ten-shilling note which had fluttered down from the man's pocket when he pulled the handkerchief out. Ciaran held his breath and waited, his heart leaping up and down. No-one came. He crept stealthily towards the doorway where the note lay defying him to pick it up.

'Is it stealing?' he thought.

He reasoned it could be divine intervention.

'What if they recognised me? What if he realises it's missing and comes back to find it? They didn't acknowledge me. I had my back to them. How would they know it was me? They'd find out. The Master knew I was up here today. It could only be me. I could deny all knowledge. He could have dropped it anywhere, didn't have to be in this room, unless he remembers taking out his handkerchief. Maybe he took out his handkerchief in other places today.'

Ciaran's thoughts took less than ten seconds. It took him two to sweep up the ten-shilling note and push it deep into his trouser pocket. He quickly finished the job he'd almost completed before the men came, collected his tools and left, nonchalantly stealing down the stairs and back into a hub of activity.

* * * * * *

CHAPTER THREE

Below deck, hundreds of frightened men, women and children huddled together. There was no sanitation and they sat on rough wooden floors, breathing in the stench from vomit and diarrhoea. Those who succumbed to the effects of the ship's undulating rhythm, or drank contaminated water causing stomach disorders, were forced to remain in a state of filth for the whole voyage.

Suffering the effects of a sea journey, fraught with the terror of diabolical conditions, Ciaran and Darina MacSweeney huddled together, struggling down the gangplank. The 'death ship' which had carried them across the Irish Sea to the port of Liverpool, floated in the murky waters of the River Mersey, a dark shadow of horror behind them. They carried their three children, wide eyed with fear, to an unknown future. Filled with revulsion, they had left behind the horrors of their past, barely surviving the hell in the hold of a tin bucket masquerading as a ship and now stood on the precipice of hopelessness.

"Where do we go now?" asked Darina.

Had Ciaran imagined a future as tarnished as that which they'd left behind, he may have thought twice.

"Surely fate won't be so cruel a third time?" he said out loud.

The family made their way to where a large group had gathered. There was an overseer counting heads. Having no idea where they should go, Ciaran guided Darina and his girls towards the throng, but the overseer had seen the stragglers arrive.

"Can't take any more," the overseer said to Ciaran and Darina.

"But we've nowhere else to go," protested Ciaran, trying to keep the older girls getting lost in the crowd as people surged forward.

"I can't help that mate. You can't come with this lot."

The overseer began assembling the rest into a long line, three bodies wide. The snake of people began to wind its way forward, following the overseer's direction. Ciaran wondered if he should just tag along at the back but a deep sense of survival kicked in and he swiftly surged his family forward through the crowd until they were no longer in the snake's tail.

'Integrating into the body of the snake,' he thought, 'might prevent the overseer from recognising us.'

Darina was struggling to keep up. Her seven month pregnancy was taking its toll. She was certain her labour would begin soon. Ciaran carried Mary in his arms, shouting to Emily and Ann to hang onto their parents, for fear they would be trampled.

The 'snake' wound its way through the shabby cobbled streets. Drunken men and women lay slumped on the steps of public houses which appeared on most street corners. Fights broke out, abuse was hurled at the 'snake', jibing and jostling to promote retaliation. The narrow streets were lined with dirty looking houses. Filthy children played in the gutters and the noise and evil smell cast a nauseous spell over the scene in front of the terrified family. The street ahead widened and Ciaran found himself looking at a road which seemed to disappear into the horizon. The overseer seemed to be slowing down. Ciaran knew in the depths of his soul this was the place they would be stopping. Again, he prayed, hoping the overseer wouldn't recognise them. As the 'snake' slowly wound its way past the houses, hordes of people came in the other direction, in a similar human snake. People came out of houses and joined the snake.

"Where are you going?" Ciaran asked a man who brushed past him.

"America lad, why don't you tag along? You'd be better off. Probably die in days if you stay here. Look after your missus and kids and come with us."

Ciaran and Darina smiled at the man and wished him well. Before they knew it, the overseer had stopped beside them. Ciaran's heart lurched. His luck held out and the overseer didn't recognise the stragglers he'd turned away. They kept their heads down while they were ushered into one of the dirty looking buildings. The foul smell hit them as they walked through the front door. Darina stumbled and involuntarily vomited. Ciaran immediately went to her aid but they were pushed along, through another door and down a flight of stone steps. The stench became stronger. Darina, holding onto her girls for fear they might slip on whatever lay beneath their feet, felt the pangs of labour begin. Ciaran's heart pounded as he came to the bitter realisation this life would be no better than the one they'd left behind. He bent his head forward onto Darina's shoulder and spoke without conviction.

"I'll get us out of here. No matter what happens, I'll get us out."

* * * * * *

Margaret MacSweeney was born in a pit of despair. The women who were capable of helping did what they could. No-one in the cramped, filthy conditions of her birthplace thought she or her mother would survive. A healthy yell emitted from the child when she pushed her way into the world and then she fell silent. For a few moments, everyone in the dark, damp and crowded basement of one of Liverpool's worst slums believed they would be adding two more to the death toll.

* * * * * *

Two days had passed since Margaret drew her first breath. She still breathed, a feisty baby, constantly hungry and barely consolable. Ciaran and Darina, terrified for the lives of their children promised each other, they would find a way to remove themselves from their purgatory. The overseer came each morning and most nights to take the bodies of those unfortunate to have lost their lives in the black hole beneath the house on Scotland Road. They appeared for the moment to be prisoners. The door above the stone steps was locked each time someone came in or out. Typhus was rife in the dilapidated, lice-infested lodging house. Food was thrown down the steps in potato sacks, a harsh and cruel reminder of that which had gone before. The stampede to access the sacks was a desperate attempt by human beings to hang on to the thin thread of life.

Ciaran asked the question of anyone who might be bothered to answer:

"Why are we being held prisoner? What do they intend to do with us?"

"They're shipping us all off to America," said one man.

"No. They're sending us back to Ireland," said another.

Despite the hunger and desperation among the occupants of the black hole, the food was shared, although disproportionately. Ciaran gave his ration to Darina and the two older girls. A few of the older women showed compassion for Darina, trying to feed her newborn child, and offered a small portion of their own, a human kindness she would not easily forget.

It was difficult to determine how long they'd been there before Ciaran formulated his plan. Terrified it wouldn't work, he hung onto the notion himself until he'd ascertained nothing had been left to chance. So accustomed they'd become to the dark, it was impossible to see when the light filtered through the open door at the top of the stairs, but Ciaran had watched. He knew how many steps there were, he knew their depth and he practised scaling them. Darina counted until they perfected the timing. Ciaran knew if he stood at the bottom and waited for the door to open, he could scale the steps before the hessian sacks were thrown down. His family's existence depended on precision and he hoped the unexpected would prove to be his family's escape route. His plan was not to kill or maim, but to momentarily disorientate. He remembered the way to the front door, which hadn't been locked when they arrived. With all his heart, he hoped it remained that way. He would share his plan with one of the older ladies who offered her food ration to Darina. He knew, beyond reasonable doubt, she would not wish to come and would seek the assistance of others to enable Ciaran and his family to escape. He had been correct in his assumptions, but could not have imagined her next move. She beckoned Ciaran to the corner of the room where it was obvious she'd been living for some time. In the darkness, she rummaged round in the straw and withdrew a small brown package. Opening it, she extracted some coins.

"I'm too old now lad. I couldn't survive outside on my own and I won't be on this mortal coil for long. I won't be needing these, I want you to have them."

She opened Ciaran's hand and pressed the coins into his palm. He smelt her breath, as she bent forward to whisper in a husky voice.

"There's a man who transports goods from Liverpool docks to St Helens on a horse and cart."

She told Ciaran the usual route the horse and cart took, and the approximate time of arrival at a crossroads.

"Tell him Annie Carson sent you and give him two of the coins. You'll receive safe passage for you and your family to St Helens. There should be enough left for food and board for a couple of days. Take care of your missus and them kids. Good luck."

The moment arrived. Ciaran stood with one foot on the bottom step, waiting to scale the steps in record time. The old lady had sought the help of two elderly men who also wished to remain. No-one else knew. Ciaran couldn't risk someone shouting out when the door opened. The wooden door creaked slightly and the tiniest filter of light could be seen where Ciaran waited below. Before the door was open fully, Ciaran had swiftly and skilfully scaled the steps, and come around the back of the sack thrower, putting one hand across his mouth. He pushed him down the stairs in front of him, threatening him with his life if he made a noise. Two men and the compassionate woman took over and held the sack thrower whilst Ciaran led his family up the stairs, followed by a few opportunist stragglers. Once outside in the hallway, he relocked the door, knowing speed was paramount.

"Ssssshhhhhh," he whispered to everyone, running as quickly as they could down the hallway, Ciaran held his breath while he tried the front door. It opened. They were blinded as the early morning sun's rays penetrated deep into the dank corridor. Holding onto their children, he and Darina left the building, Darina with her two youngest and Ciaran clutching on tight to Emily and Ann. Without turning round, they ran, hardly daring to hope they would make it to their rendezvous with an unknown man and a horse and cart.

Annie Carson was a name Ciaran MacSweeney would cherish. He'd been certain she was his guardian angel sent to protect them, and made him all the more determined to make contact with their carriage, but they had to move fast and his margin was a slim one. While he ran, his faith wavered a little.

'How do I know Annie Carson was telling the truth? How do I know she wasn't just giving me hope? Could be she owed this man some money. I don't know anything about this man I'm going to give the money to. Could be anybody. Oh God, what have I done?'

The niggling doubts troubled him as he struggled to navigate the street corners of the Liverpool docklands. Hordes of people, bustled around, the smell of cigarette smoke saturated the clothes of ragged children sitting in gutters playing with bits of old wood and stone. Huge shire horses with their immense capacity for pulling heavy weights transported wagons filled with wooden boxes of fruit. The tallest horse Ciaran had ever seen emerged from a foreboding looking building pulling a brewery wagon making its regular delivery to the local ale houses, prevalent on every street corner. Smells in the air he'd never smelt before filtered out into the sunlight from open doorways, stall holders along the road tried to make him part with the money they didn't know he had.

"Fresh fish – caught on the early tide,' they yelled

Ciaran would have loved to buy the man's fresh fish to feed his family. Instead all he could do was navigate the cobbled streets, which although credible transient passage for the large black, bay and grey shires, were not entirely suitable for a man and a woman with four children, running quite literally for their lives.

* * * * * *

Strands of matted greasy hair persisted falling across the eyes of the man holding the reins. His constant snorting as he brushed them aside became a welcome distraction for Darina, making her daughters sitting on top of the straw in the back of the cart, giggle. Exhausted, she found herself bedding into the straw with Margaret, the clanging wheels across the cobblestones, her lullaby. Ciaran, glad to see his wife and youngest daughter sleeping peacefully, cast a quick glance towards the older girls and shut his eyes, safe in the knowledge they were being transported to a new life. Annie Carson had been their saviour. The future was back in their own hands and once more, he offered up a prayer of thanks.

The cart journey was long and tiresome, there being two occasions when Ciaran inwardly punished himself for allowing his family to take Annie Carson's offering and trust this man whom he now believed may be unscrupulous. He kept his feelings to himself and Darina and the girls, despite their intense hunger, seemed to take the journey in their stride. One or two of the kindly women in the 'black hole', had shoved bits of bread into Darina's cloth bag. She intermittently broke a morsel off, denying herself and distributed the crumbs between the three older girls. Margaret, lay snuggled into Darina, comfortably feeding.

The first occasion Ciaran bethought himself, was when the 'driver' stopped the cart and delved into a bag from which he produced some bread, apples and a small piece of cheese. He uttered no words but instead tucked into his feast, sparing not a thought for his passengers and their hunger. Clearly, he hadn't taken pity on them, agreeing to take them along, only for the money. He paid no heed to the babies and young children going hungry while he ate.

The second occurrence of Ciaran's self-doubt was when one of the wheels began to work loose. The man instantly jerked the horse to a stop, jumped off and promptly sat on the grass at the side of the road.

"Your fault this," he yelled gesturing to Ciaran and his family.

"All that extra weight. Should have known better than to take you. There's some tools under the back seat. You broke it, you fix it."

The driver sat at the side of the road, tucking into yet another eating foray.

Ciaran debated whether or not to quickly fix and go, leaving the driver at the side of the road and take charge of the horse and cart himself. Despite his slight frame and lack of nourishment, Ciaran felt he'd be strong enough to fend the driver off if he attacked him. As if the thought had also occurred to the driver, he jumped up and put himself back in the driving seat, turning first to glare at Ciaran. No words were exchanged and their journey resumed.

A couple of hours later, the landscape began to change. So too, did the smell. Gone was the fresh country air through which they had travelled. This was the smell of industry in its infancy. A canal ran alongside the track. The water looked murky, a thick strange coloured mist rose from it.

"Cover your faces with something. Anything you can," shouted Ciaran above the noise of the carriage rumbling over rough terrain.

They passed a couple of smallholdings. Wisps of smoke rose from the chimneys and Ciaran wanted to weep. How he longed to have a place for his family.

The cart journeyed on for what Ciaran suspected was a couple more miles. Though the evening clouds darkened the sky, lanterns glowing in the distance enabled him to make out the silhouettes of buildings.

'I wonder if we're here. Annie Carson gave me enough money to pay for lodgings for a couple of nights, but what if .....?' he thought.

The cart rolled over cobblestones and just in front of them, they could see a row of tiny cottages. There appeared to be a number of outbuildings to the side and rear of the first property. Ciaran guessed this was their destination. The driver brought the horse to a halt and climbed down.

"Get down," he shouted to Ciaran rudely and waving his arms in a sweeping motion, indicated his family should do the same. Stood under a lantern casting a yellow glow, Darina passed Mary to Ciaran and then climbed down herself holding Margaret. Emily and Ann, though weak from lack of food, were excited and wanted to play. Darina suppressed their misplaced and failing energy, not knowing if Annie Carson's prediction of a good bed for the night and something to eat would, in fact, be the case. She was right to do so. The driver came back and spoke to Ciaran.

"Come with me. The others can wait here."

Reluctantly Ciaran followed. Darina felt uncomfortable and barely able to stand. Emily sat down at the side of the house holding Mary. Darina held Margaret who was beginning to search for food whilst Ann kept watch. A sense of foreboding hung over them, not knowing what fate had in store and fearing for Ciaran who had not yet returned.

The news was not good. Ciaran was bloodied and limping when he returned alone. His frustration and anger had given way to a surge of temper when the driver told him it would cost him all the money he had to stay in one of the outhouses. Ciaran had no choice except to hand the money over. Then, he was informed there was no food. Despite Ciaran's initial attempts to appeal to the house owner's humanity, there was no relent and Ciaran had lashed out. The driver and the house owner had immediately retaliated, beating Ciaran until he retreated, defeated. Now, Ciaran and his family had nothing to eat, nowhere to stay and penniless.

What Annie Carson couldn't have known, was the sudden demise of the usual driver, whose fight against disease had failed. This had enforced the initiation of a substitute, a disreputable character who had taken Ciaran's money, offered little in return and caused him grievous bodily harm.

Darina, distressed to the point of giving up, considered going back to the house owner and begging, but Ciaran had another plan. He had seen white smoke emitting from a large building somewhere at the back of the cottages, over in the fields. Darina and the girls turned to follow him. Emily screamed as she saw her sister collapse in front of her. Ciaran was at Ann's side in an instant, picked her up and began running, shouting at the others to follow. Darina clutching onto Margaret and Emily doing her best to carry Mary whilst running, almost collapsing herself, struggled to navigate the darkness. They had left the illuminated cottages behind and seemed to be running up a grassy incline. The large building loomed in front of them, the smoke curling from its chimneys. Ciaran found his way to the front door, one which seemed horribly familiar. Without hesitation, he took hold of the large door knob and knocked with urgency. The door opened within seconds.

The wisps of smoke from that chimney served to be their salvation. Despite Ciaran's hesitancy to step back into a life he had once left with a sickness in his heart, he now viewed as a saviour for his family's lives.

Ciaran and Darina's fortunes changed. They were grateful for the workhouse matron allowing them sanctuary that night, and not believing their luck given their horrendous circumstances, they agreed to stay until they were strong enough and had a viable plan to leave. Within two years, Ciaran had his plan, which he executed with an admirable amount of courage and a little help from some newfound friends.

On a sunny Saturday morning, the MacSweeney family left the workhouse, leaving behind many sad faces. They resembled humans, Mary and Margaret were thriving babies while Emily and Ann skipped happily alongside their parents. Ciaran's destination was a village lying just to the north of the workhouse. He believed in God and the Holy Spirit and he believed this miracle had been performed, because he believed, because he wouldn't give up his faith no matter what.

The night he left the wooden shack in search of bread to feed his family was the night which forged his destiny. His experience in the bakery would now be put to good use. In return for lodgings for himself and his family, he became the master baker for an establishment serving two villages. The MacSweeneys would survive another day.

* * * * * *

CHAPTER FOUR

The years flew by and Margaret, the last born of the MacSweeney girls, was interrogated every day by her three older sisters.

"When are you going?"

"Where is it?"

"How many bedrooms has it got?"

"Can we come and visit you?"

Margaret was excited. She felt the help she'd given her father in the bakery had groomed her for the position she'd been offered and could barely contain herself for the new life ahead. She promised to come home once a month to give Darina some of her wages. She would miss them all.

On the basis of skills she'd learnt with Ciaran, she had secured an assistant's position in the kitchens of a large house near the up and coming industrial wave of Widnes. She would be supplied with a uniform, consisting of the customary black dress, white pinafore and mob cap. Her shoes must be her own, black and serviceable with good grip on a non-slip sole. These she had procured from a friend.

The morning of her departure arrived, a happy, yet sad day for them all. Margaret was the first of the MacSweeney brood to flee the nest. Her eldest sister Ann, was helping out in the local school and Emily and Mary were now helping Ciaran in the expanding bakery.

There were big hugs all round and Ciaran made ready to accompany Margaret to the station where she would embark on a train journey to her new life. Darina felt deflated as she watched Ciaran and her daughter walk away. A new form of despair threatened to engulf her. She shouted after them "Come see us soon." They turned the corner and were gone.

Margaret had trembled a little as she left her father stood on the platform, but now excitement took over as she neared her destination. A pony and trap had been sent to collect her from the train station, her luggage strapped onto the back. The footman assured her the journey would be comfortable and take about half an hour.

Margaret's first sight of Heddington Hall near Widnes caused her mouth to drop as she stared in awe of the sheer size of the building that was to be her workplace and her home. As the driver turned sharp right and diverted around to the back of the building, the size of her new 'home' made her shiver.

'How will I ever find my way round?' she thought tentatively as nerves began to flourish.

There was no-one waiting to greet her as she stepped out of the carriage.

'Was I expecting there to be a welcoming committee? Well, no, they've probably all got chores to attend to. I wonder what waits for me inside?'

The footman dropped her cases at the back of the carriage, wished her well and said goodbye. Margaret picked up the cases and walked the few steps to an open doorway and knocked. No-one came. She knocked again. A rather large lady appeared in a servant's uniform, a wide grin forming as she saw Margaret.

"Margaret MacSweeney. We've been expecting you, come on in."

Margaret liked this lady who'd made her feel welcome and was instantly at ease. She followed the lady up some tall steep steps at the back of the building, up and up and into the servants' sleeping quarters. She had been allocated a bed in a dormitory with five other girls, none of whom were there.

"The others will speak to you at supper. They're all looking forward to meeting you. The Master says you come highly recommended. I'm Head Cook. You'll be working with me most of the time. I run a tight ship, but you'll fit in smashing. I've seen your application and you're just what I'm looking for. We'll talk about your work in the bakery later."

The large woman held out an equally large hand, and taking Margaret's hand, she shook it vigorously.

She pointed to Margaret's bed.

"This is where you'll be sleeping."

A uniform was laid neatly across the bed.

"Pop your uniform on and we'll see what it's like for size."

Cook turned her back whilst Margaret nervously undressed down to her underwear and donned the uniform.

"Are you decent?"

"Yes, but I think it's a bit long."

Cook turned to have a look.

"Ah, don't worry, it's not too bad. The seamstress will pin it up tonight and we'll have it ready for you by morning. Come on, let's go and meet everyone."

Margaret couldn't believe all her eyes wanted to take in.

'And, if this is only the servants' quarters,' she thought, 'what on earth must it be like 'upstairs'?'

She was in awe of her surroundings.

Her initiation had her reeling with excitement. The servants' hall, cook informed her, was where the servants gathered for meals. The long wooden refectory table took centre stage, with a bench running all the way along the length of each side and a wooden chair with arms at each end, which she assumed correctly, would be for the butler and the housekeeper. The table was set for a meal and three evenly spaced huge wooden candlesticks occupied the centre space. A large, ancient looking, dark oak dresser dominated one end of the room with all manner of plates and crockery on display. Margaret glanced around the walls hung with dark portraits, which she assumed could only be the ancestors of the inhabitants 'upstairs'.   Also attached to the wall on large rusty nails were some menacing looking tools from days gone by.

'I wonder if they'll give me anything to eat? Or will I have to 'earn' my first meal?' she thought.

There was no-one else in the room except Cook, who pointed out Margaret's place at the table.

"This is where you'll sit for all your meals. We always tend to sit in the same place. That way, there's no fussing."

The table was so huge, it left Margaret in no doubt there must be an army coming into dinner and she felt nervous again.

'Will the others be kind to me? Will they like me? Will I like them?' she thought.

Her experiences in the bakery with her father had equipped her with a wealth of knowledge, and an ability to communicate with others, but she felt more than a little intimidated at the prospect of all those people firing questions.

'Will I make a fool of myself?' she thought with a sudden rush of home-sickness, wishing her family would be coming into dinner as well. She was missing Ann, her eldest sister, Emily's tormenting and Mary's gorgeous hugs. Tears began to pour down her face.   Cook put her arms around Margaret and hugged her.

"Now, now, dear, everyone feels a little like this when they start out. You'll be just fine, you wait and see. Come on, I'll show you the kitchens where you'll be working. Let's see what you make of that."

Laughing out loud, Cook turned and walked out of the door with a timid Margaret following into the rest of the servants' domain.

As they entered the kitchen, cook turned and saw Margaret's jaw drop.

"Big, ain't it?" laughed Cook. "You'll soon learn the ropes. I don't take no messing, mind and you'll work hard or else."

Margaret wondered nervously what the 'or else' meant.

"It'll be up early for you my dear and you'll be late to bed," Cook continued.

"You'll be exhausted and there won't be time for dilly dallying. I don't stand for that. You be a good girl, work hard, and you'll be just right. We rise at five thirty. You're expected to have a wash. We have to get the stoves lit ready for them upstairs. If you see one of them from upstairs, unless they're talking directly to you, look away, they don't like mingling with the likes of us. Some of them are alright, but 'til you learn who's who, best to keep a low profile."

Margaret tried to take in every word. She was going to work hard. She knew she'd landed on her feet. Out on the street, word had it this was one of the better houses to work at. Not like some, where the servants' lives were little better than slavery.

'Yes, I like it here,' she thought.

The memory of Margaret's first meal at Heddington Hall would remain with her forever. She had never seen so much food in one place. Although rumour suggested servants only received scraps from the leftover meals of the 'upstairs' folk, Margaret didn't feel that was the case, and even if it was, she didn't care. A couple of the other servants sitting near her laughed.

"Have you not eaten for a month?"

"Not like this, no," she said, continuing to stuff her mouth with the various titbits on offer.

Cook had made a vegetable soup, which left her drooling for more. There was a loaf of bread and some butter at each end of the table. She had to admit the bread didn't taste as good as her father's and hoped she'd be allowed to bake some. There was lots of chatter and questions. One or two of the others seemed a little aloof but she'd expected that and happy some of the others seemed to enjoy her company, she gained confidence. By the end of the meal, she felt she'd made some firm friends and climbed into bed that night, one happy fourteen year old young lady. The room felt cold but the warm feeling inside was enough to compensate. She said a prayer for her family, closed her eyes and slept.

* * * * * *

Though the days were long and her first year was tough, Margaret settled well into daily life at Heddington Hall. Cook was a good teacher and pleased with Margaret's previous experience, they got along really well. A couple of the scullery maids were a little off-hand but she determined to win them over and tried hard to be especially kind to them. She loved the work, she didn't mind rising early, she was used to working through most of the night and her mind was kept actively engaged using her imagination to impress Cook. There was so much to learn and mistakes were made. There were telling-off from Cook, and others, but for the most part, she did her job well, learnt quickly and became an integral cog in the wheel.

A couple of the other girls took her on a tour of the 'upstairs' while the family were all out on a picnic. Margaret was in awe of the place, the priceless artefacts, the lush fabrics, furnishings and drapes. Never in her wildest dreams had she imagined she would become a part of such an establishment.

Visits home to her parents became less frequent, making the journey once every two months. Things were changing there too. Her sister, Ann, had moved away to another school, a better job, with better prospects and was courting a young man. Darina had told her, secretly, she was expecting an engagement to be announced any day. Emily had moved out and was a live-in housemaid for a local family. Mary was busy in the bakery. Ciaran and Darina found themselves scaling down a little, still bemused by their change of luck after their diabolical start in life.

Twelve months after Margaret's arrival at Heddington Hall, she fell in love.

* * * * * *

CHAPTER FIVE

Bartholomew Bradshaw worked in the timber yard in the grounds of Heddington Hall. Like all servants, his hours of work were long and tedious. He was seventeen years of age when Margaret joined the ranks and they rarely saw each other due to the nature of their duties. The attraction between them began during the long dark winter nights when the lack of daylight hours brought the groundsman and his colleagues into the house for an evening meal with the rest of the servants. They each knew the bitter consequences of conducting themselves in an inappropriate manner and for that reason their relationship was shelved, until one winter's night when Cook, feeling ill, had been persuaded by Margaret to retire to her quarters. It was late, there had been a party upstairs and Margaret had insisted Cook needed to rest and volunteered her services.

An ancient rocking chair beckoned to take the weight off her feet for a few moments. There were some dregs of ale in a jug on the table. She reached up to the top shelf of the dresser and brought down a small tankard, into which she poured the dregs and sitting in the rocking chair, she reflected on her life at Heddington Hall. She thought about Bartholomew Bradshaw. A strange feeling inflicted her the day she met him, one she couldn't shake. Servants' rules were clear. She must not socialise with a member of the opposite sex. Bartholomew was definitely a member of that fraternity. Tall, stocky, handsome with a mop of black hair, which despite the rules of the house for men to keep their hair short, he seemed to ignore and get away with, on the grounds it kept his neck warm whilst working outside in the elements. The spark was about to ignite.

Downing the dregs of the cold ale, Margaret set about her final duties for the night when she heard a commotion outside. Tired, frightened and a little woozy, she made her way across the kitchen and, standing on tiptoe on a small milk stool, peered out of the window. She stretched a little too far, the three-legged stool wobbled and Margaret fell to the floor. As she was regaining her composure and trying to sit up, someone banged loudly on the scullery door. She tried to get up quickly, but winced in pain when she put pressure on her wrist to stand up. She looked around, still a little dazed and felt her heart stop when she saw a face peering through the window. Unsteady on her feet and heart pounding, she tried to focus. Realising who it was, and that it was obviously a state of emergency for him to be knocking at this hour, she made her way to the door and quickly turned the large key with her good hand. As soon as the lock released, the door opened and Bartholomew Bradshaw, in a dishevelled state begged her to come and help.

"Bring the smelling salts."

Sensing the urgency in his voice, she hurried back into the kitchen, snatched the key to the cupboard containing the crude array of medicines, grabbed the salts, took his offered hand and they ran.

"What's wrong? You're frightening me. Where are you taking me? What's happened?"

"It's Mr Hegarty. He's collapsed. Fell on the floor in a heap. Banged his head. I think he's unconscious."

"We should get some help."

"There's no time."

"You administer the salts and I'll go and get help. Is he breathing?"

"I don't think so."

Margaret released Bartholomew's hand and screamed at him to hurry back to Mr Hegarty and she'd go for help. Forgetting her own pain and the possible consequences of her breath smelling of ale, she ran like the wind back into the house and hurtled up the back stairs to alert cook.

Cook, still feeling groggy, heard the crash when Margaret fell and they met on the stairs.

"What on earth's going on?" asked Cook grumpily.

"It's Mr Hegarty, he's collapsed and he's not breathing," answered Margaret, hoping cook wasn't too cross.

Margaret turned and flew down the stairs, almost tripping over her skirt, Cook followed close behind. It was pitch black outside. Margaret let Cook go in front, she had a better command of the pathway down to the yard. They yanked the heavy

timber yard gate open and ran inside to find
Bartholomew kneeling on the floor beside Mr
Hegarty with the smelling salts.

"I think he's dead," he yelled   "The salts
aren't working. I think he's dead."

Cook dropped down on her knees beside
Bartholomew, shushed everyone and bending her
head to the side, she put her ear down to Mr
Hegarty's mouth.   She couldn't hear nor feel any
breath.   She quickly moved her head down to his
chest and slowly stood up.   Making the sign of the
cross, she announced quite matter of fact,

"He's dead. Margaret, you stay here. I'll go
and fetch someone."   With that, she left the timber
yard. In no particular hurry, it seemed to Margaret
.

Bartholomew crossed the room and opened an
old cupboard door.   Taking out a clean brown
pinafore, he placed it as best he could over Mr
Hegarty, covering his face. He didn't speak. Once
again, he offered his hand out to Margaret. She took
it and they made their way across the yard towards
the blacksmith's shop. Once inside, there was some
warmth to be felt from the burning embers of the
furnace. He turned to face her.

"Thank you," was all he said.

The bond between them grew in strength in
that second. Both traumatised by the evening's events
and the untimely death of one of their colleagues, a
most natural phenomenon took place. The warmth of
the   blacksmith's   shop   was   insignificant   by
comparison and it was in each other's arms, locked in

an embrace, that Cook and the master found them. Despite vehement protests nothing was 'going on', they were instantly dismissed. Cook implored the master to take heed it was nothing more than a hug of consolation. She was ignored. At two o'clock in the morning, each carrying their suitcases, Bartholomew Bradshaw and Margaret MacSweeney left Heddington Hall for the last time. Not knowing where they would go or what they would do, but knowing they were inexplicably bound to each other.

* * * * * *

The fateful night at Heddington Hall had taken Margaret MacSweeney and Bartholomew Bradshaw on an unforgettable journey through the nightmare of homelessness and hunger, but thrown them together in strength and resolve. Not wishing to burden her parents with the shame of losing her position at Heddington Hall, Margaret delayed seeking help. Strong-willed and determined to overcome the trials bestowed on her by the untimely death of Mr Hegarty, she nurtured the feelings she had for Bart, and fell deeply in love with him.

Their relationship was consummated in the barn at the back of a coaching house and Margaret fell pregnant with her first-born, Mary-Ann, named after two of her sisters. Following a short period of time living in farmers' barns and old tin huts, Bartholomew stumbled upon an elderly acquaintance he'd helped out some years ago. The ragged-looking Horace Edgar took them in and gave them lodgings in return for Margaret's culinary skills and Bartholomew's help on the farm. Margaret and Bartholomew married at St Bede's Roman Catholic Church in Widnes on 16 July 1866, a quiet service with Horace Edgar and a passing stranger their only witnesses. Troubled with the anguish her parents might be experiencing, they eventually made their way home to the bakery, for the sake of Mary-Ann and their unborn child.

On a hot summer's day in August 1869, Ciaran and Darina MacSweeney, thrilled beyond belief, prepared a belated wedding breakfast for Margaret and Bartholomew. Family and friends crowded into the lodgings behind the bakery. Margaret's homecoming was welcomed by all, Bartholomew was eagerly accepted into the fold and for a while all was well.

* * * * * *

CHAPTER SIX

Amidst screams of pain and squeals of delight, Elizabeth Bradshaw, slowly but surely made her way into the world, the second daughter of Bartholomew and Margaret Bradshaw. Elizabeth's older sister by almost two years, slept peacefully at the bakery. Ciaran, idyllically happy Grandfather, had the duty of looking after his granddaughter, while his daughter produced his second born grandchild, aided by Darina and the local 'midwife'.

The bakery was full of laughter. Ciaran and Darina were delighted to have Margaret back home with Bart and the children. It was a tight squeeze, but the family thrived. Mary-Ann and Elizabeth were happy children, another little mouth was on the way and great excitement bounded in the household.

As Margaret Bradshaw moved into her final months of pregnancy with her third child, everything changed. Ciaran became depressed. Despite Darina's love and support, he became moody, angry, sometimes violent and unable to cope with life at the bakery since Mary had moved away to live on the South coast. He lacked motivation and often took to his bed for days at a time. At the same time, Darina also noticed a decline in Margaret's health. The anxiety caused her to seek medical advice and the local midwife was called in.

"She'll be fine," the midwife pronounced as she was leaving. "Make sure she rests plenty. Lots of hot broth washed down with plenty of water."

There seemed to be nothing wrong and the midwife assured Darina everything would be fine but the mood of the house had changed dramatically and Darina couldn't shake the descending sense of foreboding.

Two days after the midwife had been called out to Margaret, Ciaran lay in his bed and Darina answered a knock on the door. Her face turned to stone. She instinctively knew the visitor brought bad news. One week later, the MacSweeneys and the Bradshaws were forced to leave their home. The owner of the bakery was closing it down and moving his own family into the bakery lodgings. Ciaran had known, his state of depression, a direct result of this discovery.

'How will we survive? There's nowhere else to go,' the thought on everyone's mind.

The surrounding neighbourhood were experiencing their own problems and dwellings were overcrowded. The family was faced with a life-changing decision and Ciaran would sooner have sold his soul than choose either.

Bart had a younger brother, Edward. They didn't see eye to eye and hadn't communicated for many years. It had come to Bart's attention that Edward was also living locally. When Bart discovered news of the bakery's closure, he'd made some tentative enquiries as to Edward's whereabouts. Having located him, he had to search his heart and soul to ascertain, if the need arose, would he be prepared to bury the hatchet for the sake of his family. The straightforward answer had to be yes, he would swallow his pride and ask Edward for help. If he refused, the certainty he would knock on the old oak door of the workhouse would become a reality.

Edward slammed the door in Bart's face. Bart knocked again. There was no reply. He knocked louder. Not wishing to beg, he turned, reunited himself with the rest of the family hiding around the corner, and set off in single file towards the end of the street and out of his brother's life forever. But fate intervened, or rather Edward's wife Julia. She opened the door and shouted, "Bart!"

He turned, but turned again and continued walking away. Julia ran, breathlessly, after him. Standing face to face, she offered a hand each to Bart and Margaret.

"It's alright. He'll listen."

They took Julia's outstretched hands and the bizarre line of people wound its way back to Edward's house.

Edward and Julia listened to the family's story with astonishment. Julia excused herself and Edward while they talked privately.

Bart was overwhelmed Julia could bring about such a change in his brother in a few moments. He swore to him, he would try and get another job and the family would be gone as soon as ever was possible. He explained the situation with Margaret and her forthcoming confinement. Edward and Julia had two children themselves and were no strangers to poverty and struggle, but eventually welcomed the family into their fold. For a week or two, all seemed settled.

* * * * * *

In the early hours of 18 August 1871, an ear-piercing scream brought everyone running to the dark, cramped conditions of the grey room. Margaret's time had come and the midwife was called. As Katy Bradshaw entered the world, no-one would have suspected Margaret would draw her last breath within forty-eight hours, a direct result of a puerperal infection. Her painful death was cruelly slow, intensely heartbreaking for her family and devastating for Bartholomew who was so distraught, he would never recover. Her three young children, Mary-Ann, four, Elizabeth two and the new-born Katy would embark on a series of disturbing changes, causing shattered lives and overwhelming odds to survive to adulthood.

* * * * * *

CHAPTER SEVEN

Bart and his three girls continued to live with Edward and Julia, but it became apparent he was losing mental capacity in an ever diminishing state of health. He wasn't coherent enough to minister to his daughters' well-being and the role of guardians fell predominantly to Ciaran and Darina, whose dwindling energy heralded a new set of problems. For Edward and Julia, with children of their own and another child on the way, disaster struck in the form of a mining accident.

At about nine o'clock on the day of the accident, Edward had been hewing coal for four hours. Props had been supplied for the purpose of supporting the roof and while Edward had been in the act of digging a hole with his pick to erect them, five tons of dirt fell from the roof of the pit and buried him. Despite four men sent down the pit to dig him out, Edward was dead when they found him. Following an inquest, the coroner returned a verdict of accidental death.

The neighbourhood mourned the passing of Edward Bradshaw. He had been a stalwart member of the community. Despite his immediate reluctance to accept Bartholomew into his home, the brothers had become reunited. Edward had watched the slow demise of his brother and vowed to work harder to manage the upkeep of his brother and nieces. He paid for the extra shift with his life.

Edward's body was carried through the streets of St Helens under a dark sky and the rain pelted the gravestones lining the walkway to the field at the top where a grave had been prepared to accept his mortal remains. The ground beneath the onlookers was squelchy and once or twice the bearers had to adjust their footing. In the hearts of all burned the sharply critical loss of a man trying to raise his brother's family as well as his own. For Julia, the pain of Edward's passing was a prelude of what was to come. In the days following Edward's burial, the life growing inside her was extinguished.

Wishing to mourn the untimely demise of Edward and the loss of her child in her own house, her own way, Julia was uncomfortable with Bartholomew's presence. His inability to overcome the loss of Margaret rendered him incapable of normality. Not knowing how she could maintain support for all the children living under her roof, and ever concerned for Bartholomew's mental health, Julia sought to do the only thing left. Dressed in the customary colour of grief, her head covered in a black veil, she headed the line of her family who followed her up the hill to the building with the white smoke.

Once again, the large oak front door cracked open to allow members of this family to enter its portal. Bartholomew was assigned to the infirmary which also housed that portion of the building allocated the title 'lunatic asylum'. Ciaran and Darina were separated and Ciaran, being arguably able-bodied, was assigned immediately for work duties and the two women together with the children were ushered into the women's wing. Following a brief summary of their ability, Darina was assigned to the kitchen and Julia to the laundry room. Darina's work in the kitchens came to an abrupt end when her arthritic hands became incapable of lifting the heavy iron skillets. She was moved to the laundry.

Darina MacSweeney, whose troubled life had brought her to a Union Workhouse for the third time, reflected on her past while she scrubbed the clothes dumped into the large drum in front of her. The hard water and carbolic soap created large red blotches of itchy patches on her already twisted hands. Whilst she was grateful the family had a roof over their heads, the conditions in which they now lived were appalling. The work was arduous, the hours long and the separation from her beloved Ciaran and their family heartbreaking. She requested to see the children as often as she could. For as long as the Lord let her live, she would not, could not, ever come to terms with the death of her daughter Margaret. She had watched Bartholomew's health deteriorate from that second and couldn't yet believe their lives had been taken, once again, to an all-time low. Just a few paces away from where she stood elbow deep in hot water, sat her son-in-law, in an area which, in some cases, bore a stigma of horror for the rest of the workhouse community. Bartholomew was unrestrained, for now, but his cries of grief could be heard throughout the night, suddenly silenced, by what, she didn't know. She was thankful her older children had not succumbed to the disparaging way of life fate had created for her. Julia stood opposite her. Darina MacSweeney would remain eternally grateful to this young woman whose life, already in torment, and suffering a widow's grief, for bringing their family in from a certain state of homelessness. The bond between the two women would be Darina's strength for the news waiting around the corner.

Elizabeth's Grandfather, Ciaran MacSweeney, beloved husband of Darina and bereaved father had lived his life in the workhouse almost in silence. He had suspected the onset of his bad health almost as soon as he'd heard the news of the bakery closing down. He never came to terms with being evicted from his livelihood and his home. The death of his daughter Margaret giving birth to his grandchild disturbed him deeply and he fell into a chasm of depression. His mind didn't have the ability to cope with the anguish caused by his separation from Darina and his body was being torn apart by the growth inside him.

The end came quickly and Ciaran's body was buried beside Edward Bradshaw. Grief was etched into the faces of the two widows as they made their way slowly back towards a life they wished they'd never encountered and a family torn apart, once again, by the ravages of disease and poverty.

* * * * * *

CHAPTER EIGHT

A life beginning and a child as yet unable to understand events which forged her destiny, Elizabeth Bradshaw at the tender age of two and a half years, helped to care for her six-month old sister Katy. Together with her four year old sister Mary-Ann, they were thrown into a life incomprehensible for even the most strong of character. Three sisters, bound in a life of destitution.

Elizabeth did not retain her full title for long. Lizzie became the name she answered to, a bright little girl, totally dedicated to her siblings and with just the vaguest snippets of memory, brought alive by her elder sister, of the mother she would love to have known. Taken away by the God she would be taught to love and honour, Lizzie Bradshaw was embarking on a journey of endurance. Her ancestors had bestowed upon her, against every fibre of their will, a life fraught with a fight for survival, but somewhere along the way, Lizzie and her sisters had already developed individual characteristics which would help prepare them for their uncertain future.

Strong-willed and determined, Lizzie had a positive love of life. A mop of thick black curls surrounded her pretty face and she soon became an icon in the workhouse, with inmates and guardians alike. She was clever, with an aptitude most children hadn't acquired at such an early age. She skipped or ran everywhere, brushing aside the curls flapping around her face. She played happily with her sisters and the other children. Approaching her third birthday, she was kind, gentle, yet with a will of iron and brought laughter and happiness to those around her.

Lizzie's irrepressible high spirits were contagious but not everyone in her immediate environment looked upon it as an asset and claimed her to be an unruly and disobedient minor who needed expert management. Following these accusations, the matron requested Lizzie be sent to the school house to join those children already receiving an education. There was some controversy and unrest about the fact Lizzie was not yet of school age but the matron was a force to be reckoned with.

"Alright. I suppose we could give her a trial," said the Master reluctantly. "She can start when she turns three."

The day after her third birthday, in a class of twenty one other children, Lizzie began her meagre education. Seated with Mary-Ann, her older sister, she thrived in what was to be her learning base for the foreseeable future. Amazed at her aptitude, resilience and desire to please, Lizzie won over even the most arrogant and tyrannical of the teachers. It was this determination to succeed which came to the attention of Mr Leonard Ronald Davenport, who sat on the board of guardians. He would be keeping an eye on Lizzie.

* * * * * *

Each night, in their cramped dormitory, Lizzie lay looking up towards the roof window. Sometimes, if the moon was in the right position and bright enough, rays of light penetrated the darkness. Mary-Ann slept in the same dormitory, further along the line of beds. Across on the other side of the room was a line of cot-beds, where Katy lay screaming most nights. Once the matron had closed the door, Mary-Ann would gently lift Katy from her cot and let her cuddle up in bed with either of her two older sisters, who took it in turns to comfort her, trying to prevent the matron from removing her from their watchful eyes.

Darina and Julia continued to seek permission to see the children as often as possible. Julia's two children, a few years older, a boy and a girl had been asked to keep an eye on the three sisters and a network of care evolved between the five children. Despite the hardships and adversity, a remarkable routine developed which rendered them competent to overcome difficulties in their poverty-ridden environment and delivered the three siblings into acceptance of their existence.

Lizzie, in particular, progressed rapidly and looked forward to time spent with her grandmother and screamed herself into a temper tantrum the first time matron told her Darina couldn't come to see her, having succumbed to the current outbreak of disease. Lizzie threw herself on the cold stone floor thrashing about in an unacceptable manner. The matron in an unmerciful act of anger, scooped Lizzie up and tucking her under one arm, with legs kicking at one end and arms flailing from side to side, threw her onto the pile of empty hessian sacks at the other end of the room. Whether intentionally or not, her action caused Lizzie to sustain a serious injury, as the force with which she was thrown resulted in her hitting her head on the dirty stone wall, from which was protruding a rusty nail. Within seconds, Lizzie's clothes were blood soaked and her terrified screams brought Mary-Ann and their Aunt Julia running. One of the older girls had seen the incident. Julia scooped up the blood soaked child and ignoring the rants from the matron, took her across to the cupboard containing medical supplies. Lizzie clung to Julia, continuing to scream whilst Julia administered first aid to the seeping wound.

"Don't cry Lizzie, it'll be alright. I'll have you fixed in no time," said Julia gently to the hysterical child.

She finally wrapped a crude bandage tightly around Lizzie's head and continued to comfort her until the child's sobbing subsided. Julia handed Lizzie to Mary-Ann, also sobbing at the sight of her sister with a dirty looking turban around her head, and satisfied there was no more to be done, went in search of the matron who had disappeared. Normally a quiet, inoffensive and kindly person, the whole workhouse rebounded at Julia's reaction and what followed. Others felt the same emotion, and a unanimous and angry army of women and children set out in search of the matron, whose actions had created anarchy. Her cowardly attitude and random act of violence resulted in her exit from the room. When the army of women found her half an hour later, she was hanging by an old brown rope in a remote corner of the building. Julia was the first to see her and almost collapsed at the gruesome sight.

"Help! Someone, get some help. Quick!" she screamed urgently.

Her screams sent the woman at the back running to get help. Two sturdy men cut the matron down but when medical help arrived, it was too late.

Lizzie's wound became badly infected. She was taken into the original infirmary where she lay, feverish and completely isolated, to avoid contracting a strain of typhoid so virulent, it was named the killing machine. Meanwhile, in another ward, Bart divided his time between Darina and Julia who'd fallen foul of the worst outbreak of disease the workhouse had ever seen. He sat beside Darina with no thought for his own mortality. Her sunken eyes stared into space. She was oblivious to everything except prayers to her maker. Slipping in and out of consciousness, she waited for death. Unable to physically or mentally cope any longer, Bart wallowed in grief, and held her hand, as she went to meet her maker. The debilitating disease claimed Julia's life along with scores of others. Bart begged the Lord to take his life instead of Lizzie's. Suffering severe mental anguish about Lizzie and having had dangerously close exposure to the disease, his demise was inevitable. Bart's heart stopped beating and he slipped peacefully away in his sleep, his name added to the worst death-toll of any workhouse. Mary-Ann, Lizzie and little Katy were orphans but Lizzie's encounter with the rusty nail saved her life.

* * * * * *

CHAPTER NINE

Leonard Ronald Davenport took a gulp of beer. He was digesting the information gleaned from his fortnightly meeting for the Board of Guardians. He was deeply disturbed at the account of events and troubled more than he cared to admit about the plight of the Bradshaw girls, whom he learned had lost most of their family. He was particularly perturbed to hear Lizzie's confinement in the infirmary ward was singularly attributed to the matron, who had subsequently taken her own life. Never before had he allowed himself to become embroiled in the personal circumstances of the inmates. He was an ex officio member on the Board of Governors by virtue of the fact he was a Justice of the Peace in the borough and was also a member on the Board of Guardians at a Workhouse in Wales. Owning properties in both municipalities, he carved his time in half, devoting equal amounts to both. He made a mental note to meet with the children next time he was in St Helens. Downing the rest of his beer, he left the premises without having spoken to a soul about his deliberations.

* * * * * *

Lizzie's head was shaved. The matriarch who replaced matron forced Mary-Ann to commit the act. Her appointment had been a huge mistake on the part of the Board of Guardians who had voted for Miss Harriet Arlington. They were living with the consequences of their hasty decision. She argued the girl had the worst case of head lice she had ever encountered and it had spread like wild-fire throughout the workhouse. Twenty five children with bald heads beneath their new bonnets scampered in fear when Harriet Arlington walked in the room, lest their heads be attacked again. Her tyrannical methods of discipline always went a step too far and the Board of Guardians had to meet more regularly to deal with some of her encounters. She was hauled up for questioning on the subject of the bonnets and the material purchased to make them. She had lodged a request to the Board for a bolt of white cotton material. After much interrogation, Harriet Arlington relinquished her stance and admitted the children's heads were in such a horrendous state with bites from the lice, it would be cheaper to cover them up with articles of clothing which could be washed, than to pay for medicinal remedies to treat them. The Board of Guardians instructed Miss Arlington to do both.

Life in the workhouse continued as a hum-drum existence. Lizzie made the best of it and considered herself fortunate to have her siblings and the cousins whose home they had occupied. Incidents came and went, as normally as with life on the outside. They all suffered the usual children's diseases and built up immunity to the cold, damp conditions which fate forced them to endure. Poor rations meant their stomachs shrank and therefore did not expect much food. There were times, however, when a little extra was heaven-sent.

L R Davenport, not normally given to acts of compassion had undergone a metamorphosis. He put this change firmly on the shoulders of the lady he'd been courting for two years. He put his concern for the Bradshaw girls on there too. He wasn't supposed to discuss individual cases with anyone outside the board room, but in the intimacy of conversation with the woman who was going to be his wife, when he got round to asking her, he succumbed to the practice of 'getting it off his chest' and told her all about the incidents and controversy surrounding Lizzie Bradshaw.

"You could make random acts of kindness towards the children from time to time. Do it incognito. No-one will know or suspect it's come from you. What are you thinking about anyway? You can't give them money."

"I suppose I'm thinking about extra things to eat," he said in a childlike fashion, "but I'm not supposed to do stuff like that, it's against the rules."

Eventually, with reluctance, he agreed to Helena's proposition to 'make allowances' for the Bradshaw girls. His first attempt at qualifying Helena's wishes was the incident over the bolt of material. He had single-handedly persuaded the others the bonnets were a good idea, having felt pangs of pity for Lizzie Bradshaw's mop of black curls being chopped off by the matron he helped to hire.

He began to visit more frequently, under the persuasion he was in the area for a while. He befriended the newly-appointed cook after a kitchen accident rendered the old one incapable. His collaboration with the new cook enabled him to bring in extras, which were to be served amongst the children as rewards for hard work. Gifts occasionally came in from the more affluent members of society and he deemed he was one of those most fortunate to be labelled the same.

The workhouse Lizzie Bradshaw had known gradually began to change. Unnoticeable at first, but as surely as her hair was growing again, so was the environment she lived becoming less daunting. Her small body had become accustomed to the rigours of daily life, she had some amazing friends and everyone enjoyed her company. Even the tyrannical matron was mellowing. Before the end of the year, people began to notice the presence of Leonard Ronald Davenport. Some had even speculated about his motives, but he was never going to reveal the horrifying truth behind his kindnesses to the Bradshaw girls and his visits to the confines of this particular Union Workhouse.

* * * * * *

CHAPTER TEN

Lizzie's teacher set various tests for the children. Lizzie passed them all. An upcoming student, she was proud of her achievements in the classroom. She could read a simple book from cover to cover and showed an aptitude for arithmetic. At first she'd lacked the ability to grasp handwriting, but her arithmetic and reading skills remained remarkable. Now aged eight, her handwriting skills matched other subjects and she was way ahead of other children her own age. The extra fruit and vegetables supporting the meagre diet was bringing her hair and nails back to life. L R Davenport had introduced a new idea to the Board of Guardians and requested its implementation with immediate effect. With Helena by his side, he had put together a verbal presentation supportive of his reasoning behind his suggestion all children should be allowed outside in the grounds, under supervision, at least once a day, enabling them to enjoy daylight and the elements and thereby reduce the risk of disease from breathing in only the recycled air inside the house. Remarkably, his idea had registered impressive and a positive unanimous vote was cast.

The Master and Matron revoked the idea in the beginning on the grounds it made more work for the staff, having to put outdoor garments on the children during the colder months, but L R Davenport managed to persuade them it was time for change and that only good could come from the implementation of the 'outdoor' plan. They eventually had to concede and the plan was now in place, much to the great delight of all the boys and girls.

* * * * * *

A time was looming in L R Davenport's life which was to change the equilibrium. A vacancy arose at the workhouse for an apprentice Master. The current Master was ageing and developing poor health. The Board of Guardians recognised this at once and an advertisement was drawn up for a position as Master's assistant. L R Davenport didn't need to think twice. He ran it past Helena, who was delighted. First though, he had something to attend to.

The jeweller pulled out the trays one by one. L R Davenport had the man's undivided attention as he was the only one in the shop at nine o'clock in the morning. In fact, he had been there before the doors opened, peering in through the window to establish the approximate cost of each tray to avoid embarrassment. He had selected two trays which the jeweller now pulled out and placed on the counter. L R Davenport's eyes selected the ring he thought his future bride would wish to wear and the jeweller nestled it into its plush navy blue velvet interior and closed the lid of the tiny box. He popped it into a small bag bearing the name of his establishment. Payment exchanged hands and pushing the small parcel deep into his trouser pocket, L R Davenport raced home.

Knocking on Helena's door one hour later, he beamed at her when she opened the door and welcomed him inside, offering him a freshly made cup of tea from the blue and white bone china teapot.

"Have you written your letter of application?" she asked, sure this was the reason for his obvious elation.

"No, that's my next job," he said. "This is my first."

Retrieving the box from his trouser pocket and clutching it tight in his palm so she wouldn't see, he bent down on one knee.

"Helena Ormishaw, please will you marry me?"

A pink flush coloured Helena's cheeks and she laughed, as she took the offering and opened the box followed by exclamations of delight.

She placed the box on the table beside her and offered both her hands. Pulling him back up to his feet she looked him directly in the eyes and before melting into his arms, she whispered, "Yes, please."

* * * * * *

L R Davenport began his position as apprentice Master on Monday 18 June 1877. It was to be a fruitful move in many ways and he became a happier man than could be found anywhere. He had off-loaded his bad news to Helena some months before he popped the question so that was a worry he could now put away for good. It hadn't made any difference. She'd married him anyway. His appointment had been celebrated at the workhouse and he silently vowed to continue making the necessary changes to bring the degradation of all workhouse inhabitants to the absolute minimum and became an iconic force to be reckoned with in terms of moving the establishment forward. This, he knew he could achieve with the help of his new bride and the money from his covert operations.

Lizzie and her sisters had come to know L R Davenport well and looked forward to and welcomed his occasional visits. Discovering the news he was to become the new master added to Lizzie's happiness. When he became the official Master of the Union Workhouse he ordered a children's party to be held in the board room, an unheard of occurrence in this establishment. Staff and inmates scurried around, feeling much like the staff of a stately home, rather than the gruelling, hard working members of a poverty stricken house for the poor.

Mary-Ann was concerned about her own future, as well as that of her sisters.

'What will become of us? Will we be turned out into the world considered too old to remain in the workhouse?'

She began to think of jobs she would be comfortable with. She'd been happy now for a few months, helping out in the infirmary and had come to the conclusion she might seek employment as a trainee nurse in such an environment, though quite how she would do that, for the moment, remained an enigma.

* * * * * *

Just two months into his new job, L R Davenport was considering applying for the position of a husband and wife team to take over the role of Master and Matron in a workhouse in Wales, the workhouse where he was already on the Board of Guardians. He was torn. He'd been born and raised in the countryside surrounding the said establishment. It would be like going home to his roots. It would also mean leaving the Bradshaw girls and never seeing them again, a decision he didn't believe he could make alone. His determination to resolve his dilemma resulted in a conversation later that day with his new wife, in which he appeared to be owning up to feelings he'd been harbouring for years.

He had confronted Helena with his secret before he asked her to marry him, in order for her to make an informed decision. Surely now, in the light of the future possibly offered to them as a couple, she would see sense in his proposal. L R Davenport couldn't have children. He'd suffered an accident some years ago which had rendered him infertile, a condition he'd been assured couldn't be reversed. The plight of the Bradshaw girls had claimed his attentions and he'd wanted to take them under his wing and look after them as his own whilst developing his long-term financial plan. He hoped now, his new wife, Helena, whom he knew would have loved children, would accept his proposal and they could 'take the girls in'. They would become their personal guardians and, on the face of it, could all live together as a family.

"I've known for a long time you have a particular affection for these girls, so your proposal doesn't shock me. However, I think you should take things slowly. Perhaps we could ask if the girls could be transferred? What do you think?"

Level-headed in her thinking, Helena visualised encountering problems with a family if they were both working all day, not to mention the difficulties it might present in attaining the vacancy at all.

"You always seem to know the right things to say," he said to his wife, actually succumbing to the notion her rationalisation may well be correct. He decided to heed her advice.

They made the application and were successful. Their decision to leave the Union Workhouse wasn't taken well by the Board of Guardians and a particularly difficult two months passed whilst all the paperwork was arranged. L R Davenport requested a transfer for the Bradshaw girls to the new Union Workhouse in Wales, and subject to certain legislation, that had also been agreed, on the grounds he and his wife had become quite attached to the girls and wished to offer them a home and a better life. All that remained now was to put the question to the girls. Neither L R nor Helena wished to push the girls into a decision they didn't want to make.

Mary-Ann was a little reluctant at first. She was fast approaching a time when she would have to consider an alternative to the workhouse. Lizzie was delighted with the news and found it an exciting prelude to a better future. She liked L R Davenport and had met his wife on a number of occasions and liked her too. Lizzie's mind was made up. She would go with them and take whatever fate threw her way. Mary-Ann and Lizzie both agreed Katy should go with Lizzie. They knew they'd be well looked after, and after all, anything could happen without the Davenports at the helm. They would take their chances and take the hand offered to them. Mary-Ann, in the end, satisfied Lizzie was sure about her decision, agreed to go with her sisters, an exciting prospect and a new life looming. Of course the Davenports had not discussed the girls living with them. L R Davenport had heeded his wife's advice and was treading softly.

On 9 September 1878, Lizzie Bradshaw and her younger sister began attending an orphanage school about twelve miles away from the workhouse where L R Davenport and his wife had secured their future.

The difficulty had come not from the Union Workhouse near St Helens, but from the new one. There was severe overcrowding and because the girls didn't come from that area, the Board of Guardians decreed it would be unreasonable for locals seeking refuge to discover three places had been taken by children from another district. The answer was negative. L R Davenport had made tentative enquiries and discovered the orphanage a short distance away and approached the Mother Superior of the order of sisters who ran the orphanage. After much pleading, she'd agreed to give the three girls a trial period. The girls were accepted into the orphanage in Wales, where Lizzie and Katy would attend the orphanage school. Mary-Ann, however, was considered too old for the education offered in the school and was put to household duties in the orphanage. And so began the separation of three sisters who had suffered an intolerable childhood, and having clutched at a future they believed to be better than the one offered at the Union Workhouse, found themselves drawn into a lifestyle completely alien.

"Are they telling the truth? Have they an ulterior motive for bringing us here to this place? Will we ever see them again?'

Torn away from a familiar life and thrown into a new dimension, they could only hope it would prove a positive move.

* * * * * *

CHAPTER ELEVEN

Heralded by the onset of a flu virus, Lizzie began her new life in the orphanage. As she lay in bed, unable to properly co-ordinate her thoughts, a notion occurred to her.

'What if I hadn't been an orphan? What if my mother and father hadn't died?'

Being of an inquisitive nature, she asked everyone she thought might be able to answer her questions and discovered quite a shocking life to date. She knew her mother had died giving birth to Katy. Mary-Ann could remember remnants of a past life, living in a bakery with their mother and father, laughing, playing out in the street, and doing all the things 'normal' children did. Mary-Ann could recall memories of Ciaran and Darina, their Grandparents with whom they'd lived. Keen to learn everything she could about their past life, Lizzie asked, "What happened? What happened to spoil it all? Why did we leave the bakery?"

Mary-Ann had been barely able to answer her questions.

"I remember everyone being happy at the bakery and then something changed. Grandad began to stay in bed all day and our mother wasn't well and then suddenly we were leaving the bakery to live with Auntie Julia and Uncle Edward and our two cousins.

Soon afterwards, our mother died, the day Katy was born. I remember something happening to Uncle Edward down the mine and then we moved to the workhouse."

As Lizzie lay in her sick bed, she dug deep for memories of the relatives who'd gone to that place in the sky they called heaven, and to a God her teachers at the orphanage were instructing her to believe was a loving being.

'Why did God take them all away?' was the question resounding in her head every time she tried to understand.

'Why did God take my Mother, my Father, my Grandparents and my Auntie and Uncle? That's not what a nice person would do. Take all those people away from three children, and Katy only a baby.'

Lizzie didn't think much of God at the moment and the more the teachers at the orphanage tried to persuade her to accept the faith she'd been bestowed with, the more she struggled to understand it.

'Where's the Davenports? Have they gone to heaven too? They told us we were going with them to a new life? Where are they?'

Large tears formed in Lizzie's eyes and dripped down onto the bed sheet. She didn't normally give in to self-pity.

'It must be the flu making me feel like this,' she thought and mopped the tears tickling her cheeks.

'Never mind, Mary-Ann will come and see me later and they might let Katy in too,' but she knew instinctively, no-one would be coming to see her. Even the nun who brought her food wore a mask to prevent her from becoming infected with the virus.

Lizzie couldn't have known the Davenports had knocked on the orphanage door at every opportunity to try and see the girls nor could she have known L R Davenport had left large quantities of food on the doorstep, because they wouldn't grant him access. How could the girls know, when no-one told them? Their anguish was needless but there was more to come. Just around the corner was a day looming which Lizzie and Katy would never forget and one which would be the official messenger of things to come in Lizzie's future.

Having three more days in bed before she was allowed back into the community gave Lizzie the opportunity to think about what she was doing here in this place. The virus was leaving and the optimistic Lizzie was bouncing back. She knew she had two choices. To let it get her down and be sucked into a dark place or to fight back, to listen, to learn, to take on board all they threw at her, to be the best she could.

'I'll be ten next birthday. I'll only have another two or three years to find out as much about the outside world as I can, before I'm part of it.'

She resolved from that moment on, to work harder, to be her usual happy, bouncy self, to look after herself, to bathe frequently and to groom herself for her future.

'I'll make myself as attractive as I can. Perhaps someone might want to marry me, like Mr Davenport married Helena. Perhaps everything'll be alright in the end.'

* * * * * * *

Mary-Ann adored Lizzie and Katy and although their paths rarely crossed during the day she cherished the time spent with them at suppertime. She slept in a different wing and had made new friends her own age but she too, was troubled by the events which had occurred since they arrived at the orphanage. She wondered why the Davenports didn't come and why they weren't living with them. Whilst Mary-Ann's thoughts and concerns were genuine, her life was moving at a rapid pace towards the day she'd dreamed of. The day she would leave the orphanage to train as a nurse.

The Davenports made their mark at the new Workhouse. They continued to journey to the orphanage at every available opportunity, only to be fobbed off with one excuse or another. Being the Master and Matron of their new establishment, it was difficult for them to get out as often as they would have liked. L R was reluctant to make waves. The separation from the girls was wearing him down and although he knew they were in a better place for the time being, the situation was thwarting his long-term plan. The Workhouse, whilst providing them with a decent living, was having a profound effect. Rules differed from those with which they were familiar and the Board of Guardians with whom L R had associated for the last few years had changed. The old ones had retired from duty and new ones, young ones with a different point of view, were undermining his hopes for the future of the establishment. Two or three of them, disciplinarians, harboured the concept strict guidelines, with no room for manoeuvre was the only way forward and despite L R's protestations, it was becoming difficult, even as Master, to retain his edge. He must think also about his own future and that of Helena. He wouldn't be accepted back at the Union Workhouse; that much he knew. He had to find a way to keep the peace and retain his status as Master of his domain. That proved more difficult than he imagined.

Repeated attempts to leave the Workhouse to visit the orphanage were pre-empted by outbursts of violence in the house and both L R and Helena had to be present to deal with them. By no means was this the future he predicted when he made his application. However, he still retained the title of Guardian for the three girls and as such, could command a certain amount of communication with the orphanage. This, he decided, one morning, was what he needed to do. He would assert his authority as their Guardian and demand to see them.

'They can't stop me seeing them. What right have they to keep me away from them? None. They can't possibly know – no-one can,' he thought and vowed to set things right.

At eight thirty the following morning, he and Helena stood outside the doors of the orphanage, again. They each held a bag of surprises. L R was desperate to explain to the girls the prevailing circumstances preventing him seeing them. He needed to put it right and it needed to be today.

After knocking on the door for the third time, he decided to investigate round the back of the building and establish whether, in fact, they ever answered the front door. His intuition bore fruit. The gate which led to the back of the house had been left ajar by a man delivering supplies on the back of a wooden wagon. The shire tethered to the wagon, jerked his head up and down as L R and Helena marched past, down the entry and through the gate into the inner sanctum of the orphanage. At the far side of a courtyard, was an open door. They both scurried across the cobblestones and L R peered inside the doorway. He knocked and shouted out. A nun in a black habit appeared in the doorway at the back of the room. She introduced herself as Sister Aloysius.

"Pronounced Alaweeshus," she said. "Can I help?"

"Hello Sister. I'm the Bradshaw girls' official guardian and I'd like to see them urgently please."

L R stated the reason for his visit in a no-nonsense, matter-of-fact tone. The sister promptly informed him the girls were only allowed visitors during the hours of six o'clock and seven o'clock in the evening, Monday to Friday and from nine o'clock in the morning on a Saturday and Sunday until five o'clock in the evening. Today was Monday, so he would have to come back at six o'clock if he wanted to see the girls.

"But sister, with all due respect, every time I call, there is some excuse. I'm the master at the local Union Workhouse and it's difficult for me to come at the times you specify. I should like to see them now please. I have some important information for the girls."

Sister Aloysius wouldn't budge.

"I'm really sorry Sir, but rules are rules and I can't allow you to see the girls now. You'll have to come back tonight."

L R tried again.

"Sister, it doesn't seem to make any difference what time I call, whenever it is, whatever time it happens to be, there's always some excuse. I don't understand and I demand to see my girls now."

L R was angry. The nun standing in front of him irritated him more than he cared to admit. His face burned beetroot red and beads of sweat had formed on his forehead.

"I'm sorry, Sir, I can't allow you to see them. The children are in school. Goodbye."

With that, Sister Aloysius closed the door and left L R and Helena standing in the courtyard, angry beyond belief.

Their hearts sank. They would not be able to visit again today. It had been difficult enough to arrange the time away this morning, not to mention the hassle of procuring a horse and carriage to bring them the twelve mile journey each time they came. L

R had tried his best to reason this with the Sister and for a moment he'd thought she was going to relent. Distraught by their predicament, L R knocked on the door once more. It was opened but the Sister's facial expression left him in no doubt he was disturbing the peace and she asked him to leave. He said he would, but not before he'd written his girls a note. He begged her to give him a piece of paper and something to write with. His writing skills were one of the important factors of his position as Guardian. Without them he would have been passed by. The Sister reluctantly complied and L R scribbled a note:

My dearest Mary-Ann, Lizzie and Katy

Please understand we care for you very much and will see you as soon as we can. There is a bag for you in the stone room.

Your Guardian

L R folded up the piece of paper and handed it to the Sister, who twirled her rosary beads round her little finger in agitation. He spoke, his voice breaking.

"Please would you pass this note to the Bradshaw girls."

As he passed her the note, he deposited the bag they'd brought just inside the door.

"Please inform the girls there's something for them to collect. Thank you."

L R and Helena turned and left. They made their way to the corner of the street where their carriage driver had been asked to wait. Once seated, L R held his head in his hands and wept.

L R Davenport was never to know if the girls received his note and despite repeated attempts to see them at the allocated times, he was never allowed access to the orphanage. His name was clearly on the admission sheet for all three girls as their Guardian. He had been there and signed them in. It was beyond his comprehension why access was being denied. Frustrated, angry and distraught his plans to take the girls in had failed, he fell into a deep depression, one from which he might never have recovered if it hadn't been for the determination of Helena. She believed it was time to reflect on an alternative approach and this she did with the help of the seamstress back at the workhouse.

When Helena left the workhouse on Friday afternoon, she was every inch a nun. She wore the black habit, the wimple, the veil and the distinguishable set of rosary beads hanging down the side of her skirt. The seamstress had made a cloak which would disguise the fact until she needed to reveal herself as Sister Ambrose, seeking accommodation for the night, on an errand of strict secrecy from the Convent of Jesus the Saviour. Clutched tightly in her hand was another note she had written on behalf of her husband and one which she intended to ensure this time, the girls read.

Her ingenuity paid dividends and without question, she was invited in. The hour was six o'clock when she asked if there were any orphans with no visitors. She told the Mother Superior she would love to be able to visit them as part of her mission to embrace the lonely, the sick or the unloved people of the world. Suspecting nothing, the Sister granted her request and Helena was led to a visiting room where twenty children were brought in. She began to talk easily and while the Sister was still in the room, she had to use every ounce of integrity to hide her nerves, as she saw Mary-Ann, Lizzie and Katy amongst the children ushered into the room. Believing in her role and in herself, she began a repertoire she'd practised every night since Monday. Eventually the Sister left the room saying she would be back in a few moments. That was the break Helena needed. She moved in towards Lizzie and smiled a little. Her face was familiar to Lizzie but of course she wasn't prepared for her encounter with one of her beloved guardians. Mary-Ann and Katy too, saw through the facade. Helena pushed the folded paper into Lizzie's open hand, quickly making a movement with her own hand indicating Lizzie she should close her hand tightly around the piece of paper. Lizzie's astute nature knew exactly in that moment all she needed to. At that point the Sister in charge of the girls entered the room again and announced it was time to prepare for dinner. She asked the girls to thank Sister Ambrose for her visit and ushered them all out of the room.

Still unsuspecting Helena was a ruse, Sister Ambrose was invited into the dining room, where her nerve left her. She ran as fast as she could and huffing and puffing, she made for the doorway through which she'd entered. Slamming it shut behind her, she ran, her side hurting with an intolerable pain, but still she kept running until she reached the carriage which took off in the direction it was facing at a quick trot. Her job was done. Even if they caught up with her, the girls, by now, would know the truth. Satisfied her goal had been achieved, she sat back in the carriage and laughed till she cried.

'How marvellous to have pulled a stunt like that and got away with it,' she thought.

She laughed and laughed so much, the driver of the carriage laughed with her, even though he had no clue what she was laughing at. She laughed, uncontrollable, relieved laughter, all the way home.

L R Davenport had never felt such love for a person in his life. This single act bound him to this lady forever. He made a full recovery and awaited the outcome he knew would surely come. Lizzie would find a way, now that she knew. She always did.

* * * * * *

CHAPTER TWELVE

The girls didn't understand why L R and Helena had been denied access, but there was no hesitation putting a plan in place to alleviate their distress. Mary-Ann had made lots of new friends. One of them Doris Todd, also known as Dolly, a little slow and two years older than Mary-Ann, made every endeavour to make everyone like her. She had a male companion, a clandestine one, of course. An innocent relationship had struck up in the stone room as the boy delivering the milk to the orphanage on the back of his father's cart, had seen Dolly a number of times and enjoyed her company.

Mary-Ann and Lizzie, with Katy's intermittent jabbering, concocted a letter back to their Guardians, leaving them in no doubt, they had indeed received their letter from Sister Ambrose. They informed them they'd received nothing else. No letter, no 'surprises' and they'd no idea the Davenports had ever visited the orphanage. They conveyed their thanks and hoped the problem could be resolved. After signing the bottom of the letter as they'd been taught, they folded the note into four and put it inside another folded piece of paper, sealing it with a mixture of flour and water. Dolly already knew John delivered milk to the Workhouse and her instruction was to hand it to him and ask him to deliver it to Mr Davenport, the Master of the

Workhouse. John was delighted to be involved and doing something his girl had asked of him. The letter was on its way.

Before any consequence of the letter was known, a life-shattering occurrence for Lizzie and Katy reared its head. Mary-Ann announced she was leaving the orphanage. The Sisters ran another establishment in London and the Sisters there had been asked to listen out for any vacancies that might occur with a view to one of their children starting a career in nursing. An advertisement had appeared in a local shop window for an under nurse in the borough of Islington. The sisters at the orphanage had helped Mary-Ann compile a letter of application and two days ago, she'd received notice she was to begin work in a few days' time. There had been no question of her attending an interview. The sisters at the orphanage had vouched for her ability, her integrity and her general demeanour and Mary-Ann's name had been put forward as the number one candidate. The reference had been accepted and Mary-Ann would leave within the week.

Lizzie and Katy were dumbfounded they'd be losing yet another member of their family. Lizzie felt it particularly difficult as Mary-Ann had substituted the mother she'd never really known.

'How will I cope without her?' she thought, in despair.

Devastated beyond belief she dreaded the day Mary-Ann would walk out of her life. On 11

November 1880, a cold and misty early morning departure brought the three girls together in the stone room where Mary-Ann's suitcase, procured from the possessions of one of the deceased sisters, and one cloth bag containing some cheese and bread, sat by the door waiting to be collected. No-one else was there to say goodbye. A knock came on the door which sent Lizzie into convulsions. She hugged her sister so hard, she could have crushed her ribcage. Tears poured down her face. She lifted Katy up in her arms and offered her to Mary-Ann for one last hug. Clinging onto each other, they watched Mary-Ann and her escort walk across the cobbled yard towards the gate which would take her away into the world and out of their lives. At the gate, Mary-Ann turned and waved goodbye. She would never see her youngest sister again. She kept her promise and wrote every month, treasures which Lizzie would keep forever.

* * * * * *

A series of events over the months following Mary-Ann's departure, left Lizzie in no doubt her future did not lie in the orphanage, nor in the Workhouse. Katy had become distant and Lizzie felt she had not only lost her eldest sister, but also her youngest. Despite feeling this way, Lizzie felt an overwhelming excitement too. Her eldest sister had gone out into the world, to make her own way in her chosen field of work. The impact this had on Lizzie gave her not only a sense of isolation and desolation, but also hope and anticipation, feelings fuelled by the letter from Mary-Ann, outlining the life she was now living and encouraging Lizzie to develop plans for her own future.

Two days before her thirteenth birthday, Lizzie received another letter, this time from L R, a letter which, not only bizarrely she received, but was also allowed to act on, one which would change her world. The Davenports were taking a trip to London, a mix of business and pleasure and invited Lizzie along. She was beside herself. 'London', she thought for the millionth time.

'I might be able to see Mary-Ann.'

Rushed preparations were made for her departure as the Davenports were leaving on Lizzie's birthday and there wasn't much time. L R sent a large parcel, containing clothes for Lizzie's trip, in fact far more than she'd need for three weeks. Her excitement was boundless. A letter had also been sent to the orphanage explaining to the Mother Superior Lizzie's place should remain open as she would be returning. A large amount of money had been deposited with the orphanage with which to prepare Lizzie with anything the Davenports may have overlooked. On the day Lizzie Bradshaw reached her teenage years, she stood in the stone room, as her sister had done before her, suitcase packed waiting by the door, Katy at the side of her, sobbing, and a primeval heartbeat in her chest. The knock on the door came, she locked her arms around Katy in a tight squeeze leaving them both breathless and opened the door to the world outside. The strange thing was, only L R Davenport was in the carriage.

CHAPTER THIRTEEN

An old lady in dirty clothes sitting on the steps of a shabby building caught Lizzie's eye. The lady had a baby in arms.

'The child's Grandmother,' Lizzie thought.

There was a cup at the side of her. As the lady seemed to have her eyes closed, Lizzie peered into the cup. A few coins filled the bottom of the cup.

"A beggar," L R explained, watching Lizzie's puzzled expression.

They passed a number of stalls selling everything from second-hand clothing to smelly seafood. Lizzie's guardian advised her not to purchase from either.

"Street vendors trying to earn a living," he told her, a subject which fascinated Lizzie from that day on.

She noticed a couple of men with long black beards selling ironware. The scene revived images of the black iron pots of the workhouse and made her shudder. Her eyes rested on a man with crutches, one of his trouser legs tied in a knot beneath the knee. A small boy was wrestling with a fold out table. She asked L R to stop while she watched. The child set an array of pills and potions onto the table and leant a blackboard against the wall advertising their wares. Try our new 'Lemon Cough Syrup', 1/-, was written on the blackboard. People began to form a queue to look at the potions on the table. Lizzie wondered how many people would be able to afford a whole shilling for a bottle of medicine. She saw a chimney sweep carrying a bundle of poles, some with brushes on the end, longer than the others. He carried a bundle of rags in the other hand. She knew about chimney sweeps. They'd been to the orphanage a couple of times. She'd laughed at their soot-blackened faces. She remembered how one of them had touched her nose with his sooty finger, making a large black blob on the tip of her nose.

Children sat in the gutter chattering or dodged in between the legs of adults scurrying about their business. L R yelled at her to be more aware as Lizzie almost stepped out in front of a carriage coming round the corner, so engrossed was she by her surroundings.

'You need to look where you're going,' L R yelled at Lizzie.

She loved the sound of horse's hooves on the cobblestones, a noise which remained in her sub-consciousness and would resonate throughout her life. Lizzie observed and commented about the men going into the buildings on street corners, and some coming out, wobbling a little. L R Davenport laughed and explained they were public houses where people had alcoholic drinks. As they moved out of that street and onto another, the mood of the city changed. Down the next street, she saw a young boy on the pavement with a box in front of him. A gentleman dressed in fancy clothes walked up and put a foot on the box. Lizzie watched with interest as the boy began to clean the man's shoes. L R allowed her to watch the process and when both shoes had been cleaned, the man tossed a coin into a cup at the side of the boy. The people she saw down this street did not resemble in any way those she'd seen down the previous street.

'Posh people,' she thought. 'Their clothes are nice.'

The ladies wore long elegant gowns and linked arms with gentlemen, strolling past jeweller's shops, banks and important looking buildings with lots of steps up to the front doors.

'I wonder where he's taking me. I'm hungry. We've passed so much food and he hasn't stopped to buy any. There were other things besides seafood. I'm thirsty too. Why doesn't he stop to get us something to eat and drink? Perhaps he's taking me somewhere they'll give us something.'

Lizzie's excitement was now overtaken by fatigue and her suitcase had become burdensome, but still they walked on.

"Where are we going Sir?" she asked innocently, feeling a different manner in her guardian's demeanour.

"You'll see. Just a few more minutes."

They came to a crossroads and turned left. Lizzie felt a peculiar prickle down her spine. She didn't like the sudden uncomfortable realisation she didn't know this man at all, nor did she know why he'd brought her to London, where Mrs Davenport was, or where he was taking her.

Lizzie was not street wise, but she knew bad things happened to girls, she knew some men did bad things to children. She had heard tell of these things from children entering the workhouse. Her uncomfortable feeling turned to fear. She hadn't wanted to fear this man, she'd believed her guardian to be a good person. She thought for a fleeting second about running. Nimble and quick on her feet, she could outrun this large man who would struggle to keep up with her.

'Where will I run to? I don't know the streets of London. Why do I feel like this?'

For a few moments, fear threatened to choke her. The elegance of the beautiful shops had gone. The hustle and bustle of the ladies and gentlemen had been replaced instead, by a gloomy grey alleyway with unsavoury looking characters lurking in the shadows of doorways. The darkness accentuated her fear and tormented by the notion L R Davenport may not be all he seemed, she decided to take her chances and run for it.

L R paused for a second to tie one of his shoelaces which had worked loose. Lizzie stole her chance. Dropping her suitcase, she turned and ran for her life, back the way they'd come. Retracing their steps, her aim was to get back to the elegant street and run like the wind. There was a slim chance she'd remember the way back to the station if she could find that street. One of the Sisters had given her a pouch containing a small amount of money. She told her to wear it on the inside of her clothes and to use it only in an emergency.

'Maybe there'll be enough money to get back to the orphanage.'

She increased her speed.

'I have to put more distance between us. I need to stop and ask someone the way. The station's my best chance.'

She remembered having to navigate the corridors of the workhouse in the dark and bringing those skills into play, she paid attention to the shops they'd stopped to peruse and particular stall holders.

'If I can just find the posh street, I'm sure I'll find my way back to the station.'

She needed to stop running and draw breath, but frightened L R would catch up, she kept going. Never turning to look back she turned a corner and found herself in the street of banks and jewellers. She flew down the street to the other end, holding her skirt up so she didn't trip.

'I'm almost home and dry. The station's only a few more blocks. I have to keep running.'

There was another crossroads ahead. She remembered turning into the posh street from there, but from which direction? Slowing down a little to catch her breath, she quickly calculated the direction she needed and sprinted towards the crossroads. Still a way to go, she increased speed again, reached the corner and made her swift turn. Straight into the arms of L R Davenport, who almost toppled over backwards, but managed to hang on to Lizzie. He too was breathless and Lizzie took advantage of this fact and holding her knee up as high as she could, she stamped with all her might on his foot and he released his grip. She took flight, her feet hammering the pavement as she ran frantically trying to put as much distance as she could between them. People stared and without glancing back, she knew without doubt he was close. Beads of sweat poured down her face, stinging her eyes and she could hear the rush of blood pounding through her body. She saw the gates of the station loom before her.

* * * * * *

CHAPTER FOURTEEN

Mary-Ann licked the envelope and folded the flap down, pressing hard to make sure it was sealed. Her employer, Mrs Postlethwaite had given her a stamp.

"I'll take it out of your wages," she informed Mary-Ann.

Some disturbing news had come to Mary-Ann's attention. She had written the letter immediately and was on her way to the postbox when a large man emerged from the alley at the side of the house and nearly knocked her over. The incident unnerved her, not because he nearly sent her flying, but because he was vaguely familiar. With a sudden rush of blood, she realised who the man reminded her of and flew into a panic. Forgetting she had a letter to post, she began to run, following the man who she believed to be her guardian. She shouted, but the man paid no heed and continued running. His pace had slowed a little and she suspected he'd been running for some time and was puffing and panting, unable to catch his breath.

Combined with the news contained in the letter she'd written and this incident, she had a premonition. Revulsion set in and she unceremoniously shouted at the top of her voice.

"Stop that man!"

No-one seemed to hear.

She screamed "Police!" perturbed there seemed to be none around.

The elements had taken a turn for the worse and a strong wind forced its way through the streets of Islington. The wind carried her voice away. No-one heard her screams. She could still see the man ahead of her, though no image met her eyes of the person she thought he may be chasing. Astounded by the events of the last forty-eight hours and desperately needing someone to help, she shouted to a passer-by.

"Get the police."

She continued chasing the man she believed to be L R Davenport. The gates of the station came into view and she saw him turn in. Screaming at the top of her voice for someone to apprehend him, she flew through the gates and then she knew.

Sobbing in the arms of a policeman, she saw Lizzie. Knowing her premonition had been correct, she saw two policemen either side of L R Davenport as he was being frogmarched out of the station gates in the direction of the Police Station. She heaved a sigh of relief and ran to Lizzie, throwing her arms around her, almost pushing the comforting police officer out of the way. One look at the girl informed the officer the two girls were related. Another officer ran up to the trio and after a short dialogue, the two policemen led Lizzie and MaryAnn towards an empty waiting room. The second policeman stood outside the doors to prevent anyone disturbing his superior, who took out his notepad and began writing furiously as Lizzie related her story. He then asked Mary-Ann for her version. He informed the girls L R Davenport would be going to jail for a long time. The police had suspected him of a number of similar offences. They promised the girls they would not have to see their guardian again. They'd laid eyes on him for the last time.

Safe in the knowledge her trauma was over, Lizzie allowed herself to be comforted by Mary-Ann and the police officers who offered them tea and biscuits back at the police station, while they once again re-iterated the story from the beginning. When Lizzie finished her tale, beginning a few days ago when she'd received word the Davenports were taking her to London on her thirteenth birthday, it was Mary-Ann's turn.

She informed the officers she worked for an affluent family as a nurse maid and now believed her application had been orchestrated by her guardian. Her work as a nursemaid was infinitely preferable to the life she'd left behind at the orphanage. Despite missing her sisters, Mary-Ann had worked hard and felt she had gained the respect of her employers. But there was a darkness overshadowing her otherwise happy existence. This came in the form of the man who'd been responsible for the three girls' movements during the last few years. The man whose name she feared, creating a tremble in her soul when informed of his pending visits. So far, she had managed to escape whatever fate he may have pencilled in, and help to do this had come in the form of the butler, whom she trusted implicitly and whose attentions she would willingly have accepted.

Solomon Macavelly's parents had met coming over from Ireland on an Irish steam tramper. His Jewish mother had been a stowaway, hidden on the rickety old boat by relatives who didn't want her, her parents having succumbed to the ravages of famine. She had been sixteen and near death's door, when Solomon's Irish father found her unconscious under a tarpaulin at the front of the boat.

Solomon's mixed parentage had created a strong-willed sincere young man who took Mary-Ann under his wing from the day she was deposited in the affluent dwelling in Islington. She'd confided in him, trusting him wholeheartedly, and he hadn't let her down. Each time Mary-Ann's guardian had announced a visit, Mary-Ann had been smitten with a fever, or similar and her guardian's intentions had continued to be thwarted, thanks to Solomon's acceptance of Mary-Ann's intuitive nature. She didn't feel in any way threatened by Solomon's protectiveness, and knew an intimacy existed between them.

Mary-Ann told her story in as eloquent a manner as she could, leaving the officers in no doubt she considered L R Davenport a threat to young girls. Word on the local grapevine was that young girls in the district had been shipped off to foreign climes and sold into slavery, Davenport being the sole beneficiary. She felt he'd been priming the girls from their early days at the Workhouse. Under the auspices of a kindly nature, and further enhancing their future, he'd made provision for them to be housed at the orphanage in Wales, where he hoped to be able to keep an eye on them while furthering his own career. Mary-Ann suspected the nuns had either the same intuition as herself or some other knowledge as to his true demeanour and refused him access to the orphanage. This being the case, he'd engineered a plan to place Mary-Ann in a nursemaid position near enough to the forefront of his operation without being suspected, where the ships came up the River Thames to sail away their precious cargo from British waters forever. Without the attentions of Solomon Macavelly, whom Mary-Ann felt she owed her life to, she too could have become one of Davenport's statistics. What Davenport had in mind for Mary-Ann and Lizzie would perhaps now never come to fruition, but though he would likely face a term of imprisonment, Katy's future had already been determined.

* * * * * *

CHAPTER FIFTEEN

The policeman had retrieved Lizzie's suitcase and made plans for her return to the orphanage, an arrangement which was to be short-lived. Her sole intention had been to return, collect her sister, her few belongings and leave. To where, she had no notion. She needed to find a different life for them, her aspirations more than over-ruling her capability and all the while knowing there was nowhere else to go. Taking her sister could jeopardise Katy's life for the sake of easing her own conscience.

'Leaving Katy at the orphanage is not an option. I have to do something.'

The excitement she'd felt coursing through her as she walked through the streets of London led her to believe there was another life out there waiting to be found. The fact she'd happened to be with an unsavoury character with no scruples, hoping to sell her off to further his own advancement, was now of no consequence. It hadn't happened and she remained safe, for the time being.

Katy leapt into her arms on sight.

"Lizzie," she yelled. "I thought I'd never see you again."

Katy didn't want to leave Lizzie's side and as the Mother Superior closed the door of the dormitory and the dim light faded to nothing, Katy crept across to Lizzie.

The girls talked long into the night, trying not to disturb the others. They needn't have concerned themselves, as the girls were in deep slumber from exhaustion. Lizzie told Katy in long slow whispers of her exploits in London. She told her if L R Davenport were ever to show himself at the orphanage again, she was to scream at the top of her voice and alert one of the nuns to come to her aid, but never, ever, was she to allow him near her, or worse, 'take her out'. She didn't think that would happen because he would likely be in jail. It was a simple warning, in case. Katy snuggled into Lizzie, a little scared, but intensely happy her sister had returned. When her eyes closed Lizzie lay beside her with a tormented soul.

'What if we do leave the orphanage? Where will we go? What will we do?' she thought.

Contented they would be strong for one another, Lizzie began to hatch a plan which would ultimately take her away from the orphanage and back to the streets of St Helens where she would seek the location of any surviving relatives and beg to be accommodated with them until she could find a job.

'Yes, that's what I'll do and I'll come back and take Katy away from this place where people are not nice.'

* * * * * *

Lizzie didn't have to wait too long until an opportunity came her way in the form of a letter from

Mary-Ann, who despite Lizzie's encounter with the dark side of life had returned to her duties. Concerned for her two sisters, Mary-Ann was keen to find a way to bring them back to their 'hometown'. She recognised the hand of fate when her employers required her presence for a journey up North to see relatives. St Helens had only been a short distance from their destination and Mary-Ann had been granted an afternoon off.

Packing herself a small picnic, she travelled the short distance by train and found herself in familiar territory. She went into local shops she remembered and made enquiries about lodgings with families. Calling in at the church she remembered, she found herself in the midst of mourners at a funeral. The coffin, with its entombed unfortunate sat on a long table in the centre of the aisle near the altar, waiting to be taken to its final resting place. The service seemed almost finished and Mary-Ann was tempted to leave before the assembly moved towards the back of the church.

Something rooted her to the spot. Kneeling down with her head bowed, she said a quick prayer and decided to stay until the cortege had passed. She felt aware when the coffin itself passed by, headed by the priest and altar servers. She kept her head low, resting her arms on the pew in front, trying to concentrate on the few prayers she knew off by heart. Becoming aware the procession had come to a standstill, she raised her head a little. As she did so, she felt a gentle tap on her shoulder. Shocked and believing her presence had caused a disturbance, she slowly looked up into the eyes of the old man she had known in her formative years at the bakery. Jack Dodd had been a customer of good standing within the community and someone kind and trusted amongst the locals. She stood up and Jack took her hand and squeezed it.

"My wife," he said, wiping a tear from his eye.

"I'm so sorry Mr Dodd. I didn't know," said Mary-Ann, holding her own tears back.

"Are you back in town? I heard you'd gone away?"

"No, I'm only here for the day."

"If you ever pass this way, come by and see me. I'd better go."

He squeezed her hand again and the procession moved on and out of the church doors, their conversation cut short by the very nature of the circumstances.

Mary-Ann, whilst sorry for the old man's loss wondered if the idea running through her mind would be possible. She knew Jack Dodd and his wife had been childless and he would now be on his own. Perhaps they could help each other. Perhaps the Lord had drawn her into his presence to produce the answer to the problem she sought to resolve, whilst helping to solve an old man's loneliness. It would be totally inappropriate to seek out Mr Dodd today, but Mary-Ann left the church with a lilt in her step and headed back towards town, to ask where Jack Dodd lived.

On her way back to her duties, she reflected how fortunate the whole scenario had been. How incredulous it was her employers had relatives local to her native town and how incredibly uncanny it had been for her to enter the church where she'd encountered a friendly face who might agree to her request. Of course, there was always the possibility he would reject her suggestion, but that was a problem for another day. For now, she knew exactly what to do. And so would Lizzie and Katy. She would write the letter tonight. The three of them might be disappointed, but at least they could be excited together, for the conceivable outcome.

Lizzie stared disbelievingly at the words scrawled in front of her. At first, she thought the letter had come to the wrong recipient, but no, it was definitely addressed to Lizzie Bradshaw. It was definitely Mary-Ann's distinctive handwriting and it was Mary-Ann's signature at the bottom of the letter.

'My Dearest Lizzie and Katy,

I have news for you both. You must understand it is only an idea at the moment and there's a possibility no good will come but I wish you to join in my excitement.'

The letter went on to explain the cause of Mary-Ann's excitement and how it came to be.

'I hope you are both well and find the news to your liking. I will be visiting my friend in the near future and will let you know the outcome.'

It was signed, *'Your loving sister, Mary-Ann'*

Lizzie continued to stare. She pushed the letter down into her sock until she could share the content with Katy later when she returned from school. She could hardly bear to work for the well of optimism which burned in her soul and she prayed with all her might the outcome would be the one they hoped for. Mary-Ann had been right to presume Lizzie would jump at the chance to be free from the orphanage and in the comparative affluent surroundings of Jack Dodd's abode. When the news was imparted to Katy later that day, the two girls could hardly contain themselves and great plans were made. They had to keep reminding themselves it might be a negative response from Mr Dodd, but for once they felt hope was on their side and so too would be the opportunity for a great new life together.

* * * * * *

CHAPTER SIXTEEN

A solemn, heart-rending scene ensued as Lizzie Bradshaw left the orphanage on 27 March 1883, leaving her beloved sister in the confines of the institution where they'd lived for over four and a half years. Hugs and tears were witnessed and shared by nuns and staff alike. 'The Irrepressible Lizzie', as she had become known, was unashamedly heartbroken. Katy tugged at Lizzie's clothes, screaming for her not to leave. She was suppressed and comforted by two members of the kitchen staff as she watched Lizzie step out into the courtyard and away on over to the gate where she was to be escorted to the station.

"I'll be back to see you as soon as I can," yelled Lizzie as she turned to wave to Katy one last time. Then she was gone. Katy's screams faded into the distance as they closed the orphanage doors.

* * * * * *

Mary-Ann's hopes for her sisters' future had not gone according to plan. Jack Dodd would not consider taking both girls, but was willing to employ Lizzie. Once again, the lives of three sisters were separated and torn apart. Lizzie had received good grounding from the orphanage for the role she was now to take on. She'd been learning housekeeping and her skills were now to be put to the test. The meek and mild Jack Dodd, turned out not to be quite as placid as his persona suggested. Katy was to remain distraught and became introverted whilst Mary-Ann, doubted the very foundation of her faith.

The next fourteen months was a trying time for the three girls. They missed each other and whilst Mary-Ann's relationship with Solomon Macavelly was beginning to blossom, she still hated the separation from her siblings. Jack Dodd was a hard task master and Lizzie's life in his house was a tormented one. At fourteen years of age, she was aware of something, though she knew not what. An uncomfortable presence descended if they were in the same room, conversation was stinted and Lizzie spent most of her time busying herself repetitively or retiring to her room. Jack Dodd's rules were strict and there was little time for her own pursuits outside the house. Therefore it became impossible to see Katy or Mary-Ann more than once every three or four months.

A year passed by and as the second year of Lizzie's departure dawned, she was acutely concerned about Katy's future. Jack Dodd still refused to take her in. Mary-Ann wasn't in a position to help and the two older girls communicated their concerns to each other in their letters.

On 5 May 1884, Katy Bradshaw left the orphanage in Wales for good. She felt nothing. No elation, no sadness, just an empty shell. The nuns at the orphanage had received word from L R

Davenport's wife that Katy was to go and live with her as her housemaid. She wrote she had become infirm and in her husband's absence, she was taking Katy in as her daughter, to help with household chores and as a nursemaid. Mary-Ann, as Katy's next of kin was informed. The news rippled waves of fear through Mary-Ann and Lizzie. They'd been assured by the authorities L R Davenport would be incarcerated for many years and safe in the knowledge she wasn't out on the street, they reluctantly accepted Katy's fate, promising each other they would visit her whenever they could.

* * * * * *

The letter arrived in Islington on 21 June 1884, two days after the ship sailed, carrying Katy along with twenty-seven other orphaned or poverty-stricken children to a life of probable servitude in the Canadian province of Quebec. Mary-Ann dropped it on the floor and screamed. When her employer found her, she was on her knees shaking from head to foot. The front of her bodice was soaked with the tears pouring off her chin and it was clear the contents of the envelope next to her on the floor were the cause. Her screams rang out and her anguish reached the ears of Solomon Macavelly who leapt into action to assist his beloved Mary-Ann whom he believed had been seriously injured. He cradled her in his arms until the tears came no more.

* * * * * *

Lizzie was on her way home with Jack Dodd's fresh loaf. It was a beautiful early summer morning.

Wild flowers shook their heads from side to side in the warm breeze on the grassy slopes. She felt elated to be out of the house and away from her employer on such a day, but in her heart was a sense of something else. She couldn't have imagined the pain which would engulf her when the news arrived. She skipped past the row of terraced cottages leading to the track which would take her back to her domain, a place she would never call home. As though a darkness had engulfed the summer, a feeling of pure dread filled her heart and she quickened her pace, certain there would be a downpour even though the cloudless sky remained blue.

Lizzie could hear voices coming from within the house and wondered who'd come calling to see Jack Dodd this early in the morning. She dropped the loaf in surprise when she saw the door open and Mary-Ann stood there. Retrieving the loaf she ran into Mary-Ann's arms, delighted beyond belief to see her, but knowing instantly there would not be a happy outcome. Her tears had started to fall as soon as she saw Mary-Ann's face.

"What's the matter? Something's the matter. Tell me. Tell me."

"Come in and sit down Lizzie. Something terrible's happened."

"Is it Katy? Where is she? Oh, what's happened Mary-Ann, tell me."

Jack Dodd sat in the corner, disenchanted with the whole scene and obviously annoyed his morning toast was delayed. Both girls ignored him.

Lizzie's agony could be heard two streets away. She was inconsolable, her body racked with heavy sobs while painful tears stung her eyes. The girls clung together, disbelieving what had happened to their young sister.

"But she's just a child. They can't do this to her. They can't do this to us. Why? Why have they sent her away? Who told them they had to send her away? Who had the right to let them do this?" Lizzie screamed.

Looking across at Jack Dodd's face, Mary-Ann manoeuvred Lizzie out of the back door and away down the entry to the lane, where Lizzie could vent her anger without aggravating the worsening situation inside the house.

"I can't stay here now," cried Lizzie. "I can't. I don't want to be here, I don't like him. I want to come with you. Anywhere. We have to go find Katy. I want to go and find her."

The pain was excruciating, the injustice eating her away and the knowledge she had lost her beloved sibling was too much for Lizzie to bear.

She released herself from Mary-Ann's embrace and ran back to the house. She ran up the stairs, collected her few belongings, threw them into her sack, pulled the string and ran back down. She found Jack Dodd in the kitchen cutting a slice of bread from the loaf.

"I'm leaving Mr Dodd. I can't work for you any more. You'll have to find someone else."

She turned and walked out of the kitchen door and back into the arms of her sister.

"Lizzie, what have you done?" asked Mary-Ann,

"I'm leaving. I'm going to find Katy. I don't belong here and I don't work here any more."

"You can't find Katy", pleaded Mary-Ann. "She's on a ship on her way to Canada. It left two days ago. It's in the middle of the ocean. There's no way to get to her."

"I'll get a ship too."

"You can't. They won't let you on. You haven't got enough money."

Lizzie began crying again, "But why have they taken her? Why? Why? Why have they taken Katy away?"

"I don't know. Solomon says they've taken a lot of children. Hundreds."

"Why didn't they take me too?"

"Because you weren't in the orphanage, most likely", said Mary-Ann gently.

"But I left her there," sobbed Lizzie. "It's my fault. I left her there. I didn't want to. I wanted her to come with me, but Mr Dodd wouldn't let her come. There was nowhere else for her to go. I had to leave her there. It's my fault."

Lizzie's grief overwhelmed her and she sank to the ground with her head in her hands. Never, throughout the traumas of her short life, had she encountered the torturous sorrow she felt at this moment. Mary-Ann sank down beside her. They wrapped their arms around each other and cried until exhaustion ceased the flow of tears. They would carry the impact of this trauma for the rest of their lives.

Jack Dodd witnessed the scene from his front window. Mary-Ann had told him the reason for her visit and whilst he'd been annoyed at the inconvenience to himself, he now felt a similar sorrow he'd felt when his wife died. He walked across the room to the drawer and took out an old tin box. He took out some of the contents and put them into a small pouch, walked outside to where the girls still sat and threw it down at the side of Lizzie. Without a word, he turned and hurried back inside the house, slamming the door behind him.

* * * * * *

CHAPTER SEVENTEEN

A pair of tall dark grey metallic urns with spiral bay trees winding up towards the ancient lantern, flanked the door. A cobblestone path and stepping stones interspersed with huge white marble boulders littered the grassy area. A couple watching the coloured long-boats passing by, sat at a round rustic wooden table and benches. A large rottweiler lay looking out between the laths of the fence where a bowl of water had been strategically placed for stray animals. Chickens clucked, lambs bleated, birds sang and the sun shone as the light breeze carried the sound of the church bells up and away into the atmosphere. A spaniel ran up the eight stone steps leading to the top of the bridge, underneath which the barges meandered on their way past the pretty villages and pubs lining the side of the canal.

Lizzie purveyed the scene before her eyes with astonishment. Surely she couldn't be at the correct address. It looked far too grand, but then looking back, she had thought the address sounded grand when she received her reply.

Her advertisement had read:

"Young girl, strong and active, wishes daily employment as housemaid."

Please reply to Lizzie Bradshaw at 25 Onslow Lane, St Helens.

At almost fifteen years of age, she was quite an eligible catch for this type of work, having been trained in the stringent ways of orphanage housekeeping. Of course, she'd had a little help to write the advertisement.

The pouch Jack Dodd had given her afforded her payment for lodgings in St Helens near to her roots and it was there she currently resided with a family who knew her from the bakery and could vouch for her good-humoured nature and honesty. She had enough money to pay for the few things she needed and considered it a lucky break to have found somewhere so quickly. She'd only been out on the streets a couple of nights. It was still summertime and the nights didn't go so cold. Still grieving over Katy, Lizzie found it almost impossible to speak with people, preferring to be alone with her thoughts. It was hunger which forced her hand. She needed sustenance and to gain that luxury, she would have to speak to someone. With help from one of the shopkeepers who remembered her, they constructed the short advertisement which was put into the window. A chance stop by the driver of a carriage heading towards Widnes, his quick observation of the advertisement and a family desperate for a decent housekeeper, brought the reply back to the shop one week later.

As Lizzie stood looking up the steps, she hoped she was clean and tidy enough to secure the position she now knew she wanted with all her heart.

She had written to Mary-Ann, whom she knew would be praying for her to be successful. Armed with the knowledge she had Mary-Ann's support, her confidence bounded back. She climbed the steps and pressed the button on the large doorbell, alerting the occupants of her arrival.

Lizzie felt she'd been transported to another world. The hallway she stood in was vast. A dark highly polished timber frieze flanked the wall to the right, above which hung enormous portraits in ornate gold frames against a pale gold coloured wall. Huge Romanesque columns supported the ceiling which stretched so high Lizzie had to tip her head backwards to see it. Two huge columns to her left stood between a staircase going up and one going down. The black and white tiled floor led to a large arched opening some distance away, beyond which she could see another space of equal proportions. Half way along the hall her attention was caught by a large chandelier suspended from the high ceiling which provided light from some ten or twelve large glass domes. The whole picture before her was breathtaking. So much so, she'd barely noticed who'd opened the door for her to enter. A small cough to her right reminded her she was not in the space alone. She tore her eyes away from their feast and looked into the eyes of a tall lady with black coarse wavy hair, displaying a thin, defined bone structure and an extremely upright posture. Lizzie remonstrated she must be some sort of aristocracy to own such a beautiful house. Her romantic notion was quashed when she realised the lady wore a pinafore and was probably one of the servants, just like she hoped to be. This in mind, she instantly felt a little more at ease and smiled at the stranger beside her, offering her hand. The lady took it and shook it vigorously.

"Don't worry. I felt just like you when I first came. Welcome to Maddingley," she said. "Follow me. The master is waiting for you."

Lizzie put one foot in front of the other and tried to keep up.

"I'm Hilary. Hilary Hunter, I'm the head housekeeper," said the lady turning round to make sure Lizzie was following.

Lizzie caught a faint smile as Hilary turned left down a long corridor and up a flight of stairs, equally as impressive as the one in the hall. She noticed another much smaller staircase leading down and young as she was, her astute nature told her that was the servants' staircase and one which she hoped with all her heart she'd be treading before the end of the day.

Hilary stopped outside a large door and knocked. She listened for a moment, then opened the door and ushered Lizzie through. Lizzie had to be careful not to let her mouth drop too far and not to stare either. It was rude to stare. But, stare was what she wanted to do when her eyes fell onto the man sat on the other side of the desk in front of her. She almost felt she should courtesy. He, like the lady who'd opened the door to her, seemed strangely, predominantly upright, almost bending backwards on the chair. He had thick black hair, greying a little at the temples, combed back off his face in a kind of quiff. He and Hilary shared a quick exchange and

Hilary left, leaving Lizzie not knowing quite what to do in the presence of someone she knew without doubt was aristocracy. She became acutely aware of her own demeanour and tried to straighten up a little and brushing down her skirt, she stepped forward as she'd been asked to do. Feeling very much a small child again, she attempted a smile.

"It's Lizzie isn't it?" said the man smiling back at her.

"Yes Sir," Lizzie replied, feeling a little more relaxed.

"I believe in fate," the man said. "Do you know what fate is, young lady?"

"I think so Sir," Lizzie answered, wondering where this was leading.

"It's our destiny, a chance, a determining force. I believe you've been brought to our attention for some reason. The consequence of your advertisement is what's brought you to us. Can you work hard? Have you any experience of housekeeping?"

"Yes Sir. I was brought up in an orphanage where they taught us housekeeping and yes, I can work hard."

"Right then. I'll give you one month to prove yourself. Hilary will sort you out. I expect nothing less than your best. Don't let me down."

"Thank you Sir, I won't."

Lizzie's heart was turning somersaults. All she could think of was writing to Mary-Ann and letting her know she'd got the job. She wanted to tell her all about the place. She was sure Mary-Ann's appointment wasn't as grand as this. Amidst her joy, was the interminable sadness she couldn't tell Katy and, for a few moments, her excitement evaporated.

The man behind the desk rang a bell and within seconds the door opened and Hilary entered.

"Show her the ropes Hilary," was all he said. Hilary once again ushered Lizzie along and out of the room,

"So, he hired you?"

"Yes, I think so?" said Lizzie tentatively.

"Come on then, we'll get you settled."

* * * * * *

CHAPTER EIGHTEEN

Lizzie couldn't possibly have predicted her future, but if she could, she would have chosen Maddingley Hall as her permanent home. She had the best time of her life. Her character shone out through bad times and good and despite a bad start in life, she displayed a bright and sunny disposition and the constitution of an ox. There were twenty-two staff at Maddingley Hall and together they ran the place with precision. Lizzie had been just the person they needed to replace one of the older members of staff, who, due to ill health had retired to the country. They wanted young blood, somebody who would cherish the old traditions so desired by the owners and it was felt they'd found that quality in Lizzie Bradshaw.

Lizzie had now turned fifteen and was heading towards her first Christmas at Maddingley Hall. It was one she would never forget and despite the long hard hours of work, she was determined to enjoy every second of every aspect the house could offer. She wished with all her heart her family could be with her. Never a day went by she didn't grieve over the loss of Katy and wonder where she was and how she could contact her, nor did she ever stop thinking about Mary-Ann and what might be going on in her life. She wrote to Mary-Ann at least once a week, sometimes more if there were something exciting to tell and there were always lots of exciting things to tell about this house and the people who lived here.

Christmas invitations were sent out about six weeks beforehand and Lizzie had been asked to help with decorating the cards for which she had an aptitude. There was an air of optimism and excitement throughout the house and Lizzie still couldn't believe she was a part of something so wonderful. Looking back on her years spent in the workhouse and the orphanage, she considered herself amongst the more fortunate of young girls and never for a moment forgot her meagre beginnings nor the lessons learned during her childhood. She would remind herself from time to time that as easily as things start, so can they finish and with that thought in mind, she made the most of the wonderful time she was having, before at any moment, it was swept from under her.

The days leading up to Christmas were wonderful. She knew not what her future held but would use the skills learned in this household for the better, no matter what life might throw her way… and with this in mind, she soaked up every facet of Christmas life in a Victorian stately home, stored every conceivable piece of it in her memory and threw herself into it heart and soul. As with other eras of her life so far, Lizzie became a part of the household they never imagined could have existed without her.

A most exciting time at Maddingley was 'Christmas Pudding Day', the day head cook mixed together all her pre-prepared ingredients. This was done in the servants' hall on the long refectory table. Dinner was eaten first and there was excited chatter about the preparation and mixing of the puddings. Lizzie had been hired as a housemaid, but her skills were put to use in every aspect of life at Maddingley Hall and none did she enjoy more than life in the kitchen, watching at first, then slowly, bit by bit, helping cook. At first cook gave her menial tasks but over time, she progressed to preparation of meals for the table. During this, her first Christmas, she was shown how to peel the vegetables in preparation for cook's bouillon, a task which she thoroughly enjoyed. Lizzie's love of the simple aspects of life became her trademark. She didn't aspire to be great, although everyone perceived her talents were unlimited. She didn't desire an affluent lifestyle and was simply content to savour the simple joys of everyday life, no matter where that might be. The only thing she desired to have more than anything was a family. Maddingley provided her with the nearest she could manage to achieving that desire and she couldn't believe the God she'd yelled at for taking her family away from her one by one, had given her this opportunity for happiness. Katy remained a part of her heart and soul every day as did Mary-Ann, but life was teaching her some things were impossible to change. She didn't have to like it, but acceptance seemed the only way forward.

The aristocratic owners of Maddingley Hall spared no expense in their preparations for the Christmas festivities. Two Norwegian Spruce Christmas trees arrived the day before Christmas Eve and fresh holly and mistletoe were collected from the woods in the grounds of the hall and liberally draped throughout the house. The servants' hall was decorated with some of the foliage and the buzz of the house, mingled with delicious smells from the kitchen, provided Lizzie with a sense of belonging. Her most wonderful moments were when the postman brought letters from Mary-Ann. She had sent her a letter for Christmas, enclosing her attempt at sketching the Christmas tree and was delighted when on Christmas Eve, her name was shouted out to receive post. Tucking it into her pinafore, she couldn't wait to devour every word when she was alone.

Following a festive Christmas Eve with her colleagues and all her work for the evening complete,

Lizzie could hardly wait to read the contents of her letter from Mary-Ann.

My dearest Lizzie

First of all I should like to wish you great joy in your new life and especially at Christmastime. I received your letter and sketch which I shall treasure. I have some news which I hope you will find exciting and share in my elation. I suspect you knew it would eventually happen. I am going to become engaged to Solomon on Christmas Day. I wish with all my heart you could be with me to celebrate. He asked me to marry him only three days ago, so I hope this news reaches you before the day. Of course we will have to leave our jobs at the house when we marry as married couples are not allowed to work here. So, my life will take a turn at some point. I knew it would be him from the day I laid eyes on him. I love him deeply and I know he feels the same. I'm happier than I've ever been and I hope you'll share my happiness.

Enjoy every moment and share with me on Christmas Day thoughts of our beloved sister Katy whose memory is embedded in our hearts without question forever.

Your loving sister, Mary-Ann

Tears sprang to Lizzie's eyes as she read the content of Mary-Ann's letter over and over. She hoped with all her heart she would be given leave of absence for the wedding, whenever that might be and in fact was planning to ask if she could be allowed to go and see her sister long before the wedding, for which, as yet, there was no date. Mixed emotions prevented Lizzie from closing her eyes as she turned over the information in her mind until the excitement of the next day and the prospect of her sister's pending wedding took its toll and gave way to the sleep she so badly needed.

Christmas proved to be everything Lizzie hoped for. On Boxing Day, the servants were invited upstairs to the drawing room after dinner and were each handed a gift. Back downstairs in their own dining hall, they discovered the further generosity of their employers as a barrel of ale was rolled in and a crate of wine placed on the table. There was dancing and merriment after their chores were complete and the servants of Maddingley Hall went to bed fulfilled, happy and ever so tired.

* * * * * *

CHAPTER NINETEEN

Mary-Ann's wedding to Solomon Macavelly was a simple affair. Lizzie was Mary-Ann's only family in attendance. Solomon's parents had done what they could to make the day special and Solomon had put some hard earned money to one side to ensure he gave Mary-Ann the special day he felt she deserved. The service was held in a local church and Solomon's parents prepared the wedding breakfast at their home in London's East End. They were to spend their wedding night in his parents' spare bedroom. Provision was made for Lizzie in the front parlour. The newlyweds had relinquished their posts at the house in Islington, despite requests for their employers to abolish the old rule of no married couples. Their immediate plan was to seek alternative employment and for the time being live with Solomon's parents. Lizzie was perceptive and knew this arrangement couldn't continue for long. She hoped and prayed the pair would quickly find suitable posts and hopefully then, affordable lodgings on their own.

* * * * * *

Lizzie continued to learn new skills and was fast approaching her nineteenth birthday when she heard some disturbing news. Rumours and gossip were rife in the servants' hall and for the most part she took it with a pinch of salt, but this was different. There was fear in the whispers, fear a significant change was looming. The house had many rooms containing beautiful furniture, furnishings, mirrors, portraits, and foreign artefacts from

115

their employer's travels. As a housemaid, Lizzie was aware of her surroundings and the stunning environment she worked and lived in. At first, she didn't take too much notice, assuming the missing items had been moved to another room to be replaced with something new. The spaces the missing items left became a constant reminder of the chatter in the dining hall and Lizzie began to wonder if there was more truth to the rumours than everyone had first realised. She questioned senior staff on numerous occasions but their silence was deafening and Lizzie began to suspect the worst. Another year rolled by and the servants, by now, realised their time in this wonderful old house might be coming to an end as it became evident the rooms were emptying quickly.

The day dawned when they were called upstairs to a meeting. Each of them knew deep in their heart the outcome would be life changing and their fears were founded.

"I'll keep this brief. I'm sure you are already aware there have been some changes in the house recently. We're really sorry to inform you, we are closing Maddingley Hall. A skeleton staff will be retained. They already know who they are. The rest of you are hereby given one month's notice to leave your employment at Maddingley. You may seek alternative employment and leave will be granted for the purposes of interviews. We are sorry for the inconvenience this will cause. We've done everything possible to prevent this outcome. My thanks extend to each and every one of you for your years of service."

Lizzie was devastated beyond belief. Her life as she knew it was over. Once again, she asked herself the same question.

'Where will I go? There is nowhere and no-one. I can't ask Mary-Ann. They had to leave his parents' home and seek temporary lodgings. They're living with another family in one room above a shop.'

Housing conditions were at an all time low and people found themselves living in overcrowded spaces where sanitary conditions were appalling, job prospects almost non-existent and people suffered terribly. Lizzie hadn't had to worry about that for years but the horrors of her past were back to haunt her.

'Will I finish up back in a workhouse?' The thought made her sick to her stomach. She ached to be able to sit with her sisters and pour her heart out. The surmounting problem and the pain of separation from her family caused her to lose control. Cook found her with her head buried in her hands. Momentarily cook dropped the barrier of hierarchy between them and cradled her, stroking her hair and trying to comfort the sobbing Lizzie, the one to whom they all looked for solace themselves.

From that day on, the house took on a sombre mood. The staff no longer went about their duties with a lilt and a smile, instead looking worried. Chatter around the dining table was consistent with that mood and constituted melancholy as no-one knew how the consequences of this most dire news would impact on their lives. Lizzie wrote to Mary-Ann, not wishing to burden her with the worry, but more to inform and the day of leaving came all too soon. All but cook, the butler, the groundsman and the two longest serving members of the house were to stay. They congregated outside the front door with their belongings, where they'd been asked to wait for their wages. Mr Maddingley himself was there to distribute their finishing pay. He handed them their envelope and shook hands with each of them. His speech had been short and it was clear to everyone he too was distressed beyond belief at the circumstances which forced him to release the staff who had served him and his family well for many years. Maddingley Hall would be closed within the next couple of months. The building would remain empty and the Maddingleys were to take up a small residence in the South of England. It was a sorry line of people who walked down the drive towards the gates they'd all arrived at many years before. There were plenty of hugs and wet faces. No-one looked back.

Lizzie stood on the platform peering into the distance as the train came into view. The train which was going to take her away from the life she'd loved and force her to step back in time to relive a life already lived. She sat on a torn seat staring out of the window as the train sped along, not really looking at anything, just staring into a void. She was better equipped to cope with the smoky atmosphere of the carriage than the vacuum of despair which enveloped and threatened to choke her. Her thoughts couldn't focus on anything positive. She looked back on her life, her losses and her sadness engulfed her.

The train was nearing the station where she was to disembark. She considered staying on. There was nothing to get off for. There was no-one here, no-one to comfort her, no-one and nothing. Struggling to stand, she made her way slowly to the doors, swaying with the motion of the train as it chugged along, finally grinding to a halt at the station platform. As she was stepping off the train, she felt a tap on her shoulder.

"Is this yours Miss?"

She turned and looked up into the bluest eyes she'd ever seen. A man stood there with her bag in his hands. She wanted to stare.

"Oh, yes. Thank you. I don't know what I was thinking. Thank you very much."

She didn't want to get off. She didn't want to leave the stranger who'd handed her bag to her. Despondency hung over her as she forced herself to put her foot down onto the platform and move the other foot in front. She turned round again, but the man had gone.

Lizzie forced herself to move along the platform and handed her ticket in. Her bag was heavy and part of her wished she'd left it on the train. It was mid afternoon and her main priority was to find somewhere to stay for the night. There were a number of public houses offering rooms and she'd have to enquire if there were any vacancies. She had enough money for one or two nights. Without any particular reason for doing so, she found herself walking in the direction of the bakery.

'Familiar territory,' she told herself.

The shop window as she knew it had disappeared. There were no sweet treats on trays in the window and she couldn't see beyond the net curtain which now hung there, completely obscuring the view. She walked on past and turned left at the next corner. There had been a public house down that road which sometimes let rooms for the night. Lizzie wasn't at all shy but the thoughts of walking into a public house alone sent shivers down her spine.

'I've no alternative,' she mused, 'I'll have to.' The response from the publican was negative and the following two yielded the same discouraging reply.

Lizzie was weary and frightened, hoping she wouldn't have to sleep on the streets. She knew there were more alehouses to try but there was another option, one which was becoming more appealing. She headed back towards the bakery and knocked on the door which used to bring customers into their happy domain. She wondered if they would remember the family they evicted and give her sanctuary for one or two nights while she looked for work and lodgings. Momentarily her mind drifted into a dark place. She felt completely and utterly alone in the world and almost wished she was back in the orphanage, not stuck on the streets of St Helens with her worldly goods packed into one small bag and looking for somewhere to stay.

The door opened slightly. It looked to be quite dark inside what was once a thriving hub of the community. The person at the other side of the door asked, "Who are you? What do you want?"

Clearly a child's voice, Lizzie asked, "Are your parents at home? My name's Lizzie Bradshaw. Can I speak to someone please?"

"I'll fetch my mother," said the voice as the front door banged shut.

Lizzie stood and waited for the door to re-open. It didn't. She knocked again and waited. A few seconds later, the door opened wide.

"Lizzie Bradshaw? The Bradshaws who used to live here?"

"Yes," said Lizzie, "We lived here and my grandfather Ciaran MacSweeney ran the bakery."

"Come on in. What brings you back to St Helens?"

Lizzie stepped inside and was surprisingly given the welcome she'd been hoping for but not expecting.

"I'm really sorry to come knocking like this but I don't know where else to go".

Somebody fetched Lizzie a cup of tea and a thin slice of cake which she devoured hungrily and began her story. Even to Lizzie's ears it sounded incredulous so much had happened to one family.

When she'd finished her story, with an audience of six, the lady who introduced herself as Hilda Marshall, told Lizzie she could put her up until the end of the week. That was three nights away. Lizzie was overwhelmed by her generosity and glad she'd had enough courage to knock on the door. She would be sleeping on the floor in the parlour. An old dog's blanket would be her pillow but she was elated. She'd be happy to give Mrs Marshall some of her wages and would spend the three days looking for work.

'Surely someone will have work for me around here? Won't they?'

By the end of day two, Lizzie was beginning to think her optimism had been foolhardy. Her candid approach everywhere she enquired about work was met with a mocking sarcasm. The obnoxious alternative would be despicable, she couldn't bear to go back there, not alone, not without Mary-Ann or Katy.

Lizzie woke up on the last morning of her stay. Despite lying on the cold floor with her head on the dog's blanket and feeling she could sleep for hours, she sprang into action. Splashing her face with cold water she felt herself come alive. She knew today was the day she had to sort out her life. Serving herself a couple of scoops of the porridge Mrs Marshall had left in the pan she hungrily gobbled them down, threw on her coat and left the old bakery. She'd exhausted enquiries for work at local shops, she'd knocked door to door for lodgings and come up with nothing. Wishing with all her heart Mary-Ann could be with her, she ran back to the bakery. Somewhere in the back of her mind was an idea. The last letter she'd had from Mary-Ann was tucked down inside her bag. She retrieved the letter and shouting to Mrs Marshall she would collect her bag later, she ran back out of the bakery and sat on the front step to devour the contents of the letter once more. There it was – laundry. The word she'd been trying to remember. Mary-Ann had some work in a laundry.

'I wonder if there's a laundry somewhere? If I could get some work there, I'll be able to pay for lodgings.'

With a spring in her step and optimism in her soul, Lizzie set off on her quest, en route to where, she didn't know. She asked herself why she hadn't thought of it before. She scoured all the shop windows again, in the hopes someone had posted an advertisement. She didn't mind what or where, but today had to be the day or she was out on the street.

'I could try the coal pit,' she thought. 'Women sometimes get jobs there.'

Then, it came to her. She chastised herself for not having thought of it before. It would be a long walk and the distance between the two would take hours. There were factories nearby, a fairly long way from where she was now. She ran back to the bakery and collected her bag.

Mrs Marshall was more than surprised to see Lizzie back so soon.

"What's up Lizzie? Why are you back again?" she enquired in a motherly tone.

Lizzie explained.

"Good luck. Let me know when you get settled. I'm really sorry I can't let you stay longer. There just won't be room when my brother and his family arrive. We'll be overcrowded as it is."

Lizzie reached deep into her skirt pocket and pulled out the coins she had left. She offered them to Mrs Marshall who told Lizzie to keep them.

"Just in case," she said smiling at Lizzie.

Lizzie's eyes moistened as she crossed the space between them and hugged Mrs Marshall.

"Thanks for everything. I'll let you know."

Lizzie picked up her bag and left. She turned and saw Mrs Marshall waving. She waved back, turned the corner and set off at a steady pace towards the nearest factory. It took her a good hour and a half to reach the gates. She wasn't sure she knew what they manufactured there. Somewhere in the back of her mind, she thought it might be medicines. She thought the building looked quite daunting. Looking up at the sky she guessed it was coming up for lunchtime.

'Maybe I'll see some of the workers coming out for lunch.'

Before the thought had fully formed, she heard a loud ringing coming from within the walls of the building in front of her. A stream of people surged out of the building, some running, some sauntering, chattering to the person next to them. She was encouraged to see both men and women coming out of the building.

'Shall I stop one of the girls and ask them?' she thought, a little scared.

'I don't look my best. Don't want them thinking I'm a vagrant, though technically I probably am.'

She didn't have to think about it very long as a group of girls approached the gates where she was standing. Before she knew what her mouth was going to do, she stepped out as the girls approached. She directed her question to the one she thought would be most disposed to speak back.

"Excuse me, could you tell me where to go to enquire about a job please?"

"Through the gates, across the courtyard and ring the bell on those doors we just came out of," the girl said, pointing behind her. "You might just be lucky if you go now. Good luck."

The girls hadn't really stopped and Lizzie shouted "Thank you," after them. The girl who'd spoken raised her arm and carried on chattering with her friends.

Lizzie straightened her skirt, tried to tidy her hair, lifted each leg, spat on her shoes and rubbed them clean with the bottom of her skirt. Feeling she could do no more, she passed through the open gateway. Some stragglers were still coming out, a few young men amongst them. She almost choked when one of them spoke to her.

"You still carrying that bag around?"

It was the man off the train, the one she hadn't wanted to take her eyes off. 'My, he's handsome,' she thought. She smiled at him, it was all she could do, and carried on walking towards the doors ahead of her. Ringing the large doorbell brought a man in a tired looking suit.

"Yes dear, what can I do for you?"

"I'm looking for work please."

"You'd better come with me then young lady. I don't know if they're taking on, but it won't hurt to ask."

He seemed a kindly man and she instantly liked him. She hoped there would be something she could do here and offered up a quick prayer.

'Please God, please let there be a job for me here and please let me find somewhere to live too, if you could, that is.'

* * * * * *

CHAPTER TWENTY

Lizzie told her prospective employer about her work at the orphanage and Maddingley Hall and he listened intently.

"You can start straightaway. Can you stay for the afternoon?"

"Yes please," replied Lizzie, hardly daring to believe she'd got the job.

"How far away do you live? Will you be able to get here on time in a morning?"

Lizzie decided to tell him the truth.

"I have nowhere to live. I needed to get a job before I could look for lodgings."

God answered the second half of her prayer too. The man gave her an address.

"Go to that address and knock on the door. Tell them I've sent you. There'll be somewhere there for you. It might not be much good, but it'll do 'til you get on your feet lass," he said.

"Don't you go getting yourself pregnant! That's why there's always jobs going here. All you young ladies finish up with babies."

"I won't Sir," Lizzie replied, wondering if she really knew *how* to get pregnant.

Lizzie wanted to hug him. Instead she simply replied, "Thank you."

The man had been right. The place wasn't up to much. Conditions were appalling and overcrowded but Lizzie was accepted into the fold and shown her sleeping arrangements.

'At least I have somewhere for the time being,' she thought, pleased with the day's outcome. Most of the girls seemed nice enough. One or two cast her a side glance without speaking but on the whole, she thought she'd done well.

Work began at six o'clock every morning including Saturday. She would have Saturday afternoons and Sundays to herself. Lizzie began to feel she'd landed on her feet. Work at the factory was arduous but no more than other work she'd done. She interacted well with her colleagues, did her job well and once again, made a huge impact on those around her. Lizzie had been 'in training' during the first week, sorting bottles and boxes into which someone else would deposit the products. She'd been having lunch with a couple of other girls who started around the same time and in the evenings the girls took turns preparing something to eat.

At almost twenty years of age, Lizzie had developed into a stunningly beautiful young woman. Her black hair had thickened and hung in long ringlet type curls around her shoulders, except when she was working and forced to wear a mob cap. She had perfectly structured facial features with high cheekbones, stunning eyes and an enigmatic smile. Her demeanour was dignified and gracious and hadn't escaped the notice of many of the young men at the factory and in particular, the man she'd met on the train, Arthur Longton. It was during Lizzie's second week at the medicine factory when she bumped into him again. It wasn't an accident, he'd been looking for her. When he found her, she felt she looked a lot better than she had the last time they'd met. There had been an instant chemistry between them and Lizzie wondered if being 'in love' felt like this. She knew she'd never felt this way about anyone before and was delighted when Arthur Longton asked if he could walk her home. She accepted and their relationship began.

There was much joviality amongst the girls that night. They found it difficult to comprehend a pretty girl of Lizzie's age hadn't experienced feelings like this before and Lizzie became the brunt of giggling and much taunting. She'd had no-one to talk to of such things. Her mother and grandmother had died when she was very young and the nuns at the orphanage hadn't discussed anything of that nature. Katy had been too young and Mary-Ann had left for Islington so there'd been no talk of the subject within Lizzie's earshot. Not until she moved in with the girls, and she was too embarrassed to tell them she didn't understand their banter.

The day she'd had her first period at the orphanage, she thought she was dying. She'd told one of the older nuns she was bleeding and very sick. Lizzie had been told all females had to suffer this burden once each month and there was nothing she could do about it except use rags until the bleeding stopped. There had been no explanation about why and Lizzie was none the wiser. The subject had never reared its head again. Until now. Slowly, the truth was dawning on her. She would have to make sure it never happened to her.

'How on earth would I cope with a baby when I've no money and nowhere of my own to live. No, I'm definitely not having sex with a man if that's how you get a baby. Not a chance. But ..... I do like Arthur Longton. I wonder what having sex with him would be like.'

She'd heard the girls talking enough to know men looked different to women and it all seemed to be the normal thing to talk about and do.

'But I don't want babies. How would I look after them? No, it definitely won't be happening to me. I wonder if I only did it once, would that make me have a baby? The girls say all the boys want to do it and if you won't let them, they don't like you any more. I don't want Arthur Longton not to like me. Maybe I'll do it just once, if he wants me to. He hasn't asked me to yet though. Maybe he doesn't like me enough.'

Lizzie didn't want to think about it any more. It seemed more trouble than it was worth. She'd forget all about it until someone asked her to. Nonetheless her sleep was troubled that night. Her mind wandered back to the streets of London and the uneasy feeling she'd had when she was with L R Davenport.

'Could that have been what he wanted to do?' she thought.

Astute in every other aspect of life and perceptive in many ways, Lizzie was not yet street wise and certainly not au fait with the ways of the world. She would just enjoy being in Arthur Longton's company and hope the situation didn't arise. Inevitably, the situation did arise and sooner than Lizzie thought.

Their courtship gathered momentum. He was a hard working fellow, polite, well groomed and Lizzie felt totally at ease in his presence. She had felt it when she saw him on the train and the feeling hadn't left her.

'Am I in love?' she kept asking herself. 'Is this what it feels like? To want to be with someone all the time? How strange that he works at the same place I do.'

Her romantic inclinations towards Arthur Longton seemed to dominate her days. She couldn't wait for lunchtime when they'd walk out together. There was a small park not too far from the factory. Most of the courting couples made their way there to sit on the benches and eat their sandwiches. Lizzie seldom had sandwiches but Arthur shared his. They talked and laughed and she found herself unable to think about anything but him. She began paying particular attention to her appearance. She watched the girls putting powder and rouge on their faces and borrowed some to try. Looking in an old hand-held mirror, she could see a different reflection looking back at her and she liked what she saw.

The factory was moving into a new phase of 'outings' and Arthur asked Lizzie to accompany him on the next charabanc trip which was taking the workforce to Blackpool for the day. To Lizzie, this was a dream come true and of course agreed to go with him. Never in her wildest imagination, would she have thought this could be happening. Her heart was bursting with love for this man in whose company she felt truly alive. He was taking some of the pain of the past away and encouraging her to look forward instead of back. He complimented her appearance and made her feel like a lady. He was gentle, kind and loving. When he took her in his arms he was tender and when his lips sought hers, she melted into a delicious consciousness she never wanted to end. For the first time in her life, Lizzie was deliriously happy.

The day of the trip arrived. Lizzie borrowed a dress from one of the other girls which accentuated her sylph-like figure to perfection. After brushing her cheeks with powder and dabbing a little rouge on her lips, she felt a million dollars. A couple of the other girls were also going on the trip and the three girls walked to the factory gates together, causing quite a stir amongst the young male population. Arthur was waiting at the gate and took Lizzie in his arms. The charabanc was waiting and they all climbed aboard and took their seats. The day proved to be an unforgettable one. Lizzie and Arthur had a wonderful day walking along the promenade. The weather was clement and the sun shone all day. They paddled in the sea and laughed till they cried. Arthur was attentive and loving and her head was in a whirl about this wonderful man she'd met by chance on a train.

On the way home, Lizzie sat with her head on Arthur's shoulder, their hands clasped. He moved slightly and nuzzled into her neck. Moving his mouth up towards her ear, he whispered, 'Will you come home with me tonight?' It took Lizzie a moment to sift through the question to the hidden meaning and then she froze.

'Oh God, no. This is it. This is where it could all go wrong. He wants to do it. Do I want to? Do I say yes and risk having a baby or do I say no and risk losing him? Which would I rather do?'

Lizzie knew she didn't want to live without him in her life. She knew there was a slight chance there could be a baby, but also a chance there might not. Without consciously deciding one way or the other, she nodded her head. He buried his face into her neck and his hand tightened around hers.

'You don't have to, if you don't want to,' Arthur said, uncertainly.

Lizzie did want to. She wanted to more than anything she'd ever wanted in her life before. She wanted to feel what it was like. She wanted to be with this man for the rest of her life, no matter what. She'd thought when it came around to him asking, it would repulse her, but it didn't. After the initial shock, she felt excitement, anticipation.

'I want to make love with Arthur Longton. I do want to. I do.'

* * * * * *

Lizzie was never to truly know what prevented her losing her virginity to Arthur Longton. A change in his attitude was a contributing factor. The adorable soft-hearted man she knew and had come to love deeply, to the point of giving herself up freely to his amorous attempts, had suddenly lost control, becoming agitated and angry. The wonderful experience the girls had described hadn't manifested for Lizzie. The man she had faced, wanting to lie with and feel his hard body against her soft flesh, became someone to fear. Anger burned in his eyes and, quickly evaluating her intuition she could sense violence in his manner. Feeling alone, vulnerable and frightened, she acted upon her instincts and grabbing some already discarded clothes, she ran. Terrified of him giving chase and slamming the door behind her, she ran like the wind and for the second time in her life, straight into the arms of a policeman. He had the situation summed up in seconds and pushed Lizzie for information on the perpetrator of her anxiety. Lizzie, fearing for her life, wouldn't disclose Arthur Longton's name. She knew she'd had a lucky escape. Instinctively she had known her fate, had she stayed. In an instant, she knew she wouldn't return to the factory. Her life was about to take another twist of fate.

* * * * * *

Forlorn and entirely discouraged about men, Lizzie remained in bed the next morning, telling her housemates she felt poorly and wouldn't be going to work. She tried to eradicate the memory of Arthur's abrasive behaviour and terminate the carnal thoughts which had occupied her mind for weeks. Determined she would not return to the factory to face him or any sneering jibes which may have ensued from his lies, as soon as the girls left for work, Lizzie jumped out of bed. She prepared herself for one last attempt at finding somewhere to live before she delivered herself back into the fires of hell.

Lizzie packed her few belongings, threw cold water over her face and scribbled a few words on the inside of a discarded cigarette packet. Propping the message up on the mantelpiece, she cast one last glance at her surroundings and with an impartial toss of her head and a phlegmatic mood in her heart, she closed the door on another chapter in her life.

* * * * * *

CHAPTER TWENTY-ONE

Daunting memories of other large buildings flooded Lizzie's head as she stared at the factory towering in front of her. She'd heard tell of this workplace and wondered many times if she should have come here first, believing her dignity might have remained intact. She sat down on a low wall which ran around the whole compound. She felt the air change and watched the sky darken. She summoned up the strength to go forward and seconds later, in an almost tropical rainstorm, Lizzie ran through the main gate towards the front entrance of the factory. Her thin dress clung to her legs, strands of hair whipped up by the sudden wind, stuck to her cheeks with water dripping from the ends of her curls, tightening, the wetter they became.

A bedraggled young woman dripping over the porch floor, was the scene in front of the man who'd seen her running towards the building, when he opened the door and found Lizzie. She would be twenty-one in a few weeks and that meant autumn was just around the corner. She needed to find work and lodgings before then. The streets were no place to be during those months and the alternative was too much for Lizzie to bear.

Hoping the employers here were as forthcoming as her last employers, she asked intrepidly,

"Are there any jobs Sir, please?"

Lizzie was ushered along the corridors and into a waiting room where she remained standing so as not to wet the chairs. Moments later, someone opened the door and led her down the same corridor and through another door where she found herself in a plush room with a huge glass partition and through which she could see the workforce in the factory down below. Trying to concentrate on the job in hand, Lizzie forced her gaze to land on the person behind the desk. She attempted a smile and an apology for looking the way she did.

"What can I do for you Miss?" said the man behind the desk.

"Is there any work please?" asked Lizzie.

"As a matter of fact, yes, we do," said the man. "Problem is, whether you're strong enough to do it."

"Oh, I think I will be, Sir," said Lizzie.

"What makes you think so young lady?"

Lizzie proceeded to furnish her would-be employer with a brief summary of her working life so far.

"My my", he said finally. "A proper feisty lass. You've got the job. Can you start in the morning?"

"Yes. Thank you." Lizzie humbly replied.

"How far away do you live?"

"I don't have anywhere to live," said Lizzie again, feeling uncomfortable.

At that point, there was an urgent knocking on the door. The man shouted, "Yes?"

The door opened and a red-faced girl, a little older than Lizzie stood there, hands on her hips.

"There's another fight broken out down there, Sir. I've tried to stop them but they're ripping lumps off one another. Can you come?"

The girl turned and looked at Lizzie, standing there, still dripping slightly onto the polished floorboards.

"Can't be. Lizzie Bradshaw?"

"Yes. Oh no, I don't believe it. You're my Auntie Julia's daughter aren't you? I'm sorry I've forgotten your name."

"I'm Teresa."

"That's right. Teresa."

A little uncomfortably, Lizzie added, "How are you?"

The reply came quickly and sarcastically, "Fed up of those beggars down there. Always fighting they are. Come on Sir, or they're gonna kill one another."

Teresa was almost out of the room and she turned back to Lizzie.

"You coming to work here?"

"I think so."

"Hang around 'til I've finished. I'll show you the ropes before you start."

"Thank you," was all Lizzie could say.

Teresa and her employer raced out of the room. Lizzie made a few tentative steps towards the glass partition and watched the scene below unravel.

'I wonder if I'm doing the right thing. It looks a bit dangerous down there with all that glass about. The women are all but rioting. Shall I just leave?'

Within a few minutes, the situation was under control and the women had returned to their workplaces. All was calm again. The man returned and closed the door.

"It's not always like this," he said and smiled, sensing Lizzie's apprehension.

He smiled again. "You'll be fine. See you in the morning at six o'clock. Don't be late. Teresa will be finished in half an hour or so. I've told her to collect you from the waiting room if you want to make your way back down there."

"Thank you Sir."

Lizzie couldn't believe her luck. Once again, fate seemed to have swung in her favour. Though she still had nowhere to live, she had another job. 'Straightaway, just like that,' she thought. 'How marvellous.'

Teresa found Lizzie in the waiting room looking out of the window. She went up to her and gave her a big hug. Lizzie hugged her back tightly, two young women who'd shared their formative years in the horrors of the workhouse with their families dying around them.

"Do you have to leave straightaway after I've shown you round?" asked Teresa

"No, not at all," said Lizzie, wondering why Teresa had asked.

"Well, why don't you come home with me and have a cuppa and a chat?"

"I'd love to," was all Lizzie could say, tears stinging her eyes.

* * * * * *

CHAPTER TWENTY-TWO

An outstretched hand, inviting Lizzie in from the certain cold and homelessness, Teresa seemed to be Lizzie's saviour. They chatted over a cup of tea, reminiscing about their observations and emotional memories from a dark time in their past. Lizzie was glad to have someone to talk to, someone who could identify similar experiences, someone she'd once shared her life with. Teresa offered her some clothes which no longer fitted her and by the end of their chat, they were firm friends again.

Teresa was living in the top room of a three-storey house about five miles from the factory. Big enough for two people, she invited Lizzie to share the costs with her and another era in Lizzie's life began. They had to cycle to work and home each day. Teresa procured a bicycle for Lizzie from an old man who no longer needed his.

It was a mundane existence without the man she'd believed to be her soul mate. Many times she considered confronting him and asking him 'Why?' Self preservation prevented her from making that foolish mistake. 'Life goes on, there'll be someone else soon,' she'd been told. 'Little comfort,' Lizzie thought, when all she wanted to do was wrap herself up in the memories she had of their good times together and forget the monstrous behaviour of a man she didn't know at all.

Lizzie's life at the factory proved little better than workhouse life. Her colleagues weren't of the same calibre as her previous employment. They fought and argued, making life uncomfortable for everyone who wanted to get on with their jobs whilst enjoying each others' company. This didn't happen. Lizzie's twenty-first birthday came and went. Teresa baked her a cake. There was no-one else to celebrate with. Occasionally Teresa's brother, Peter came for tea, but Lizzie paid him no attention, nor he her.

Life continued in this predictable pattern until the spring of 1893. Lizzie was twenty-three, still single, still frightened of relationships with men, and disenchanted with life at the factory. She knew there were no other options available, but a notion niggled in her head. She wasn't prepared to live this way forever and the idea had come to her to seek an alternative path. Again, she considered going back to Wales and asking to be admitted to the order, continuing to live her life of chastity, whilst also helping others. This thought was short-lived when she considered the considerable joy she'd once felt in the arms of a man. She wanted to feel that joy again. Living here with Teresa and working at the factory was not going to bring about that dream.

Lizzie considered applying to work down the coal pits, but the horrors overwhelmed her and she knew she'd be miserable, and so, she made her decision.

'I'll look for work similar to Maddingley Hall. The factory shutdown's due in a few weeks. I'll be a free agent for two whole weeks.'

She'd saved a little money from her wages and would have enough to travel back to the area she knew and loved and ask around for vacancies in one of the other big houses. Armed with her decision, she broached the topic with Teresa. Her announcement was met with stony silence. Lizzie knew in that moment she was making the right decision. Despite the fact Teresa had invited her in to her home, all Teresa had been concerned with was finding someone to share the cost of living. Her sullen behaviour and unwillingness to do anything but remain in her room had been a contributing factor to Lizzie's decision to move on. Now she knew she'd made the right one. She also knew if her plans went astray, she wouldn't be coming back. It was make or break.

The day Lizzie was leaving, Teresa left the house in the early hours of the morning. There was no note, and there were no goodbyes. Lizzie felt a certain thrill when she closed the door for the last time and hurried to the train station.

* * * * * *

"Oh my! Lizzie Bradshaw!"

Cook stood there flabbergasted for a few seconds and then pulled Lizzie into her arms and hugged her so hard, she almost crushed Lizzie's ribs. She was a little larger than Lizzie remembered, but the feeling remained the same. Warm, inviting and definitely pleased to see her. Lizzie couldn't believe this was happening. It was either her lucky stars or the God she learned about when she was little really did exist. Either way, she couldn't believe she was standing in Maddingley Hall with Cook's arms around her. Even if it turned out there was nothing for her, she was glad she'd made the journey.

It had happened when she was pulling into her destination station. There was a poster on the railings of the station platform. It had read: 'MADDINGLEY HALL – OPENING TO THE PUBLIC - MAY DAY 1893. Come and browse our stately home. Enjoy walking around our beautiful gardens and grounds. Reasonable rates.' Lizzie's eyes had nearly popped out of her head.

Thankfully, the train was pulling slowly into the station and Lizzie was able to read it a couple of times while she waited for the train to stop.

'May Day,' Lizzie thought, 'that's only a few days away.' There was no procrastination, her decision was made. She enquired at the ticket office about transport out to Maddingley Hall, thinking if they were inviting the public, some form of transport must be available. The ticket master told Lizzie a bus had been laid on to take visitors. It was available two or three times a day and was operational due to the amount of interest. He added, "You won't be able to go in today though, it only opens to visitors on May Day."

"Thank you," said Lizzie, smiling inwardly, hoping against all hope she most definitely would be able to get in today.

* * * * * *

"So," said Cook, "Where've you been and what've you been doing? Come on, come with me, we'll find somewhere and have a good old natter."

When Lizzie had finished her story, Cook's eyes were glistening.

"You've certainly been through the mill young lady, haven't you? But look at you! You're a fine looking young woman. Any man would give his eye teeth to have a chance with you." A big smile broke out on Cook's face. Lizzie wondered what she was thinking. 'Does she know someone?' thought Lizzie. 'Someone who might like me?'

"So you want some work then?"

"Yes, if there is any, please."

"There's plenty of work Lizzie. I can't believe you've just turned up on the doorstep. We wanted to try and contact you to let you know we were re-opening, but we had no forwarding address. Didn't know where on earth you were. The Gods have sent you to us child.

Now, we can't pay any more than before. The family can ill afford the upkeep of such a house. Between you and me, a Canadian relative of the master died a few months ago and left some money, enabling them to return. That's what May Day's all about. For some strange reason, he wanted them to open the house to visitors, beats me why. You'll be at home here, you'll get board and lodgings and a small income to help with personal items. Are you still interested?"

Lizzie hadn't needed to answer. Cook could see in her eyes the answer Lizzie was incapable of making.

"You can stay in your old room. You'll be sharing again. The duties will be varied and because you know the ropes, you'll be expected to muck in everywhere. There's some new rules and regulations but I'll make sure you know them. It'll be great Lizzie and I'm so glad you're here."

Cook came forward and hugged Lizzie again, the two of them locked in an embrace for a few seconds. In those few seconds, Lizzie knew without doubt she'd made the right choice.

'Life's going to be better from now on. I just know it,' she thought.

The Maddingleys had moved back from the South of England and taken up residence again in the magnificent building Lizzie had come to know and love. She knew life would be different than before but her adventurous nature and amazing ability to take on situations and cope admirably with them, despite her jaded past, would be put to the test in the coming months.

The May Pole, traditionally decorated with a variety of coloured ribbon, was erected with the use of long poles. Long coloured ribbons hanging from the top had been secured to the pole awaiting the festivities, when females, young and old, would take one of the ribbons and dance around the pole to the strains of music played by a local brass band. Standing tall and proud in the gardens of the Hall, the May Pole took centre stage, visually and in the minds of all who worked there. Mr Maddingley had made it clear the success of the day depended upon their hard work and he expected nothing less than perfection. Each member of staff had additional duties in preparation for the day and the hall buzzed with anticipation and excitement. The seamstress busily prepared crowns of flowers for the children who would perform the May Pole Dance and rosettes for the winners sat waiting to be pinned onto their recipients.

Cook had spent most of the night baking simple biscuits along with edible prizes for the winning dancers. Jugs of water flavoured with an elderflower syrup had been prepared in the still room and stood in rows on the wooden draining board waiting to be taken outside. Sunshine was breaking through, its first rays of warmth beckoning the festivities to begin. Colossal pans of stew were ready to be carried out to the two long wooden tables the carpenter had made. The puppeteer of one of the side shows put his final touch to the Punch and Judy booth while his assistant practised his rather loud drum roll.

Mr Maddingley declared the event open and was shocked and pleasantly surprised to find more than a hundred people waiting at the gates. Two of the footmen directed the surging guests round to the back of the house, whilst Mr Maddingley hurriedly reported to Cook, they needed more biscuits.

The staff at Maddingley Hall declared it one of the most exciting and interesting events ever. A box had been left on the table with a notice asking people if they would like to leave a donation, for the upkeep of the hall. Their entrance fee had been nominal and the request was well intentioned and well received. The visitors who could, gave generously and the day was a resounding success.

The overall management plan for Maddingley Hall would prove to be fruitful for its owners and initially, the employees were kept so busy, Lizzie hadn't time to dwell on events of the past. Once again she proved herself an asset to the hall's staff and despite the strict rules, found herself pursued by many of the young men. She enjoyed their attentions but there was no-one who took her eye the way Arthur had. Her beauty together with her good-natured characteristics continued to entice men of all ages, but she let no-one in close enough until Albert Harris was hired. The spark ignited immediately but Lizzie conducted herself in the fashion to which she had become accustomed and much as she was drawn to this good looking man, she kept him at arms length. She couldn't risk losing her job.

Albert Harris was besotted with Lizzie. Two years older, he was employed as an 'odd job man'. He too, was making an impact at Maddingley Hall. His charming persona and willingness to work hard at whichever task he was given, gave rise to talk amongst the servants he would soon become a footman. But, Lizzie Bradshaw was getting in the way of his aspirations. His most difficult task was to be in Lizzie's company at times when his duties required it, and not make it known he adored her. The epitome of restraint, he didn't think he was capable of prolonging.

Lizzie felt the same. Having thought she would never look at another man in the same light as Arthur Longton, there was a stirring deep within her. She wanted to be in his arms. She longed to feel his breath on her face, to feel his body close to hers, to succumb to an urgent need as yet unfulfilled. Her endeavours to remove herself from his company when they were forced to work together only served to increase Albert's yearning for her. She found it difficult to communicate coherently without revealing her emotional state and the need to confide in someone overwhelmed her. She wished with all her heart she could speak to Mary-Ann or Katy. She thought of Katy every night before she closed her eyes.

'Poor Katy, my beloved baby sister. Why did they send you away?'

Lizzie practised, with precision, the art of keeping a distance from Albert. She refrained from close contact wherever possible for fear she would lose control and brush her lips against his. Her thoughts, however, could not be controlled and regardless of the mounting criticism from Cook that she was daydreaming, she couldn't help herself. She pictured herself running through the garden, playing hide and seek, hiding behind one of the large topiary trees. Albert would come up behind her and put his arms around her waist. She would nuzzle her head in towards him and turn round, joining her lips with his and they would fall to the ground in a passionate embrace. It was one such daydream, her mind wandered a little further, when she was jolted out of it by someone. When she turned to respond, she found herself face to face with the subject of her daydream. Feigning a coughing fit, she ran from the room in a flustered state. Cook, standing at the other side of the kitchen, saw the incident and irrevocably knew the cause of Lizzie's coughing fit. She smiled inwardly, whilst also concerned with the possible outcome.

Lizzie and Albert exercised self control for a further six months. Christmas was almost upon Maddingley Hall once again. Lizzie remembered with affection her first Christmas in this fascinating house and was already making plans for this one. She wondered if this one could surpass the joy she'd experienced last time, the added bonus being, the man of her dreams would be present.

Albert had eyes for no other. Lizzie Bradshaw evoked in him feelings he'd never known before. She shone above every other girl he'd ever known; her personality, the way she looked, the way she smiled and laughed, everything. He was head over heels in love with her. He knew the reason for her aloofness. They both had jobs to hold down and neither could afford to lose that privilege. He'd achieved his goal and the master had awarded him the status of Footman. He was, ever so slowly, moving up the ladder in the servants' world. He couldn't risk losing that. To lose his job would mean losing Lizzie. Knowing he couldn't have both was torture, but he'd sooner have her near than never have her at all. He therefore conducted himself accordingly. The love inside each of them grew daily. Tormented by the circumstances of their love, they tried to believe dreams come true. They were about to find out.

* * * * * *

CHAPTER TWENTY-THREE

Christmas was looming fast and Maddingley Hall was in full swing, the workload for Lizzie and Albert all-consuming. Lizzie felt drained at the end of each day, her dreams of Albert thwarted by the intense throbbing of her pain. A little over two weeks before Christmas Day, Lizzie collapsed on the kitchen floor. Cook almost fell over Lizzie's slumped body and screamed for help, a scream which brought everyone running. They stared down at Lizzie who was ghostly white and motionless, her facial expression etched in pain.

"Get the doctor," screamed Cook.

Everyone scattered. As an able rider, Albert had already mounted one of the horses. He rode the horse at break-neck speed to the village two miles away. He knew the way. He'd been called upon for a similar duty some months ago, when one of the visiting aristocrats had taken ill. He leapt off the horse outside the doctor's house and hammered on the door with an urgency that couldn't be denied. He prayed the door would open. A well informed interpreter of knocks on his door, the doctor grabbed his prepared emergency bag. His horse always saddled and ready, he rode behind Albert, making a good attempt at keeping up with Albert's horse. They quickly dismounted and ran inside to find Lizzie had been moved and raised up to a bench, where her head rested on a pillow. Cook informed the doctor she had vomited violently several times.

Everyone was ushered out of the kitchen and the door closed. Only Cook and the doctor stood beside Lizzie. In a low voice, the doctor mouthed to Cook, "Is she pregnant?"

"I don't think so", answered Cook cautiously.

"Has she shown any signs of fever recently?"

"No, she's been fine, though we've been exceptionally busy. I'm sure she was tired like the rest of us."

"Do you know what she's eaten in the last twenty-four hours?"

"Same as the rest of us", said Cook, bristling slightly at the notion her cooking had anything to do with Lizzie's plight.

"And what would that be?" the doctor asked, also picking up Cook's train of thought.

Cook gave an account of the day's food intake whilst the doctor examined Lizzie's abdomen, smelt her breath for any sign of alcohol, checked her temperature which was raging and ordered Cook to get cold cloths and apply them to her face, neck and wrists to try to lower her temperature.

"Open the windows please."

Lizzie seemed to have drifted away again and Cook was asked for smelling salts. After a few moments, Lizzie opened her eyes. They were glazed and unfocused. The doctor was unable to determine the cause of her symptoms.

"She needs to go to bed in a darkened room. Thin cotton sheets and make sure she drinks plenty. I'll come back tomorrow."

"What do you think it is doctor?" asked Cook, becoming increasingly alarmed.

"I suspect it's a case of food poisoning, but I can't be sure if it's the onset of an infection. Come for me if there's any change for the worse." With that, he was gone.

Cook was beside herself with worry. Lizzie was carried to her bed where she lay for three days and three nights in a state of delirium. Doctor Ash, medical practitioner for the Maddingleys, had been called back twice. There was no sign of improvement. He was reluctant to transfer Lizzie to the ward of a local hospital, fearing she could contract an additional illness far worse than the one she was currently suffering.

Albert, out of his mind with worry, sought the nearest Apothecary, and furnished with the merest hint of information about Lizzie's condition, it was concluded a dose of 'Bitters' could not worsen the poor girl's malady and may in fact help to fight it. Hurrying back to Maddingley Hall with the small brown bottle tucked inside a pocket, he burst into the kitchen and asked for a word with Cook, who had her own suspicions about Lizzie's condition. She firmly believed Albert may have been the cause of Lizzie's collapse, violent vomiting and therefore the cause of his obvious concern. She looked at Albert with some disdain, but without speaking, she took the bottle and with the help of a metal funnel, administered two teaspoons of the foul tasting liquid to her patient. Lizzie spluttered as the liquid hit the back of her throat, making her cough it back up. Cook tried again, after mopping up the regurgitated foul smelling medicine. This time, the medicine went down. The Apothecary had informed Albert to administer the medicine three times a day. Containing herbal plants he had grown himself, together with a fair amount of alcohol, he recommended the potion be administered until the bottle emptied. If there were no sign of improvement, Albert should return for a stronger concoction.

Maddingley Hall was renowned amongst the servants as one of the better houses to work in. The master showed an interest in the people who looked after him and his family and as such he was anxious about Lizzie and the cause of her 'lying in'. Both the master and Doctor Ash had questioned Cook about her methods in the kitchen, concerned particularly with her techniques for cooking raw meat. Although no-one else in the house had become ill in any way, their concerns were valid. Cook was finding it hard not to pass on her own thoughts on the matter. She knew it would mean Lizzie's and Albert's instant dismissal and she wasn't sure enough. She kept her silence and suffered the indignation of relating her methods of preparation and cooking to those who asked. All was found to be well.

Albert, whilst trying to avoid questioning from the other servants, continued to enquire about Lizzie. At the end of the second day of administering the bitters, Cook announced to the servants at dinner that Lizzie Bradshaw was beginning to show signs of recovery. Doctor Ash had been informed of Albert's visit to the Apothecary and had concluded Lizzie's condition had a number of contributing factors. He suggested her sudden collapse could have been due to severe pain from an ear infection coupled with an extreme menstrual cycle causing exhaustion due to lack of iron. An exacting diet was drawn up for one month and the Maddingleys compensated Albert for the bottle of bitters. One further bottle was ordered from the Apothecary. Lizzie was to remain in bed for a second week to fully recover.

Lizzie, now out of her delirium and feeling much better by the day, objected to this further convalescence and begged to be allowed back to her duties. She was denied that privilege and by the time Doctor Ash allowed her to return to light duties, there were only three days until Christmas. Deprived of her input towards the festivities, Lizzie found it incredibly difficult to remain focused on her full recovery and threw herself back into servants' duties with audacious enthusiasm. She'd been almost mobbed the first time she entered the servants' hall, no-one more pleased to see her than Albert who wanted more than anything to take her in his arms. The unbearable pain of not doing so was witnessed by Cook who was delighted to discover their love may not yet have been consummated and therefore she wouldn't be losing Lizzie Bradshaw.

'Well, perhaps not just yet,' she thought.

* * * * * *

CHAPTER TWENTY-FOUR

A sustainable relationship developed across the distance between Lizzie and Albert. Their inevitable entrance into the portal ahead was only a few days away. Christmas at Maddingley Hall was everything Lizzie remembered, from the beautiful Norwegian Spruce Christmas Trees, to the servants' party in their own hall on Christmas Day. Having thrown herself into her duties, she had recouped some of her precious skills and memorised the format necessary to provide her Master and her fellow servants with an unforgettable Christmas. Albert watched from a distance. The pain of not touching her was unbearable. Knowing they would both lose their jobs if their relationship was suspected and the anguish it would cause Lizzie, was the only thing preventing him from declaring his love. The torturous silence between them when their eyes met gave him hope.

'There has to be a way, there has to be,' his soul cried.

The memories made at Maddingley Hall that year resounded in the hearts of both the servants and their masters. Lizzie's talent around the place, whilst retaining the art of discretion around the ladies and gentleman above stairs, rendered even the most particular of tastes in awe of her skills. She placed the exquisite decorations with precision, according to her Master's wishes. She decorated the Christmas trees with fashionable expertise, helped by three of the other girls, who all enjoyed the direction engaged by Lizzie's leadership skills.

Cook and Lizzie, skilfully created a meal for their employers far surpassing anything they'd done before. The laughter emanating from the guests above stairs promoted the ethos for a spectacular Christmas downstairs. As was the usual format at Maddingley Hall, the servants were called upstairs on Boxing Day to receive their gifts.

Albert, in his role as footman stood beside a table, filled with small boxes, at the end of the Maddingley family line-up. Lizzie caught his eye as she stood with the others, excited to receive her box. She smiled nonchalantly, lest anyone caught the glance and interpreted it correctly. Albert handed each box to the Master or his wife accordingly. Lizzie felt a sudden shyness as she was called up to receive her gift. It was the closest she had been to Albert since before her illness. She'd been made aware it was he who had ridden to the Apothecary for the medicine which everyone believed had been her saviour. She could almost touch him, if she reached out.

'I can't. No-one must suspect, no-one must see.'

She received her gift and curtseyed. Wishing she didn't have to return to her line, but instead, stand beside the man she'd grown to worship from a distance. She felt she was in slow motion as she trod the few steps back to her place, her feet seeming like lead. She hoped she wasn't going to collapse again. She felt a little light-headed but this time she knew it was the blood pounding through her body at the thrill of his closeness and made it back to her line, steadying herself between two of her colleagues.

Mr Maddingley informed the line-up his wife had an announcement to make. The servants stood with great anticipation waiting for her speech.

"*In acknowledgement of services rendered throughout the year, and particularly over the festivities of this wonderful Christmas, I should like to inform you we shall hold a ball on New Year's Eve to which you are all cordially invited. You may dress in clothing of your choice, which must be appropriate to the occasion. You will have no duties on that day. We have hired help to cover each of you for the day. For this day only, you will be allowed upstairs in the ballroom and enjoy the privilege of dining, dancing and merriment with the rest of the house.*"

When Mrs Maddingley stopped speaking, they waited a few seconds. The butler instigated a loud cheer. "Hip Hip ...."

"Hooray" everyone shouted at the tops of their voices.

Laughing and chattering loudly, the servants all curtseyed together and left the room in an excited frenzy. Never before had they heard of anything like this happening amongst a serving fraternity in a large house. Lizzie's joy came not only from that announcement but the fact she'd caught Albert looking at her. He'd been discreetly casting his eye over everyone in the line-up so it was unlikely anyone noticed he lingered when he came to Lizzie. Cook had.

* * * * * *

New Year's Eve 1893

The day dawned. It was an odd sensation. Lizzie woke at five o'clock as did most of the other girls. Completely unaccustomed to being able to lie in bed and chatter, there was much giggling. A pillow fight broke out at the other end of the room but Lizzie's dream was haunting her. Delicious notions of Albert remained in her consciousness and try as she might, she couldn't rid her mind of the dream she'd been having.

"Come on dozy," shouted one of the other girls.

"What you wearing tonight Lizzie?" shouted another.

Lizzie was jolted back to the present and remembered it was the ball tonight. She leapt out of bed and grabbed the dress she'd set aside to wear. Everyone stared at it, disbelieving their eyes.

"Where did you get that?" one girl asked, jealousy burning, obvious to everyone.

"A friend of mine gave it to me," Lizzie replied, remembering the day she'd arrived at Teresa's house for a cup of tea.

"It's beautiful," said the girl stood beside her, touching the fine material. "You'll look like a princess," she added.

Lizzie blushed. "We'll all look different tonight."

In a flurry of anticipation, Lizzie and her companions organised their clothes for the forthcoming evening. Maddingley Hall was one of the larger stately homes and excluding Cook and the Housekeeper there were ten girls with duties ranging from Head Nurse down to Scullery Maid, whose drudgery cleaning passages, pantries, kitchen and the scullery, as well as a million other duties, was made more bearable by Lizzie's presence. They shared conjoined rooms at the top of the house, in small rather cramped conditions, but today the overwhelming excitement of their evening with the gentry totally outweighed any gripes they had about sharing their belongings. Clothes-swapping consumed the morning, until everyone felt satisfied in their chosen outfit. Lizzie had a small stash of rouge, courtesy of the factory girls and others were willing to share whatever accoutrements they had to ensure everybody looked and felt their best. Lizzie had a particular affiliation with the Mistress's seamstress who'd agreed to warm the irons.

By lunchtime, spirits were high. An unceremonious luncheon had been laid on in the servants' hall by the hired catering company. The meal consisted of a vegetable soup and freshly baked bread rolls. The delightful smell reached them as they came down the stairs, giggling and laughing, to discover the butler, Cook and the entourage of footmen and valets, together with the groundsmen already in the party spirit. An air of optimism generated throughout the hall and there was much laughter as everyone chattered excitedly about the pending party upstairs.

Lizzie glanced at Albert to find him smiling across the room at her. She smiled back at him, their eyes locked together in a wave of affection. On this occasion, no-one saw and no-one cared, each filled with their own aspirations of the evening ahead. Cook was jabbering animatedly with the butler and Lizzie pondered the notion perhaps it wasn't a singular romance skimming the surface of the servants' hall that day. Spurred on by this concept, she felt slightly tempted to catch Cook's eye and wink at her, but the impulse lasted only a second, as lunch over, everybody scrambled back to their rooms to prepare for what they hoped would be a night to remember.

When Lizzie emerged from her ablutions late that afternoon, she was transformed. Beauty radiated from deep within her. Her youthful exuberance created an iridescent glow, possessing a mysterious quality, and sure to captivate all who gazed on her. Her excitement and laughter were contagious and it was a happy group of Maddingley Hall female servants who entered the ballroom upstairs, astounding their male counterparts and impressing their employers.

The man stood beside Albert told him to close his mouth, re-iterating it was rude to stare. But stare he did. He couldn't divert his eyes from Lizzie. Her striking beauty was dramatic and took his breath away. She was dazzling. Her long black naturally wavy hair hung loose around her face and shoulders, the curls cascading down against the fabric of her simple dress, accentuating the curve of her back. There were no adornments, no jewellery, no hair combs, simply exquisite beauty.

Lizzie felt alive, as if born to a life of affluence. Her genteel manner didn't go unnoticed by her employers. When the music began to play, young men gathered round her, requesting the first dance. Albert wasn't one of them. He stood in the background watching Lizzie, listening to her laughter and wishing he'd had the courage to request the first dance.

The musicians played with amazing virtuosity. The romanticism of the waltzes as the master's guests swirled in their resplendent colourful gowns, together with a little of the amber liquid from the punch bowl, made Lizzie lightheaded. Guests and staff alike ate their fill from the luscious array of food and the magical party spirit continued until the bewitching hour. Powerful music, laughter and an undeniable flutter in Lizzie's heart made the ambience unforgettable and for everyone, a hugely successful evening.

Mr Maddingley announced the last dance. Some of the girls were stood chattering and Lizzie took a pace toward them. She felt someone brush past her shoulder and Albert came and stood in front of her. He held both hands out to her. She took them. The distance between them magnetised and he drew her into his arms as the music began. Lizzie felt his strength in taking the lead and followed him, glad of the recent tuition in dance moves given to them by Cook. Tonight she was perfecting them. Albert could scarcely contain himself. His fingers played with her soft curls. He felt her body beneath the fabric of her dress and longed to feel her skin against his flesh. He lived a lifetime in those few moments in Lizzie's arms and knew she was the one. No-one could surpass the beauty emanating from inside her and he knew in those few moments while they danced to the haunting music, oblivious to everything else, they would be together. The music stopped playing and the party drew to its conclusion. They moved off the dance floor aware they were still holding hands and Lizzie withdrew hers from his grasp. Tearing himself away from her, Albert crossed the dance floor to the other side and took a half empty glass of wine from a tray a waiter was carrying. He raised the glass to his lips and swallowed. The full-bodied earthiness of the pungent liquid increased the delectable sensation he'd discovered, whilst holding Lizzie in his arms.

The Maddingleys made a short speech and prompted by the butler, the servants lined up in front of their employers and their guests. The servants bowed and curtseyed their acknowledgement and thanks for a wonderful evening. The double doors opened and they were ushered out to head back towards their room. Life for Lizzie and Albert could never be the same. Their fate was sealed. In the early hours of the next morning, restless and wanting, Lizzie climbed out of bed and walked across to the door, having no idea why she was doing it. Gently opening the door so as not to awaken any of her colleagues, she peered outside along the corridor. Albert was sitting on the top step of the staircase which led down to the servants' hall. He hadn't heard the door open. His brain was trying, against the effects of the alcohol, to calculate how he and Lizzie could ever be together. Lizzie walked over to the staircase and throwing caution to the wind, sat down beside him, an unspoken knowingness between them. If they were caught now, that would surely be the end for both of them. For now, it was enough they each knew. Looking around to make sure there were no other late night wanderers, Albert gently brushed his lips against Lizzie's. A swell of blood flooded to her head as they sat there in the dark and kissed gently. Albert's self-control was ebbing. He stood up, kissed her gently one more time and left. Lizzie went back into the bedroom, climbed into bed and dreamt, about the most wonderful night of her life and the man whom she knew she could now never live without.

CHAPTER TWENTY-FIVE

Two days after the New Year's Eve party at Maddingley Hall, the servants' hall remained a buzz of chatter about the evening. Lizzie hadn't seen Albert since, the crushing emotional pain threatening her capability to function. Her colleagues sensed a change in her and on numerous occasions, questioned her.

"I'm fine," she answered reluctantly, realising she was anything but fine.

Cook knew. She had known for a while Lizzie was trying to hide her feelings for Albert. She also knew Bert, as she called him, carried the same feelings for Lizzie. She hadn't wanted either of them to lose their positions at Maddingley Hall and had cunningly requested Bert be sent on an errand, keeping him away for a few days, to let them both simmer down. Her actions had an adverse affect, serving only to enhance their emotional attachment. Lizzie's disturbing melancholy reminded her of her separation from Mary-Ann and Katy. Heartache once again bore down on her and she asked for leave. Believing her request to be an indirect result of her recent illness, Mr Maddingley granted her four days. She would leave in the morning, bound for Islington, not knowing if she would find Mary-Ann. It had been Cook's day off and she would have no knowledge of Lizzie's leave until she returned for work, by which time Lizzie would be well on her way.

Reliving memories of past departures, Lizzie rode in the carriage to the station, where she would continue her journey by train alone. A lone figure, standing on the station platform, she pondered about the wisdom of her actions.

'What if Mary-Ann can't accommodate me?' she thought, fearing the consequences.

She had enough money to make the return journey but this was a foolhardy expedition. She hadn't heard from Mary-Ann for a few weeks.

'What if she's moved? What if I can't find her?'

All these questions and more pounded in her head as she heard the gentle chugging of the slowing train in the distance, steam billowing out of its chimney and whistle blowing as it eased its way into the station. The guard jumped down onto the platform before the familiar smell of the old locomotive and the grimy carriages shunting behind it, finally came to a grinding halt. Lizzie picked up her bag and took a step towards one of the carriages and waited for the guard to open the door. A side glance up the length of the train to locate the guard produced a heart-stopping moment as she thought she saw Albert walking towards her. She straightened up and smoothed her skirt.

'No, can't possibly be him,' she reproached herself and turned back towards the carriage where the guard had opened the door for her embarkation. She caught a movement out of the corner of her eye and once more turned, to see Albert running towards her.

"Lizzie?" he shouted, as disbelieving as Lizzie herself.

"Albert!" she said. "What are you doing here?"

"Never mind me. What are *you* doing here? Where are you going? "

Coming over quite faint, Lizzie explained she was going to see Mary-Ann.

"Why? You're not leaving me are you?"

A loud whistle rattled through their ears as the train prepared for departure. Loud bursts of steam emitted from the front of the train, where the engine strained to get underway. Lizzie and Albert were struggling to say what they wanted to. He didn't want her to go. She didn't want to leave and burst into tears, Albert opened his arms and she fell into them. The whistle sounded again. The guard came running up the platform, closing doors as he went.

"Are you getting on Miss?" he asked agitatedly.

Lizzie looked up at Albert, who answered for her.

"No Sir, the lady won't be boarding the train. Thank you."

Slamming the door shut, the guard bolted back along the platform and sounding his whistle again, jumped back onto the already moving train, which slowly and surely, began its journey South without Lizzie.

* * * * * *

It had been a sunny morning when Lizzie left Maddingley Hall but the sun was not responsible for the warmth kindled in her heart, as holding hands, they made their way along the platform with new vigour. Lizzie had been brought back to life and navigating the reasons wasn't difficult. Albert was totally responsible and the love emanating right back at her, told her she'd found her soul mate, but what were they to do with that knowledge? Albert had a little money put aside but not enough. They would have to continue at Maddingley Hall, at least for a while. The initial problem was what to do with Lizzie for four days. She was supposed to be away visiting her sister in Islington. Albert had returned from an errand he found inconceivable he'd been sent on and was already late. The train on which he'd returned from London, hadn't stopped at his station and taken him another five miles down the track to its terminus. He'd then had to buy a ticket back as far as the platform they were now just leaving and Mr Maddingley would be anxious Albert hadn't yet returned to the Hall. They needed a plan.

* * * * * *

"Hey Bert, is that you? Bert Harris?"
Albert stared in disbelief and momentarily released his hold on Lizzie's hand.

"Well you look like you've done well for yourself,' said the man now standing in front of the two of them. He offered his hand out to Lizzie, who embarrassingly shook it.

"Sidney Offington. Pleased to meet you ma'am."

"Lizzie Bradshaw," said Lizzie a little cautiously.

"We were mates at school," Albert reassured Lizzie.

"Oh, nice to meet you," said Lizzie, relaxing a little.

"What you up to these days my friend?" asked Sidney.

"I'm at Maddingley Hall. So is Lizzie. Just come to meet her at the station. She's been visiting her sister in London. What you up to these days?"

"Got me own place now. Married, three kids."

"Where's that then?" asked Albert, a semi-plan formulating.

"Just up the road from 'ere. You'll have to come and see us," said Sidney, inching his way towards the edge of the platform.

"We'd love to come, meet the wife and kids, have a good old catch up," replied Albert adding quickly, "When would be convenient?" not wishing to miss the opportunity.

"Well, I'll be home around teatime this evening. Why don't you come then? Wife's always got enough food to feed the five thousand."

At that moment, Lizzie could once again hear the now familiar chuffing coming down the line.

They exchanged a few more words. As Sidney was boarding the train, Albert shouted, "What's the address?"

"21 Poppy Lane."

"See you later. Great to see you," shouted Albert, his voice almost lost against the wind, the steam and the sharp shrill of the Guard's whistle.

* * * * * *

It hadn't taken Albert more than a few seconds deciding whether or not he would visit Sidney Offington. Poppy Lane was located in an affluent area of the town and he wondered if his old friend Sidney would let him rent a room on an ad hoc basis. He knew Lizzie was the girl he wanted to be with for the rest of his life. Neither of them could risk losing their jobs at the Hall, yet their love could not be kindled within its confines. Sidney Offington had come along at precisely the right moment in Albert's life.

'Yes, we'll definitely be there at teatime,' he thought.

Albert took hold of Lizzie's hand again, and squeezing it tightly, he leaned in towards her. He was intoxicated by the smell of her. He longed to lay beside her and Lizzie's body language suggested she felt the same.

"Come on," he prompted, breaking into a run. "I know a little teashop not far from here."

"But, won't Mr Maddingley wonder where you are?" asked Lizzie beginning to worry about the consequences of them being seen together.

"I'm already late. Might as well be hung for a sheep as a lamb. Come on, I'll race you to the end of the platform."

The tea-shop, nestled between a butcher's and a greengrocers in the old cobbled street, provided a sweet haven for the afternoon. They ordered a pot of tea for two and in a secluded corner of the shop, they sat opposite one another, holding hands across the table, barely able to take their eyes off each other. Their fingers entwined, they whiled away the hours, chattering excitedly. Lizzie had fallen in love with Albert Harris. She wanted to be with him more than anything she'd ever wanted in her life. Tears were already forming behind her eyes in anticipation of their separation. The honesty between them was overwhelming and the touch of his hands left her wanting more.

They'd discussed the possibility of the outcome of a visit to Poppy Lane. Albert had needed the certainty Lizzie understood the path on which they were about to embark. The time came for them to leave the tea-shop and make their way to Sidney Offington's house to put forward their proposal. Lizzie was nervous. What would his wife think of her? Of course, they would have to make it look like an off-the-cuff remark once they were engaged in conversation with their newly-found friend. Lizzie's heart fluttered and her body trembled slightly when she realised the full implication of their intended purpose, but she knew there was no other way. She was totally committed to this man with whom she'd found a profound happiness. She knew with certainty her destiny would somehow be forged by the visit, no matter what the outcome.

CHAPTER TWENTY-SIX

The house in Poppy Lane took Lizzie's breath away. In a town she'd become familiar with as an industrial area filled with smoke, steam, grimy streets and grubby front doors from the constant mud-flinging hooves of passing horses, she found herself in a secluded leafy lane, once again, thrilled with the concept of the chapter in her life about to unfold. Astonished Albert's friend Sidney could live in such an awesome house filled her with hope for their future and she gazed at the building sprawled out in front of her at the end of the winding driveway.

'Surely this can't be a single dwelling? There must be some mistake,' she thought.

She let go of Albert's hand and ran back to the large pillars flanking either side of the gateway and looked again. The number 21 was clearly engraved on a metal plaque embedded in the gate-post and she knew it was Poppy Lane because she'd checked that too.

Albert turned Lizzie to face him. "Please may I kiss you? Properly?" he asked knowing and anticipating her response. Lizzie didn't answer, but instead moved her face towards his and looking up into his eyes, saw what his mouth wasn't saying. Locked in an embrace, Albert sought her lips. Lizzie finally closed her eyes as Albert's lips brushed gently at first, against her mouth. Shocked by her own response, she found herself yielding to the exhilarating experience. They both knew irrevocably in those few moments they were approaching the point of no return. With full knowledge of Albert's intent and willingly succumbing to his advances, they began to move up the drive towards the front door of 21 Poppy Lane.

Boasting a large facade of interesting proportion, 21 Poppy Lane seemed to have two entrances. The door to the main house sat beneath a canopied roof sloping down towards the first floor windows. On the ground floor and opening almost as though to welcome them inside, was the beautiful oak front door flanked either side by shuttered windows. Tall chimneys rose either side of the roof and the two stained glass windows situated within the roof space sported their own canopies. The smaller attached building to the left of the property also had a sloping roof containing one white painted tudor-style window and a smaller chimney, beneath which stood a white painted door set back behind a stone built facia with a small shuttered window to the side. A tall silver birch stood about eight feet from the front of the property, lowering its branches towards the larger roof. A beautifully manicured lawn encompassed the ground around the house and a lone terracotta urn containing an exotic-looking palm stood to the left of the steps leading up to the front door.

'There would certainly seem to be enough room,' Albert said to himself. 'He said he had a wife and three children. I wonder if they all live in the main house and the smaller building is used for something else?'

Somewhat mesmerised, Lizzie ambled behind Albert, taking in every detail of this wonderful place. As she walked towards the beckoning front door, the delicious scent of old English roses carried on the air evoking a sense of hope and well-being.

Albert stretched out from the bottom of the two steps and knocked on the open door, shouting 'Hello,' as he did so. A large Scottish Deerhound bounded past him, down the steps and nearly knocked Lizzie flying. Unafraid of animals, she held out a hand when she heard a voice from the house shouting, "Daisy. Daisy. Come."

Daisy had a quick sniff around Lizzie's feet and bounded off, back into the house.

"Well, someone's pleased to see you!" Albert said, laughing.

"Albert Harris! I didn't think you'd come. Come on in," said Sidney from the doorway, his head almost touching the top of the door frame.

Albert, feeling a little nervous now, reached out and helped Lizzie up the two steps and in through the door. The smell of baking pastry wafted towards them.

"Martha's made steak and ale pie. Would you like to join us?" asked Sidney.

Lizzie, feeling decidedly too comfortable hoped and prayed Albert would say yes.

"Yes please, if it's not too much trouble," replied Albert, beginning to relax a little.

Sidney invited them both through into the kitchen where he introduced them to Martha, his wife and to the three children, who were already seated around the country farmhouse table. A huge stone fireplace dominated the room and was where Martha was busying herself stirring the contents of a pan suspended above the flames licking around it. The scene, to Lizzie, was one of domestic bliss, adding to her repertoire of differing ways of life and one which she memorised.

The kettle was boiling fiercely next to the pan and Martha carefully drained its contents into a huge enamel teapot which she placed in the middle of the table on a trivet. She lifted two more pretty cups and saucers down from a dresser and placing them next to the teapot, she offered her guests cups of tea. The contents of a large pitcher of juice was poured into glasses for the table and whilst Sidney and Martha continued their final preparations for the meal, Albert and Lizzie struck up conversations with the children.

There was an eager moan of anticipation when Martha brought the delicious looking perfectly cooked rustic pie to the table. Next to it she placed a large earthenware bowl full of buttered mashed potatoes. A selection of steaming vegetables was revealed, when she removed the lid from the pretty pink and white tureen.

"Come on everyone, tuck in," encouraged Martha. scrumptious

Daisy sat in the corner sniffing the air.

'Obviously well-trained,' thought Albert.

There was a comfortable ambience around the table. Sidney and Albert chatted about their school days, reminding each other of acquaintances they remembered, whilst Lizzie was busy complimenting Martha on the feast and listening to stories about the children. After a scrumptious sponge pudding made with seasonal fruit covered in custard, Lizzie and Albert played with the children while Sidney and Martha cleared away the pots. Despite Lizzie's offer to help, Martha wouldn't hear of it. The children were sent to get ready for bed and the four adults sat around the table. Sidney produced a flagon of beer and four tankards and began the post-dinner conversation.

"Now, Bert, tell me about you. What are you doing with your life? What brings you to my village? And how did you meet this beautiful young lady?"

Bert began his story. Most of it, he'd already told Lizzie, but there were snippets new to her. Fascinated, she soaked up every syllable, savouring them all. Sidney turned to Lizzie.

"How do you like working at Maddingley? I hear it's a nice place to work. I've been there a couple of times on business with Mr Maddingley. Seems like a nice chap."

"I love it," said Lizzie unashamedly. I feel I belong there. Everyone is so .... so warm, and friendly. I began as a housemaid when I was fourteen. I placed an advertisement ..... ." She looked up at Sidney and smiled, " ...... with a little help."

Sidney smiled back, recognising Lizzie possessed no airs and graces.

"And so?" Sidney pushed Lizzie to continue.

"So, a passing stranger saw the advertisement. Maddingley Hall required a new housemaid. I got the job."

"And what kind of work do you do there, if I may ask?"

"Yes, of course," said Lizzie, enjoying Sidney's interest in her work.

"I was hired as a housemaid and I do a lot of housekeeping, but I love my work in the kitchen best."

Lizzie presented a virtual picture of life at Maddingley including the Hall's closure and re-opening. Sidney and Martha listened intently to her story, fascinated by her portrayal of life below stairs in a large country house.

"There's a lot to learn. I'm just helping out at the moment," ended Lizzie, a little shyly.

"I'm sure Mr Maddingley considers he found an asset, Lizzie. Well done."

"Thank you," said Lizzie.

The two men poured themselves another tankard of beer.

"You have a beautiful place here," said Albert. "How did *you* come upon such good fortune?"

Sidney raised his tankard.

"Yes, I've been lucky Bert, in many ways. After my parents died, I lived with my Uncle for a while. When I was sixteen, he joined the forces and was drafted to India. I lived in his place for a while. I was working for a local businessman."

"Doing what?" asked Albert

"General run around, at first. It was a haberdashery store." Sidney laughed.

"Never would have seen myself doing anything like that. Imagined I'd probably be down the pit when I left school or in the mills. It was just a chance encounter. Anyway, he was the sole owner of the business. We got on really well. Like I say, at first I was the assistant, cleaning up the place, brushing up, making tea. One day, he began teaching me how to do other stuff. I liked the job. He liked me. He told me I was good. That gave me confidence. Gradually, I began doing more of the important stuff. He asked me if I'd be interested in a full time job with him. I said yes. We became a great team and the business thrived. Eventually, he began to have a day off here and there, and left me with the shop.

One day, right out of the blue, an official looking envelope dropped on the mat at my Uncle's house, where I was still living. It was a telegram, informing me my Uncle had died, some kind of tropical disease. I was the sole beneficiary of his estate. There was lots of coming and going, for meetings in stuffy offices, but eventually it was all sorted and I received a large sum of money."

Sidney took a large gulp of his beer. Albert did the same.

"Was there a funeral?" asked Albert

"The army sorted all that out over there. I suppose one day, I might go and visit his grave."

"That's quite some story," said Albert.

"There's more. A few months rolled by and Mr Thorpe, my boss, became ill. He was in hospital for a couple of months. He asked me if I could run the business for him till he was better. It was quite a daunting prospect, but I took it on. When Mr Thorpe came out of hospital, he was sent for convalescence for another month, somewhere by the sea. He became ill again and died while he was there. The next thing I know, a man in a suit and tie walked into the shop and asked for me. My presence was requested at the reading of Mr Thorpe's will. He left the lot to me, his business, his house, his money, everything. I couldn't believe it. I kept the business on. Martha was one of my customers, that's how we met. We got married a year later and I sold the two houses and bought this."

"And the business?"

"Yes, I kept it. It's a gold mine. I realise I'm most fortunate."

Albert, whilst delighted to hear Sidney's good luck story, wished to bring the subject around to the reason for his visit. Waiting for the appropriate moment, he sat enjoying his beer and their chatter.

Lizzie's constant brush with the elite only served to enhance the poor conditions under which she'd spent her life so far. Though she considered herself a step or two up from the workhouse, she knew with certainty it was only a heartbeat and bad times could once again inflict themselves upon her. For that reason, she wanted to jump up and run away from Albert, almost wanted to run back to Maddingley Hall and forget she'd ever met him, so distressed was she about the thoughts of being caught and having nowhere else to go but back to a life of poverty. In that moment, she had been willing to give up Albert for good, but something she couldn't explain, drove her on. Her intense love and passion for this man would not let anything get in the way of the promise of a better life with him. A life she felt would give her more happiness than the one she'd have without him.

Albert glanced across at Lizzie, certain she was having second thoughts. He need not have worried. The Gods were indeed on his side this day. A quick nod of her head spurred him on to finally ask Sidney the question which would determine their future.

"Sidney, can I ask if you have a room we could rent, please?"

An alarmingly long minute later, he was shaking Sidney's hand, a big grin from ear to ear. Lizzie was crying tears of joy and Martha mopped up her own tears after hearing their heartfelt story. The attached building had once been used as a lodging house for the groundsman. More recently it had been used for Martha's ailing parents who had now passed on. The building stood empty. Albert explained their time off together was limited and Sidney granted Albert and Lizzie use of the building whenever they wanted.

"We might not be able to use it for weeks at a time, but knowing we have somewhere of our own to go if only for a few hours is enough. It'll spur us on to go back to Maddingley Hall. We'll work hard, try to save up and hopefully be able to look to a better future together."

As a shrewd businessman, and mindful of Albert's pride, Sidney wasn't offering the building for nothing, but he was certain they could accommodate the small fee he would charge. They took the key Martha offered and the two of them, ran excitedly, into their private oasis to celebrate their good fortune.

* * * * * *

CHAPTER TWENTY-SEVEN

Mr Maddingley gave Albert a dressing down when he arrived back at the Hall. He and Lizzie had staggered their arrival so as not to be seen together. Cook was more than surprised to see Lizzie appear half an hour after she caught a glimpse of Albert running up the driveway and disappearing round the back of the house. Her suspicions had been raised many times over the past few weeks but none more so than today. She'd heard from the head footman that Albert had not been seen all day. Lizzie was supposed to have been going to Islington to stay with her sister but had returned within half an hour of Albert.

'Something's definitely going on,' she thought. 'I only hope they can keep it under wraps or the master will sack them both.'

Cook was fond of both of them and would have hated to see either of them lose their job. She remembered fondly having the same dilemma in her youth. She believed she had chosen the wisest route and lived without her love. Lizzie, she knew, would follow her heart and if Albert had won that, their days at Maddingley Hall were numbered.

Lizzie and Albert had refrained from consummating their relationship at their bolt hole. They both wanted the time to be right, slow and unhurried. Despite their desperate need for each other, they had put the key in the allocated place and returned to Maddingley Hall to face whatever awaited them. Lizzie hated telling lies, but there was nothing else she could do but tell Cook she had changed her mind about going to Mary-Ann's and just had the day off.

"So, you didn't go to London then?"

"No, I changed my mind."

"Why?"

"Just thought it seemed a bit daft," replied Lizzie, hating the lie.

"So what did you do with your day then?" asked Cook, unrelenting.

This time, Lizzie could answer truthfully.

"I went to a little tea-shop in town."

Cook was about to ask Lizzie if she'd spent the whole day in the tea-shop but decided she was wasting her time. She believed she knew the truth and Lizzie wasn't about to tell her. Not until she was ready. Cook's facial expression was enough to put Lizzie on alert.

'She knows,' Lizzie thought and returned to her duties without further conversation.

Two weeks later, by a quirk of fate, Lizzie shared the same day off as Albert. It had been a most difficult fortnight, each knowing they wanted to be together, but knowing they could not. They tried in vain to avoid each other in case any suspecting eyes caught their glances. When the rotas were given, Lizzie could not believe her eyes.

'We're off on the same day. Oh goodness, I wonder if this will be the day. I wonder if we'll be together, in our little house. I wonder if ....'

Albert's heart was racing. The very thought he might be able to hold Lizzie in his arms with no restrictions, no-one who might be watching, just the two of them, was enough to send him crazy. He was crazy, crazy for Lizzie. The woman he would spend the rest of his life with, no matter what.

Albert was the first away from Maddingley Hall. He had told no-one what he intended to do with his day off. Cook watched with interest as Lizzie nonchalantly ambled down the drive an hour later with a bag slung over her shoulder. Lizzie and Albert both knew they would have to return to the Hall before dark to avoid arousing suspicion. Excitement beyond belief sprang in their hearts as once out of sight of the Hall they met and, holding hands, ran towards their destiny. This time, when they closed the door behind them, when their laughter subsided, the silence was electrifying. Their eyes locked together and they moved in closer, their inhibitions lost as their bodies responded to the urgency.

The intensity left them breathless and idyllically happy. They lay in one another's arms, their bodies still entwined, kissing, laughing, teasing and wanting. Passionately crazy for one another, their love-making continued long into the afternoon. The sun was low in the sky and it was time for them to leave. Lizzie cried onto Albert's shoulders.

"Why do we have to go back to the Hall? Why can't we stay here forever?"

Albert, almost losing control to his own feelings told Lizzie he would do everything in his power to make it possible. They declared their love for one another one more time and it was later than they'd planned when they left Sidney's house. Lizzie had swilled her face with cold water from the butt outside. Her hands were freezing and Albert covered them with his own, trying to impart some warmth. The evening became chilly. But there was something else. Lizzie felt a chill in her heart. She couldn't explain it. She was happier than she'd ever been in her whole life. She loved Albert more than life itself and she knew he felt the same. They had just consummated that love and no-one knew about them except Sidney and Martha, but there was a foreboding in her heart, which refused to go away.

They managed to get back to Maddingley Hall before dark and once again, arrived separately. No-one saw either of them return. They crept up the servants' stairs and into their own rooms, into their beds and slept. A sleep with delicious dreams of their time together, a sleep which would give them the strength to carry on hoping something would happen to enable them to be together forever.

* * * * * *

The following day, the Maddingley's were celebrating an early spring picnic. Lizzie was helping Cook prepare the hampers. Whole chickens and a couple of pheasants had been cooked and prepared, and together with a large ham, sweetbreads, potted beef and chicken jelly, these made up the savoury element of the picnic. Cook had baked the last of the apples into two of her delicious pies, made her famous shortbread and baked half a dozen small loaves of bread. Lizzie loved the smell of the kitchen when cook was baking bread and vowed when she and Albert were together, their kitchen would smell of all the mouth-watering delights she had become accustomed to at the Hall. Cook had had to reprimand her for daydreaming on more than one occasion this morning.

"Lizzie Bradshaw, have you put the champagne flutes in their holders?"

"Doing it now Cook," replied Lizzie, grinning back at her.

Their banter in the kitchen had become legendary and made for an easy working life. Lizzie knew her boundaries and Cook knew she did.

Albert's duties today would consist of assisting the stable lads with the horses. Three carriages each pulled by two horses would leave the cobbled yard and head over the fields towards the edge of the forest, where blankets would be laid down for the family's picnic. This would be followed by the races across the field. On this day, anyone who could ride could take up the challenge to win the race against Mr Maddingley, an accomplished equestrian veteran. The challenge could also be taken up by the servants and any wishing to participate would be sent for later.

Albert busied himself with his normal duties until it was time to breech the horses. Once ready, the family were informed and the ladies and gentlemen were escorted to their respective carriages, the picnic hampers were loaded onto the back of the carriages and the convoy began its journey across the field. Albert was asked by one of the visiting guests if he would be taking up the challenge. He hadn't previously considered it, but today, he decided to take the bait and accepted.

A couple of hours later when all the feasting and champagne drinking was finished, Mr Maddingley sent one of his footmen to bring along any aspiring challengers. Albert was prepared. He hadn't seen Lizzie to tell her but he knew she'd have disapproved.

His time to ride was announced and as quite a talented rider himself, he thought he may have a chance of winning the race. The prize had not, as yet, been disclosed, but in previous years, it had been quite substantial, although no-one had ever claimed it.

His horse was brought to him, one he was unfamiliar with. She must have belonged to one of the visitors. The chestnut mare, Andrina, was champing at the bit and he felt no reluctance as he mounted into the saddle. A starting gate had been erected and a single strand of wire attached to a spring at either end. The device was activated, the barrier sprang up and the horses were off. Mr Maddingley took the lead and raced his Arabian towards the other side of the field, a good half a mile away. Albert, close behind, felt the breeze blow through his hair, a totally invigorating experience. There was a point when he thought he was going to overtake the Arabian and steal the place but Mr Maddingley was an astute rider and surged his horse on to the finishing line. Just a nose behind him Albert and Andrina finished second. Mr Maddingley was so impressed by Albert's expertise on horseback, he offered him a second challenge back across the field. Albert took up the challenge. This time there was no starting gate, nor string. Just a three, two, one countdown from his employer. Albert held the position to the right of Mr Maddingley's horse. Both horses surged forward on cue. At the quarter waypoint, they were neck and neck. Galloping along, Albert had designs on winning. He felt Mr Maddingley's Arabian pull back a little and he surged Andrina on until he was a head in the lead. Then disaster struck. From a patch of undergrowth to Albert's right, a raven flew up and across the path of Andrina. The sudden flapping of wings in front of her made her skittish. She reared up on her hind legs while Albert hung on for dear life. Andrina bolted, veering off towards the forest and the river beyond. Despite trying to rein her in, Andrina gathered more speed, heading straight for the river. Albert tried to control his terror as he attempted, in vain, to bring Andrina under control, but the more he tried, the faster she ran. They'd reached the forest and still the horse ran, darting past the large trunks with amazing alacrity and heading straight for the river. Albert knew the river was deep and knew he had to stop her somehow. He considered throwing himself off but knew that was certain injury. Within two feet of the river's edge, and without warning, Andrina stopped dead in her tracks and despite using all his force to remain on the horse's back, she unseated Albert with one violent movement. The severity threw him over the top of Andrina's head, crashing him down with headlong velocity, onto a pile of sturdy rocks in the water. Blood immediately gushed out of the gaping wound on the top of his head. Albert lay motionless, his blood forming a pool of red water around his head.

* * * * * *

CHAPTER TWENTY-EIGHT

Lizzie drifted in and out of consciousness. She lay in a darkened room, the heavy drapes shielding her eyes from the light she did not wish to see. Bathed only in melancholy, she was inconsolable. She had confided in Cook. It hadn't mattered any more. Nothing mattered any more. She had not attended the funeral. Cook had told the master she had a severe case of food poisoning and the doctor had prescribed complete bed rest for two weeks. Cook had known. It hadn't come as a surprise when Lizzie rambled in her unconscious state. Cook knew Lizzie would need someone to confide in, someone to talk to, or the loneliness and the grief would likely drive her mad and they would be burying her too. And so she had questioned and Lizzie had been grateful. She'd cried on Cook's shoulder. Her life story had come pouring out. Maddingley Hall had been her saviour. She had found Albert, a truer love could never be found. She sobbed loud rasping sobs, not caring if she caught her breath in between. She didn't want to stop crying, she just wanted to stop breathing. She didn't want to continue life's journey without Albert. She couldn't. He was her heart, her lungs, her arms and legs, her soul. Her grief was total, her thoughts awash with misery.

"How can someone so beautifully perfect, so gentle, so funny, so sincere and so all-giving be gone? How can I think about going on without him?"

Cook didn't need to ask the question burning inside her. She knew. Deep down, she knew. She just hoped and prayed their love would not now betray Lizzie.

181

Riveted by the spring flowers swaying in the breeze outside and dreaming of what might have been, Lizzie stood on the second floor of Maddingley Hall gazing out of the window. Straining to see the rooftop of the little house in the distance was becoming something of an impossibility now the leaves on the trees were interrupting the view. She had found this spot quite by accident when she was still in shock. She needed something to remind her of their time together. Cook had demanded she get out of her bed and take a walk along the corridor. The masters seldom took that path to their rooms and it would be unlikely she'd see anyone. Following Cook's instructions, she'd complied and believed she could see Sidney's house from this spot on the landing. Four weeks on from Albert's untimely death, Lizzie had been given light duties away from the kitchen. As Lizzie stood by the window, a wave of something coming up from her boots overcame her. She thought she was going to faint, but then realised with astonishment the feeling had momentarily stopped in her stomach. The wave washed over her again and in stark horror, she grasped the situation and ran for the nearest exit.

Cook had known. Long before Lizzie's morning sickness had hit, she had known. She also knew the long-term consequences for Lizzie were dire. She could cover for her for now, but the inevitability of Lizzie's demise at Maddingley Hall would be mercenary.

On 30 June 1894 Lizzie Bradshaw stood at the back doorway of Maddingley Hall for the last time, her few meagre belongings packed into her small suitcase. Cook was crying with her. No-one else was allowed to say goodbye. Cook had organised her transfer to the Union Workhouse near her hometown, where she would be put to task and given board and lodgings prior to the birth of her baby. Mr Maddingley had publicly denounced her as a message to all servants who dared to cross the line, informing them in no uncertain terms that Maddingley Hall rules existed to be obeyed. There was to be no recognition for the years of hard labour Lizzie had endured with dignity, integrity and a happy disposition, helping to make the pleasant ethos Maddingley Hall was famous for.

Cook had organised a carriage to take Lizzie to the station platform where, once again, she would return to her life of poverty alone. Except for Albert's child growing within her, Lizzie had no-one. She existed now, only to give life to the love she and Albert had shared. The baby would be her life-giving saviour. She would treasure every moment spent with the tiny miracle inside her. She would have a reason to live again.

The train journey was hampered with a feeling of mixed emotion. Distraught beyond belief about Albert's death, saddened by taking her leave of Maddingley Hall, terrified of the next few months at the workhouse, and yet her heart leapt with joy for the life she and Albert had created. A life for whom she now had sole responsibility, someone to care for, love and share with. A tiny, living breathing entity she would devote her entire life to. Lizzie had already begun to pat her tummy, gentle tiny movements, which to any unsuspecting witness, would be simply passing time, as some would drum their fingers on a table. There was comfort for them both in the gesture, a reassurance everything would turn out right.

Lizzie's arrival at the workhouse was fraught with the usual stringent rules of admission. The master and matron had already been informed Lizzie was with child.

Her embarrassment at undressing was therefore minimised, as she took on the regular workhouse uniform once again and was shown to her dormitory. There were few words spoken and Lizzie guessed her time here would not be an easy one. Finally in her bed at the end of what seemed an endless day, Lizzie reflected on her life so far. The emotional agony gave way. She buried her head beneath her pillow for fear of waking others, and sobbed herself to sleep.

Lizzie found the days long and arduous, the work infinitely more demanding and physically challenging as her baby continued to grow. Spring had turned into summer and the days became warmer, intensifying the strain on her exhausted body. Despite her difficulties, Lizzie captured the hearts of those around her, assisting the older inmates whenever help was required and making herself an almost indispensable cog in the wheel of industry at the Union Workhouse.

The fatigue of a non-stop work regime was to take its toll and Lizzie collapsed, narrowly missing hitting her head on the handle of an iron pan full of boiling water. A doctor was on duty in one of the infirmary wards and came to assist. Once again, two weeks bed rest was prescribed and Lizzie was subsequently confined to a bed in the infirmary ward with nine other patients, suffering minor ailments. She struck up a friendship with an older lady in the next bed who was recovering from a miscarriage.

"I told them," she said to Lizzie. "I told them it was happening, but no-one believed me."
"What do you mean? asked Lizzie wishing to hear more.
"I'd had pains all morning. Doubled up I was. Kept telling them something was wrong but they told me

to stop moaning and I'd be alright. I knew I wasn't going to be alright."

"How far on were you?" asked Lizzie, feeling quite flushed and more than a little scared.

"The doctor reckoned about three months gone. I know you're pregnant. One of the nurses told me after they brought you in. Out cold for hours you were. You caused quite a stir lass. How far on are you?"

"About six months, give or take", answered Lizzie, relaxing a little as she spoke. She'd heard once you were past the three month mark, you had a good chance of a full term pregnancy.

"What will you do after the child's born?" asked the older lady.

"They say I'll have to leave."

"Where's the father?"

"He .....," Lizzie found it difficult to carry on speaking.

"He's dead," she finally spluttered out, tears dripping down her face.

"I'm sorry. How? How did he die?"

"A horse threw him. He hit his head on some rocks. They said it was instant."

"I'm so sorry lass. We both have a story don't we?"

The two women chatted long into the afternoon when Lizzie realised she didn't know the lady's name.

"What's your name?"

"Lottie Morgan, the lady smiled, "what's yours?"

"Lizzie Bradshaw."

They both laughed. Lizzie knew with certainty she had a friend in Lottie Morgan, who already had one child, Molly-Ann, from whom she was separated in the workhouse. Lizzie could relate to Lottie's pain and both women knew they would become firm friends.

* * * * * *

CHAPTER TWENTY-NINE

The pain gripped Lizzie in the small hours of an early August morning. She thought perhaps she'd over-indulged in the fish-pie the cook had prepared for a fortieth birthday. She sat bolt upright in bed clutching her stomach.

"Ouch," she grumbled angrily, the word lingering, realising something else was wrong too. "Have I wet the bed?" She whispered to herself, feeling the space around which she was sitting. Realising the sheet was wet, she swung her legs off the bed, inched her bottom along and felt again.

'No. I can't have done. I've never done that before.'

Barely had the thought transmitted from her brain, when she caught her breath as another pain came, sharper than the last and more prolonged.

"Oh no," she said out loud. "No, it can't be. It's not time yet."

Her suspicions were confirmed after a visit to the small space at the end of the dormitory. Thankful for her conversation with Lottie Morgan, she knew it was time. Her baby was coming and he was early.

* * * * * *

Sidney Bradshaw weighed three pounds five ounces. Lizzie's labour, sharp and intense had lasted only two hours from the onset and the little mite hadn't been expected to survive. Once again, Lizzie found herself confined to her bed, but this time, she could have lain there forever, watching her son. Hers and Albert's tiny miracle. Lost for words when she held him for the first time, the tears had dripped down her face, her body in convulsions, sobbing for the love she'd lost and for the indescribable love she now felt for the new life in her arms. A makeshift cot had been prepared and Lizzie was permitted to keep her baby with her, a ruling of the matron who'd been informed the child would probably die. Sidney didn't die.

"He's going to be fine, isn't he?" Lizzie asked Lottie, when she came to visit.

"I think you're going to be very lucky Lizzie Bradshaw," said Lottie, smiling at her friend.

Lottie hugged Lizzie, who was delighted to have found someone she could talk openly to without fear of reprisal or judgement.

Sidney continued to thrive, despite his low birth weight and premature arrival. Lizzie's providential interlude at Maddingley Hall had provided her body with the much needed sustenance to ensure Sidney had the best chance. The worrying thing now, is where she would go once her confinement was over and Sidney was considered strong enough to leave the workhouse. This opportunity came out of the blue. Lizzie hadn't known what the future held for an unmarried mother with a young baby, and in particular a mother who would sooner have died than part with her baby. She had already consciously made the decision that if the authorities deemed she were to be parted from Sidney, she would leave in the dead of night with her child. She would never give him up. He was the only part of Albert she had left and that, she would never relinquish.

Almost three weeks after Sidney was born, Lizzie received a letter. It was clear on the envelope it had previously been sent to Maddingley Hall. She didn't recognise the writing and cautiously opened it with a degree of anticipation. Its content knocked her sideways. It was from Solomon Macavelly. The letter read:

My dearest Lizzie

It is with deepest regret I'm writing to inform you of some dreadful news. Mary-Ann was almost six months pregnant. Twins. She wrote to you at the Hall, but there was no response. We assumed you had moved on. We knew you had no address to write to us, with us moving about. Mary-Ann stumbled and fell down the stairs and as a consequence we have lost our babies. She remains very poorly in hospital so I am trying to contact you again. I wrote to Maddingley Hall asking them to forward this letter to you. I am so sorry to bring you this news but hope somehow, the letter will find you. If it is at all possible, Mary-Ann would like you to come to the hospital. I think you should come as soon as you can when you receive this letter. There will be a bed for you to stay at the infirmary if you wish.

Love and best wishes

Solomon

Lizzie stared at the letter in utter disbelief. Her brain incoherently collated the information, refusing to accept yet another tragic event in their lives. She quickly located a pen and paper from her travelling bag, and putting aside the traumas of her own life, wrote straight back to Solomon.

After much deliberation by the 'midwife' who delivered Sidney, and after having noted the contents of Lizzie's letter from Solomon, it was decided to end her confinement. Lizzie had secreted a small amount of savings from Maddingley Hall, which had been for setting up house with Albert. On 4 September 1894, Lizzie Bradshaw, clutching her baby son, set out on a journey of mercy and love.

Lizzie's train arrived twenty minutes late. Solomon had been about to leave without her. He didn't want to waste a precious second away from Mary-Ann. At the last minute, as he was turning out onto the street, he heard the train in the distance and ran back onto the platform.

The inconceivable emotions about bringing Sidney with her, to two people who'd recently lost two babies, was all-consuming and Lizzie had considered turning back, but by now there was nowhere to turn back to. The workhouse in all probability wouldn't have her back, unless she once again became destitute and she desperately wanted to be with Mary-Ann. Despite the difficulties ahead, she couldn't bring herself to a decision other than the one she'd already made.

Solomon was standing, back against the wall, when the train pulled into the station. She saw him before he saw her. The carriage door was opened and she stepped down onto the platform clutching Sidney in one arm and her bag in the other. She almost felt she should conceal Sidney's presence.

'He knows about Sidney from my letter. If he hadn't wanted me to come, he wouldn't have asked me,' she thought.

Solomon spotted Lizzie amongst the commuters and strode forward to greet her. She could see the lines of sorrow etched in his face and her heart went out to him. They kissed each other's cheeks and silently she followed him out of the station and down to the waiting carriage. Apart from the odd word or two, the journey was undertaken in an awkward silence. Solomon had moved Sidney's shawl to peek at him when they first met, but apart from that, he wasn't mentioned. Lizzie found the journey and the silence between them perplexing.

'Will Mary-Ann really want me there with Sidney?' she kept asking herself.

'Or is it just Solomon doing what he thinks is the right thing to do by asking me to come?'

As the thoughts raced around her head, she hadn't noticed the carriage had pulled up outside a large conglomeration of buildings. Solomon handed some coins to the driver, took Lizzie's bag and helped her down from her seat. She stared in dismay as she realised the buildings had the same overall appearance as the one she'd just left and her heart sank. Once again, she walked into what she believed to be the corridors of horror. At first, she was pleasantly surprised. The walkways seemed clean and polished and there was a smell similar to that she'd experienced at Maddingley Hall when cleaning was in progress. Maybe her sister was more fortunate in her location. Hope sprang in her heart though she remained sceptical as they moved through the long corridors away from the entrance into the vast building. It was barely noticeable at first, but the deeper into the bowels of the workhouse they walked, a bigger the foreboding. She could hear screams and noises in the distance which unsettled her. Sidney was hungry and began to cry. She needed this journey to end.

Solomon pushed the double doors open for Lizzie to pass and then it hit her, a wave of nausea. Dumbstruck by the dramatic change from a feeling of fundamental well-being to stark horror, she numbly followed Solomon into a corridor which nurtured her fear. She no longer wanted to take Sidney into this environment. She wanted to turn and run. She involuntarily pulled his shawl up around his tiny face and held him closer. His cry for food was gaining momentum and she grabbed Solomon's arm.

"Can we go back and find somewhere for me to feed him? I don't want to take him in to see her while he's crying. It'll be better for everyone, if I can feed him first."

Solomon sensed the urgency in Lizzie's voice.

"Yes," was all he said and turning back, he walked quickly back to the double doors, through to the other side and knocked on a small door on the left of the corridor. There was no answer. He ushered Lizzie inside.

"You'll be alright in here. I'll go and see Mary-Ann and come back for you in half an hour."

Lizzie suckled Sidney undisturbed but her fear escalated. She didn't want to take Sidney back through those doors. He was so tiny and should still have been inside the warm safe haven from which he came. Lizzie pondered the problem. There was only one thing for it. She would ask Solomon to look after Sidney when he returned.

After delivering her sleeping child into the arms of Solomon Macavelly, she took a deep breath, headed back down the corridor and pushed open the double doors.   Following Solomon's directions, she approached the entrance to the infirmary. A young girl came forward to greet her.

"Lizzie   Bradshaw?"   she   asked,   obviously expecting her.

"Yes. I'm here to see Mary-Ann Macavelly."

"Come this way. She's sleeping at the moment."

Lizzie found herself in the longest room she'd ever seen, lined with beds either side. Surprisingly, the room looked clean and tidy and the smell was less pungent than before. Her spirits lifted a little. The young girl stopped beside the last bed on the left, above which was a huge window, stretching up almost to the high ceiling. A shaft of sunlight played on Mary-Ann's face. Lizzie gasped. Her sister was thin and gaunt, a ghostlike creature, lying motionless, arms stretched out alongside her body. The emotion was too much and Lizzie burst into tears.

'How could this have happened?' she wanted to shout out.   'How could our lives have brought so much torment and sorrow?'

The young girl put a hand on Lizzie's shoulder.

"My name's Polly.   Shout me if you need anything."

"Thank you," said Lizzie, continuing to stare down at Mary-Ann.

A history of memories flooded her mind as she held Mary-Ann's hand. She began to talk about them. She pulled her chair closer so she was near Mary-Ann's face and slowly and gently rubbing her sister's hand, she poured out her memories.

"It's Lizzie. I'm just remembering things. The times we've been through. Some good, some not so good! The Workhouse – you told me so many stories. I think I was too young to remember them but I remember the things you told me. The day the matron threw me across the room. Do you remember that? Awful for you that must have been when you found out what she'd done. The day we started at the orphanage and they wouldn't let you come to school 'cos you were too old. L R Davenport, rotten old man. Wonder if he was to blame for our Katy leaving. I liked him in the beginning 'til he took me to London. Don't really know what made me stop liking him. Just got scared really. His wife tho. Do you remember her? When she came to the orphanage dressed as a nun to give us that message. That was funny. We laughed and laughed about that. The day you left. We were all stood in the stone room. I lifted our Katy up for you to kiss goodbye. That'd be the last time you saw her. We watched you walk away. It was awful. Then in London, when the police caught L R. Lucky I managed to get away. He stopped to tie his shoelaces and I ran. Couldn't believe you were there too. Then you meeting Solomon and me going to old Jack Dodd's. Don't know if I ever thanked you for that, but in the end, he wasn't such a nice man. Then you came and told me about our Katy. Broke our hearts. My heart will never mend. I still miss her terribly. Then I went to Maddingley. You were still a nursemaid then. I loved it at Maddingley. Felt at home there. Christmas times were the best. Then you got married."

Lizzie stopped her ramblings and stared at Mary-Ann. She lay almost lifeless in the bed. She hadn't flinched the whole time Lizzie had been talking. Lizzie crossed to the other side of the ward to have a chat with one or two of the patients who had waved to her. She could hear a commotion in the corridor outside the ward and excused herself, going back to Mary-Ann to continue her reminiscences before it was time to go. Rubbing Mary-Ann's hand, she continued her ramblings.

"Maddingley shut down and I had to leave. I went back to the bakery, which wasn't a bakery any more but they let me stay for a few nights. I got a job in a factory and met Arthur. I thought I was in love but he turned out to be a wrong'un. I went to stay with Auntie Julia's daughter, Teresa for a while. She was a funny one she was. Had a new job too. Then Maddingley re-opened and I went back. That's when I met Albert. Oh Mary-Ann, I loved him. Can't believe he's gone. He's Sidney's father. They threw me out of Maddingley when they found out I was pregnant. That's when I had to go back in the workhouse. Then I heard about you. I had to come Mary-Ann. I had to. Please get better. We need you.   Me and Solomon. We need you."

Lizzie leaned over and kissed Mary-Ann's forehead. It felt cold and clammy. Feeling a sense of despair creep over her, Lizzie stood up. The nursing staff were beginning their rounds and she knew it was time to leave. She remembered Solomon had said there would be a place for her to stay. She wondered if that were still true. She approached the most senior looking nurse to ask about Mary-Ann's condition.

In a rather brusque manner, she told Lizzie, "She's been like that since she lost her babies. We don't know how long she'll remain in a coma. She lost a lot of blood and we're doing the best we can. It's up to the good Lord now."

It was time to leave and Lizzie crossed back over to Mary-Ann. Bending down, she whispered in her ear.

"Come on Mary-Ann, you have to get better. We need you. You're all we've got. Come on, you can do it. Come back to us."

She kissed her sister once more and hurriedly left the ward before the tears came. Hurrying back to Sidney and Solomon, instead of the despair she should be feeling, Lizzie felt light. Deep down, she knew Mary-Ann would recover.

Despite her optimism about Mary-Ann's recovery, she felt something else was about to change. What she couldn't have predicted was that something, would be dramatically, horrifically life-changing.

* * * * * *

CHAPTER THIRTY

Lizzie had nowhere left to go, yet this fact didn't deter her excitement. She pleaded her case and the guardians at the workhouse infirmary permitted her to stay for a short while with Sidney. An arrangement had been reached which suited all parties. Lizzie had requested to help out in the infirmary if her son could be cared for during her stay. She was allowed to see him at feeding times and the room Solomon had taken her to when she first arrived was designated for that purpose. It was a temporary arrangement and the date for Lizzie's departure back to the North of England was set for the 24 October. Solomon remained in the male section of the workhouse. She didn't see him every day and felt he was impartial to her presence.

'Perhaps it's Sidney,' she thought. 'The wounds are too raw.'

Her premonition regarding Mary-Ann's recovery proved correct and she was at Mary-Ann's bedside when she opened her eyes. An ecstatic moment existed between them, as Mary-Ann recognised her and tears filled the eyes of both women. Lizzie knelt down beside the bed and propped her head up on her hands staring at Mary-Ann, searching her sister's features for signs of pain. She found none.

"Lizzie!" said Mary-Ann softly.

Lizzie couldn't speak.

They held hands. There was no need for words.

Within a few days Mary-Ann was allowed to be propped up against her pillows. She watched in awe as

Lizzie exercised careful attention on the other patients. Lizzie's presence with her cheerful disposition brought happiness to those suffering a dull and painful existence.

Mary-Ann continued to grow in strength, not least because of Lizzie's positive influence. The next few weeks saw Mary-Ann returning rapidly to her healthy self. Solomon was beside himself and despite his earlier impartiality towards Lizzie, he realised Mary-Ann's full recovery was in no small part due to Lizzie's presence and for that he would remain eternally grateful.

The day Lizzie Bradshaw and her son Sidney left the workhouse in London, the two sisters clung to one another. Lizzie, full of anticipation for her chosen career back in the North of England and Mary-Ann thrilled to be alive and feeling well again. Lizzie's departure and the loss of her twin babies would leave a hole in Mary-Ann's life that could never be filled, but they both knew their destiny was not to be together.

Lizzie made her way to the station for the return journey, a track into the unknown. She cuddled Sidney and spoke softly to him, ecstatic to have him with her, a tiny life, developing his own personality and one whom she loved more than anything in the world. Happy and with a spring in her step, she boarded the train and finding an empty carriage, surrendered herself to the joy of her son.

Lizzie re-entered the Union Workhouse that same evening. She put forward her intentions to be discussed at the next Guardian's meeting. This time, Lizzie's return to the workhouse was purely voluntary. Her time in the London workhouse spurred her on towards a possible nursing career.

'If I gain further knowledge and experience, perhaps I can apply for training.' She thought. Following the Guardian's meeting, Lizzie was brought in front of the Master and Matron.

"Lizzie," the matron began.

"We have discussed your proposals. Your training in the Infirmary Ward will begin immediately. Your son will remain in the children's wing and you will have full access once your duties have been fulfilled."

Lizzie's delight was fuelled with optimism and her confidence grew daily. Her ability to encourage patients' recovery astounded the infirmary staff and guided by the long-term experience of her older peers, she learnt quickly how to deal with the ever-growing balance of motherhood and work life. Surrounded daily by dire poverty, she overlooked her own dismal life, instead working towards creating a happy environment for her son and her patients. A positive ethos resounded throughout the buildings. She was an inspiration to many and the Guardians discussed the possibility of opening up a small unit for medical training. Lizzie was approached and asked if she'd like to assist in the training unit. She declined, preferring to be hands on with the patients and spend time with Sidney, her life and soul.

"Thank you for the opportunity, but I prefer to tend the patients and be with my son," was her response.

* * * * * *

The winter was fast approaching and the cold seeped in through every crevice of the building. Lizzie's concern for Mary-Ann continued to grow as newspapers reported widespread flooding in the South following high rainfall during October and the early half of November. The cold damp conditions of the workhouses had a profound effect on older patients in the infirmary wards and there were many deaths in the first two weeks of November. Lizzie was tired and wanted to spend more time with Sidney. At every available opportunity, she ran to the children's ward to be with him. Concerned for her small son and the cold wet winter upon them, she needed reassuring at regular intervals he was being well cared for.

On 18 November 1894, a visiting guardian from the South, informed staff the River Thames had burst its banks, causing wide-spread flooding and pandemonium. Lizzie listened intently to the chatter about the abhorrent conditions people were dealing with and wanted to go straight to Mary-Ann. She went in to see Lottie to talk it over with her. Lottie was the more sensible one of the two women.

"I know it's hard Lizzie, but you have to think about Sidney. I don't think you should go chasing off down to the other end of the country with a young baby. Solomon will take care of Mary-Ann."

Lizzie had to admit defeat.

"Your place for the time being is here with us," said Lottie, smiling.

Lottie had recovered from her miscarriage and was now back to her normal duties. The two women had become what they hoped would be lifelong friends and Lizzie was grateful she'd met Lottie whose friendship she valued. Giving Lottie a quick hug, Lizzie left her to go and see Sidney, her duties for the day finished.

Sidney lay in his cot sleeping. Lizzie touched his head, he was hot. Alarmed as the building was so cold, she wrung out a cloth in cold water and lay it across his tiny head. He didn't flinch, he didn't cry, he didn't do anything. She bent down and taking him out of his cot she nuzzled him into her neck. His body felt too warm.

Cradling him in her arms, she sat down beside his cot and rocked him, singing gently which usually brought a happy response. She held him close to her breast so he could suckle but there was no movement.

'He must be getting a fever,' Lizzie thought.

Lying him back down in his cot and assuring herself he was breathing normally, she raced back to the infirmary to find a doctor or senior nurse. The doctor could find nothing abnormal and reassured Lizzie her baby would be fine. As his mother, Lizzie knew Sidney was not fine and pushed time and again for someone to come and look at him. The result was always the same.

"Nothing wrong with him."

Lizzie did everything a mother could do to ensure Sidney's comfort. but he remained hot and despite administering cooling cloths, his body heat remained high.

On 25 November 1894, at just over three months old, Sidney Bradshaw passed from the shores of this life to a new one. Somewhere innocents cannot feel the pain life inflicts on them in this world. He was in his mother's arms, where he felt safe and warm when he drew his last breath. There had been no other contra-indications to suggest anything life-threatening. The scream which emanated from Lizzie's mouth could be heard throughout the building. People came rushing from all quarters to the sound of a mother's terror. Lizzie dropped to her knees clutching Sidney against her, rocking him in the hopes she'd imagined what had just happened.

"He just stopped breathing," was all she was capable of saying. The doctor on duty together with two of the nursing staff finally managed to release Sidney from Lizzie's clutches to examine him. A definitive conclusion as to the cause of death was unable to be established and Lizzie was encouraged to believe the most likely cause had been an infection.

With Lottie on one side and a member of the nursing staff holding her other arm, Lizzie allowed herself to be escorted to the place where her son would be buried. A small moving ceremony was performed by the workhouse chaplain. Lizzie was incoherent, her body racked from head to foot in agonising pain, as the tiny crude coffin was lowered into the ground. Nothing had ever or could ever have prepared her for the excruciating ache in her heart. Nothing would ever feel or be the same again. The heart and soul of Lizzie Bradshaw was buried in the ground with Sidney, a part of her she knew would never resurface.

* * * * * *

CHAPTER THIRTY-ONE

Lizzie's inconsolable grief had an overwhelming effect on the people around her. Lottie did everything possible to help raise Lizzie's spirits. It didn't matter Lizzie didn't respond, Lottie never stopped trying. She was there for her the whole time, even if it was just sitting with her, not speaking. She read light-hearted stories to her. It didn't matter, just so long as she was with her friend, a comfort for her if she needed it.

The staff and inmates were making preparations for the forthcoming Christmas, three weeks away. Lizzie didn't take part, she didn't care, there was no point. There was nothing to celebrate any more. Christmas was meaningless without Albert and her son. Only twelve short months ago, she had been on the brink of a new life, an excited young woman about to take the plunge into the realms of love. Now, almost one year on, she was left with nothing but a wound in her heart so deep, it could never heal.

* * * * * *

Lizzie reached out for her bag and took out her pen and a piece of notepaper. She began to write the letter she never dreamed she'd have to write.

My dearest Mary-Ann

I am writing to inform you the saddest news. Sidney passed away on 25 November. I have not been able to bring myself to write to you, such is my grief. I know you'll understand and share my grief as you have suffered the same. I will be leaving the workhouse shortly. After leaving you, I had been so inspired by the work of the nursing staff, I thought I may have a future in nursing and approached the guardians here. I have been working in the infirmary as well as caring for Sidney and managing the two quite nicely. They say Sidney's death was possibly due to an infection. I miss him so terribly, I can't bear to be in this place without him. I have to leave. I've a few coins left and aside from the excruciating pain in my heart, I am well enough to look for work elsewhere. When I am settled, I will write again and let you have an address. I think about you every second of every day and hope the flood waters have subsided a little. Please take great care.

Your loving sister Lizzie xx

Christmas came and went without any assistance from Lizzie Bradshaw. Lottie was with her every conceivable spare minute she had. Two days after Christmas, Lizzie told Lottie she was leaving. Lottie broke into sobs.

"Where will you go? I don't want you to go. No-one will. We all want you here, where you belong."

"I don't belong anywhere now Lottie, I'm a free spirit, I can go where I please. Somehow I will make my way in the world. I can't stay here reliving the memories of my sorrow each day. I would go insane. You don't want to come visiting me in the 'other' infirmary ward, do you?"

Lottie smiled. She was pleased as punch. A flash of the old Lizzie had surfaced and she was delighted.

"No, but I don't not want to see you every day either. Will you ever come back this way?"

"Who knows Lottie? No-one but the Lord himself and he won't talk to me, 'cos I near disowned him for taking my Katy, Albert and Sidney away. No, he'll not talk to me."

"Well, perhaps you could visit now and again?" begged Lottie, determined not to give up.

"Depends what happens next."

"Do you know what day you're leaving yet? Have you somewhere to go. You can't go wandering the streets, there's all sorts could happen if you do that."

"Yes, I'm leaving on New Year's Eve. I'm leaving this sad and sorry year behind and starting again. The beginning of a new year. Can't think of a better day to go. Leave it all behind. I know I'll always have my memories, imprinted on my brain forever they are. I'll never forget you Lottie Morgan, you've been my most treasured friend ever."

They fell into one another's arms and wept.

"Do they know yet?" asked Lottie.

"No."

"When are you going to tell them?"

"Right now", quipped Lizzie and with that she patted Lottie's arm and left the room.

* * * * * *

The evening before Lizzie left the workhouse for the last time, the inmates together with some of the staff gathered to say their goodbyes. It was an emotional evening, as despite the life of poverty in the workhouse, Lizzie knew without it, she would have been out on the streets. In the quiet aftermath of her 'send-off', she reflected how Katy must have felt the night before she left the orphanage. A young life dragged through a motherless childhood to be cruelly torn away from the only life she knew, and never to see her siblings again.

'Damn the ravages of this poverty-stricken life,' she thought. 'I won't be ground down by servitude and grief. I'm going to survive. I'm going out there and I'm going to show them all, they can't stop Lizzie Bradshaw.'

With that thought, she closed her eyes and slept.

The bitter cold wind howled through the cracks in her window as she rose the next morning and prepared herself for the next phase of her life. She knew exactly where she was going and what she was going to do. At precisely ten o'clock, she made her way to the station, to stand on the platform once more and wait for the train to take her back to Mary-Ann and from where she would put the second part of her plan into effect.

Lizzie worked in the infirmary of the London workhouse for almost a month, waiting to hear if her application to become a trainee nurse at one of the local hospitals had been successful. Her role as domestic servant at Maddingley Hall and her references from the guardians from both workhouse infirmaries would certainly help towards the positive answer she required. This, she hoped, would put her on the right road to a future, where her love of humanity could blossom. She could devote her life to helping the people who most needed it. She would have little reason to consider her own needs and could throw herself into the role fully and wholeheartedly. Her long-term plan was to return to the North of England. The letter arrived promptly and Lizzie jumped up and down with delight when she discovered its contents.

"Yes, I'm in," she said aloud.

Mary-Ann laughed. "You're a force to be reckoned with. I hope they're prepared for you, Lizzie Bradshaw!"

Lizzie began her training at the nursing hospital the following Monday. Bitter cold wet conditions still prevailed in London and she was happy to note in the letter she was being given board and lodgings at the hospital.

Life was tough. She received a meagre allowance which barely covered the cost of essentials but she knew the end result could be the beginning of the rest of her life. As was always the case, she quickly made new friends. Her beauty was astounding, yet despite there being a plethora of requests to take her out, she wasn't interested. She denied them all her company, preferring to retire to her small room at the end of her taxing days or to spend time with Mary-Ann.

Solomon had become almost a recluse. He kept himself to himself and rarely visited Mary-Ann. Their life together as a married couple had ceased to exist. He didn't interact with any of the other male inmates, preferring to spend his time alone. He always refused to see Lizzie, who hoped to bring about a reconciliation. She never gave up trying, but she had seen Solomon Macavelly for the last time. He contracted a respiratory disease, rife in his quarters at the time and passed away in March 1895, leaving Mary-Ann widowed and childless. Lizzie remained with Mary-Ann on compassionate leave for two days following Solomon's funeral and with a heavy heart, returned to her training.

Exhausted at the end of each day, Lizzie retired to her room, wrote up her nursing notes, completed any projects she'd been given and slept. She had a small appetite, was particularly trim and agile and had indeed beauty from the inside but although the temptation was sometimes great, she denied herself the privilege of male company. Apart from the feeling of guilt if she were to spend time with another man, she didn't want the complication to interfere with her devotion to nursing. She wanted more than anything, now, to care for the less fortunate, to help give them hope and a better quality of life and absorb her thoughts on others instead of the dire alternative to wallow in her own self-pity.

Her training concluded and Lizzie received her certificate of proficiency. It was time to begin looking to the future. She had spent as little of her allowance as possible and had a small amount saved to enable her to return to the North and find lodgings. She visited Mary-Ann and amidst the tears which ensued, they said their goodbyes. The parting was at best difficult for them both as they spoke of Katy who would always be a part of their lives and whose memory would stay with them forever.

"Promise me you'll come back soon," begged Mary-Ann.

"I will. I promise."

Lizzie packed her travel bag and made her journey back to the North of England hoping her qualification would secure her a position in the nursing profession. She scoured the local newspapers for advertisements and finally selected the one she believed to be the most suitable. Not too far from the workhouse where she hoped Lottie still lived.

In March 1897 Lizzie began to work and lodge in a small local hospital. She threw herself into her work with ease and in a short period of time became renowned for her expertise and bedside manner. Her life slowly began to improve. Interacting with confidence to requests for 'walking out' she began to enjoy the company of men but none came close to replacing Albert. Her ability to make people laugh was infectious and everyone loved her company, patients, colleagues and friends. She visited

Lottie often and it was on her way to one of these visits, the bolt came out of the blue.

* * * * * *

CHAPTER THIRTY-TWO

William Casey entered Lizzie's life dramatically, like a shower of fireworks shooting through the night sky - spectacularly. With a thick set face, clear blue eyes and a large nose beneath which sat a dark wild moustache, at a little over twenty one years of age his youth and rugged good lucks belied the inner man.

William was in a hurry to leave the tobacconist's shop. Dragging his fingers through his slick dark hair, he threw his money onto the pitted wooden counter and dashed back to the open doorway clutching one packet of tobacco and shoving the other deep into his pocket, the only thing on his mind now, to make it to the bookies. Slightly hung over from his drinking binge the night before, he still knew the way blindfold and without looking, he made a sharp left once out of the doorway.

Lizzie was on her way to see Lottie, strolling along, humming her favourite tune, the one she used to sing to Sidney, oblivious to the world around her. William hadn't seen her. He was too busy in his dash to the bookies, whilst attempting to roll a cigarette from his newly purchased tobacco. Head down, almost at a run, the impact was inevitable. Both yelled in shock as Lizzie crumpled onto the pavement. William attempted to regain his balance as he tried to avoid tripping over her. The pouch and tobacco went flying into the road but he managed to stay upright, annoyed this someone had been in his way, an inconvenience he wouldn't forget. He turned to hurl a tirade of abuse as Lizzie was gaining her composure, pulling her dress back down over her knees and attempting to lever herself from the floor.

With his mouth agape, he tried to utter the words but they wouldn't come. Instead, he threw himself to his knees at the side of her, offering her a helping hand to grasp onto. Their eyes met.

"I'm so sorry, are you hurt?" he said, eventually. "Here, let me help you up."

Lizzie wanted to yell too and reprimand him severely for not looking where he was going but she couldn't. She wanted to yelp "Ouch!" but she couldn't. Ashamedly, all she could do was put her hand into the one he offered and let the tall, stocky stranger help her up. They stood face to face staring, taking in each delectable facet of each other. They wanted to fall into one another's arms, feel the warmth of the beauty before them and immerse themselves in pleasure.

Lizzie spoke first. "I'm okay now, thank you."
William found himself speechless again, desperately searching for something to say which would keep her there.
"Are you sure? Can I escort you anywhere? I'm so sorry. I didn't see you. I wasn't watching where I was going."
Lizzie, still a little dazed and totally dazzled by William's good looks made her decision in a split second.
"Well I am a bit wobbly. I'm going to see my friend. It's a couple of streets away."
Lizzie smiled at William and he took his cue. Holding onto her elbow to support her, they slowly made their way towards the end of the street. William's suave manner had Lizzie reeling.

'How can I possibly feel like this about someone I've just met, someone who knocked me to the floor, someone I was going to yell at. This can't be happening.'

Carnal thoughts flooded her brain, but something far more urgent was surging through her body. Following her intense love for Albert, something she thought she'd never feel again.

Intoxicated by her beauty and genteel manner, William was smitten. He'd never experienced the flood of emotion which overwhelmed him. It confused him. His usual train of thought was not at play here. He couldn't deny the sexual attraction, but this was something else as well. By the time they reached the corner where Lizzie would turn to walk down to the workhouse, Lizzie had agreed to see William again. She was to meet him beneath the clock at the train station at one o'clock on Saturday afternoon. Their parting was awkward. They each wanted more but William didn't want to spoil his chances. Lizzie didn't want to appear desperate, so William took his leave and Lizzie walked the rest of the way to see Lottie in a haze of bewilderment.

'William Casey, I think I'm in love,' she mused and having regained total balance, she almost skipped the rest of the way to the workhouse, so excited was she to sit and discuss the events of the morning with her confidante.

* * * * * *

"I don't believe you Lizzie Bradshaw," jibed Lottie. "Men are supposed to fall at your feet, not you at theirs!" Both girls laughed.

"Is he really that handsome?" questioned Lottie, wanting Lizzie to elaborate every detail of the man responsible for her contagious excitement.

"He's more than that. He's got the looks, but there's something else, something daring me to find out more."

"Well, I hope you know what you're doing. Don't go doing anything stupid."

"Well, I'm not promising Lottie. He's so, so ...."

"Interesting......?" quipped Lottie.

"Absolutely," replied Lizzie.

The two women talked non-stop about William Casey until Lottie had to return to work. The call from the matron shook them, neither realised how long they'd been sat talking.

"I'd better go," said Lottie, standing up to hug Lizzie farewell. "Let me know how it goes on Saturday."

"I will," promised Lizzie, already making her way to the door.

* * * * * *

The next time the two girls met, Lizzie was five months pregnant with William Casey's child and Lottie didn't need an introduction to Lizzie's plight.

"Is he going to marry you?" she asked a little disdainfully, expecting a negative response.

"Oh yes, Lottie. That's why I've come. We're getting married in May. Will you be my bridesmaid? Please?"

Overwhelmed by her friend's presence, after a long absence, Lottie stretched out her arms and Lizzie fell into them. They hugged and cried and when their elation subsided, Lizzie began her story.

"I don't really know where to begin."

"The beginning is always a good place," said Lottie, smiling at the friend she was delighted to be reunited with.

"Well, that Saturday afternoon, I was supposed to meet him, beneath the clock at the station, at one o'clock."

"Yes, I remember," said Lottie, inwardly digesting with horror how long ago it had been.

"Well, he didn't turn up. I waited and waited. I was in a dreadful state by four o'clock. It had been a dismal day and the night was setting in and murky. I was worried sick what could have happened to prevent him from coming. I thought something awful must have happened."

"How much longer did you wait?"

"About another half hour. I left the station about half past four. It was raining and the sky was darkening fast. I didn't really want him to come by then. I didn't have an umbrella, my hair was all messed up and I'd been crying. I walked back to the nurse's home and cried all night."

"Why didn't you come to see me?" Lottie asked. "How awful it must have been. To have been so excited for nothing."

"I was ashamed of myself. I couldn't believe I'd been willing to be unfaithful to Albert's memory, and after losing Sidney too."

"But you wouldn't have ...... would you?"

"Yes, I believe I would. I was besotted with him. A stranger, a man who'd knocked me over, flying in his hurry to get to the bookies. Someone who I thought was as taken with me as I was with him."

"How did you know he was going to the bookies?" asked Lottie, sensing Lizzie's sinister tone.

"I'll get to that later."

Lottie bit her tongue and sat patiently waiting for Lizzie's story to unfold.

Lizzie began to cry. Her pent up agony and frustration began pouring out. Lottie put her arm around her and waited for Lizzie's tears to subside.

"After that night, I tried not to think about William. He clearly didn't want me. He didn't try to contact me and after a month or so, I took some leave and went to see Mary-Ann. I just needed to get away, to think things through. I realised I didn't want to spend my life alone, but the only man I've ever felt for since Albert, had let me down. I didn't think I could go through that again. I know I could have come to you, but shame prevented me. I was unsure what you'd think of me. When I got to London, Mary-Ann wasn't at the workhouse. They gave me a forwarding address at the other side of London. I made my way there, but she'd gone."

Lottie handed her a clean rag. Lizzie wiped the tears aside and continued.

"The landlady told me Mary-Ann was in hospital. When I got there she'd been moved to the tuberculosis isolation ward and they wouldn't let me in to see her. I told them she had no-one else, I was her only family but it made no difference. I wasn't allowed in. I didn't know what to do."

Lizzie faltered again and Lottie squeezed her. "Come on, I'll see if I can make us a nice warm drink."

Refreshed a little, Lizzie continued.

"I went back to Mary-Ann's address and asked the landlady if I could stay a couple of nights. She said I could stay until the end of the week but then I'd have to leave because she'd re-let Mary-Ann's room, not knowing if, or when, she might come back. I was worried sick about the awful trouble I'd be in at work, but I couldn't just leave."

"So how had Mary-Ann managed to leave the workhouse and get lodgings?" asked Lottie, not understanding how Mary-Ann could have paid rent.

"She was sharing with two other girls but they'd been a bad lot and moved on with their boyfriends leaving Mary-Ann with all the rent to pay. The landlady felt sorry for her and said she could have the room a bit cheaper till she found something else. She got a job as an apprentice sewing machinist in a textile mill but she became sick and needed to be nursed. The landlady said she was near death's door when they came for her.

I stayed in Mary-Ann's room for three nights. It was cold, damp and miserable. I got a fever and the landlady went for a doctor. I was taken to the same hospital. I stayed for a month but they didn't move me to the TB ward. I recovered but had nowhere to go. I couldn't come back up North, I had no money left. I couldn't go back to the lodgings as the room was no longer available. I went to the textile mill where Mary-Ann had worked and they gave me a job but I had an accident on the first day. I still don't really know what happened. Someone had left a box of bobbins out in the middle of the aisle. I didn't see it and fell headlong over it. Broke my right arm. They sent me back to the hospital. They asked me if I had anywhere to go. I told them I didn't. I asked them if they'd write to the nurse's home to let them know where I was. They said I could stay until they received a reply. They did reply and wanted me to go back. I didn't want to, I didn't want to leave Mary-Ann alone again, but I had no choice."

"What happened to Mary-Ann?"

Lizzie burst into tears again. "The disease was in advanced stages. She was terribly ill, coughing up blood and stuff they said. They told me she wouldn't really know me and she most likely wouldn't recover, that I'd be best to pass on my farewells before I left."

Lottie listened to Lizzie's tale in utter disbelief.

Lizzie continued. "They gave me my train fare and I came back to the nurse's home. I had to tell them everything that had happened. They were angry with me for not writing to let them know. To be honest Lottie, I don't know why I didn't. Anyway, they agreed to let me come back. My arm continued to heal and at least I was somewhere where they could look after it for me. I know I could have come to see you then but I was still so ashamed. I couldn't bring myself to come and I was frightened if I did, I'd find you gone too.

One day, I was out walking with one of the other nurses and I saw William Casey. My heart stopped beating. I tried to hide myself. I didn't want him to see me, but it was too late. He came running over. Despite everything, those feelings were still there and I couldn't hide them. He asked what had happened to my arm and Martha, who I was with, realised we knew one another and went off by herself to do a bit of shopping. William and I walked and talked for a while. He apologised for not turning up that day but said he'd felt ill all day. I believed him.

We'd been going out for about ten weeks. I should have seen the signs but I didn't want to. We still hadn't, you know, done anything, but I thought that was because of my arm. But that was healed by then so I couldn't understand. One day I saw him with another girl, kissing her behind the butcher's shop on Olive Street. I was devastated. I decided that day, I never wanted to see him again. I didn't go out with him again, but my feelings were still the same. I was torn. I went out on a home visit with one of the trained nurses one night and saw him coming out of the tavern. He was drunk and disorderly, making a show of himself. He didn't see me.

One night, there was a knock on the door of the nurse's home. One of the other trainees answered the door and said it was for me. I wondered if it might have been you. It was him. He begged me to come out with him. Said he was really sorry for what had happened and he really wanted to see me again. So the following night, I met him and he took me to the tavern I'd seen him coming out of that night. He bought me a couple of beers and I got a bit tipsy. I kept telling him I needed to get back home, but he paid no attention, just kept coming on to me. I didn't want it to be like that, but I wanted him. I wanted to love someone and someone to love me. I needed him. He said there was a room upstairs we could use. I protested. I didn't want it to be like that, I wanted him to love me."

Lizzie was crying, garbling the words over and over. Lottie was crying too. She wanted so much for there to be a happy ending for this lady, her best friend, who had been through so much torment, lost so much love and yet had so much to give.

"I agreed to go upstairs, but when I was in the room, I got scared. He changed and became rough with me. Oh Lottie, I didn't want to, but he made me do it. I did want him, but not like that."

Lizzie's sobs became so loud, other people began to come over to see if she was alright. Lottie assured them Lizzie was alright and they left them alone.

"So, this is the result?" asked Lottie, patting Lizzie's bump.

"Yes, the little one is William's."

"And you and William? How is it now?"

"Sometimes it's good and sometimes it's awful. He drinks like crazy and then it's awful. When he's not been drinking or gambling, he's a good man.

"Do you love him Lizzie?"

"Yes."

Lottie wasn't convinced.

"And you're marrying this man whom you love to hate?"

"Yes. Will you be my bridesmaid?"

"I will, if you tell me why you're doing this."

"I'm doing it for the baby. I don't want to go back into the workhouse with this child. I don't want to lose another baby Lottie. I don't want to lose anyone else."

"And you think marrying William is the answer?"

"Yes."

"Then yes, I will help you. Just let me know what you need. It's yours."

* * * * * *

CHAPTER THIRTY-THREE

In the parish church of Saint Ambrose Barlow, Elizabeth Bradshaw and William Casey pledged their vows. The small gathering, scattered amongst the first three pews, knew Lizzie was six months pregnant, despite her attempt to disguise her ever growing bump beneath the dress Lottie had given her. The rays of the early morning sunshine caught the vibrant colours of the stained glass windows, casting tiny shafts of coloured light across the dark interior of the church. Dust particles showered like remnants of confetti over the couple stood before the altar. Mrs Casey snuffled a lot into a hanky and Mr Casey's breath smelt like a vat of whisky. A few people coughed when the chaplain asked for anyone who knew of any impediment. Lottie wondered why. She wondered a lot of things about William Casey.

At twenty-eight years of age, Lizzie Bradshaw was stunning. She didn't stand there in the light of God and the Church, in a white gown, claiming innocence. She didn't clutch a cascading floral arrangement with its fronds of greenery skimming the silk and taffeta of a beautifully designed dress. She didn't have on her tiny feet a silken pair of shoes befitting a princess and nor did she have a honeymoon or a future to look forward to. But Lizzie Bradshaw was the most beautiful bride in her stunning simplicity. Standing there with pride and dignity, her dark ringlets cascaded where the flowers might have done, a small ring of daisy-like flowers crowned the top of her head and innocent hope shone from the glow on her face and in her eyes when she looked at William. She tried to believe they may have a future together, that they might be the perfect married couple, despite the bitter gossip. She smiled, denying all the horrors of her life as she proclaimed her love, honour and obedience to the man who'd all but raped her and brought her to this moment, for the love of her unborn child.

Lottie had seen inside Lizzie's soul and loved her like her own flesh and blood. She knew Lizzie's heart inside and out, and stood before the altar on that sunny May morning in 1898, she prayed Lizzie's life, together with the new life inside her, would prove to be rich in the happiness so deserved by this lady whose friendship she cherished.

The previous evening had been a mixture of happiness and grief. Lizzie on the brink of married life had chosen to spend her last night as a single woman in the company of her best friend. The nursing staff had paid for a room at a nearby hotel for the two women to prepare for Lizzie's wedding day. There had been laughter and tears, sadness and joy, but Lottie had been the only person with whom Lizzie would have shared her emotions, on the eve of her wedding.

William Casey had been at the tavern with his father. He had occupied the room upstairs for two hours with the woman Lizzie had seen him kissing and returned home to drink whisky with his father until the small hours when Mrs Casey found them in a drunken stupor on the floor of her front parlour.

Mrs Casey hadn't been able to sleep. William was bringing his new wife home to a temporary life with them until they got on their feet and could afford a place of their own. She was nervous and agitated. Bullied by a drunken husband and son, she knew she should have left them years ago but couldn't bring herself to leave. During the two men's absence that evening, she had made William's bachelor room as homely as she could for Lizzie, trying to impart a more congenial atmosphere in the room, fitting for her son's bride. She was nervous for Lizzie and hoped the young woman might be able to succeed where she had failed. She doubted it. She wondered whether the new bairn would bring about the change in her son she hadn't been able to. Only time would tell.

Lottie's prayers for a lovely day for Lizzie were answered. On the surface, the day went off without a hitch. The sun shone, the service was pleasant and the buffet at the nurse's home delicious. William had showered Lizzie with guilty attention and the undertones of his conceited and audacious nature had gone largely unnoticed, except by Lottie.

Lottie also underwent a change of circumstances. She had bumped into an old friend visiting the workhouse looking for a relative. They had begun a relationship some years ago but it had fizzled out before it had time to ignite. She had often wished he had been the father of her children instead of the man who'd abandoned her when she told him she was pregnant again. Her first-born, Molly Ann was now four years old and attending the school in the workhouse. Molly-Ann had been looking forward to her new brother or sister but Lottie had told her the baby had to go and play with the angels instead. Molly-Ann was now looking forward to the arrival of Lizzie's new baby and had jumped up in the classroom one day and proudly announced to the teacher and the rest of the class that her mother's friend Lizzie was going to have a baby soon and she'd be able to play with her, convinced the baby would be a girl.

Lottie's newfound relationship with Edward Gallagher began to blossom. Edward had done well for himself, holding down a managerial position at one of the local engineering companies. Lottie felt she'd been waiting for this moment all her life. She'd always burnt a candle for him even though the flame was extinguished before it flourished. Now it was burning strong again and she knew this time, it would burn bright. Lizzie was, of course, the first person she told and delighted for her friend decided to delay informing her of the bruising sustained on her arms, dealt by a vicious blow from William following another drinking binge.

Mrs Casey, long bewildered by the behaviour of the two men in her life had opted to confide in Lizzie, reproaching herself every day for not informing her before the wedding that her son was a dead-leg no-good drunken, gambling womaniser. She had hoped Lizzie's good heart and vivacious appetite for life would transform her son and that the love of a good woman would bring him to his senses. She'd been wrong.

Lottie moved out of the workhouse at the end of June, following a whirlwind romance with Edward Gallagher. Lizzie followed her down the aisle in a wedding ceremony she could only have dreamed of. Lottie, Edward and Molly Ann moved into 158 Boston Road at the beginning of July to begin their new life together as a family. Following a brief discussion with Edward, they agreed to share their joy after an initial period of time on their own, with Lizzie and William. William was reluctant. He didn't want to go somewhere else. He wanted to stay in his parents' home, where he could continue his reign of tyranny without reproach from interfering busy-bodies, but his strong-willed wife, having suffered on more than one occasion the effects of his drunken nature, informed him she was going anyway. He could either go with her or their marriage was doomed. Besotted with Lizzie in his few sober moments, he reluctantly agreed.

The house was three stories and Lizzie and William's room was on the top floor. The two men left the house for work early each morning, Edward to his office at the engineering works and William to labour in the local copper works, making a reasonable wage to fuel his dark habits. For a short while the arrangement was acceptable to all and in the days leading up to Lizzie's confinement, they lived a reasonably settled existence.

Mary Alice arrived in the world in the early hours of a mid August morning in 1898 amidst a frenzy of excitement in the household, fuelled mainly by Lottie's daughter, Molly Ann, who at almost five years of age couldn't contain her excitement and ran about the house wanting to help everyone. The lady who 'attended' had been sent for, the men were packed off out of the house earlier than usual and Lottie carried boiling water by the bucketful for the dutiful 'midwife'. Having been delivered of a healthy baby girl and all the arrangements down below attended to, Lizzie basked in the presence of her 6lbs 8oz baby girl, the pain of her labour now evaporated. Mary Alice was a name derived from Lizzie's sister and Mrs Casey, whose first name she had heard William's father yell in one of his inebriated rants. She knew Mrs Casey would be delighted her granddaughter had been named after her and Lizzie couldn't wait to show Mary Alice to her grandmother and the world. Neighbours they hardly knew donated items of baby clothing and both

Lizzie and Lottie were overwhelmed at the extent of kindliness shown by everyone. The lady next door came knocking with a matinee coat, bonnet and mittens she'd been knitting since she discovered her neighbour was expecting, together with an apple pie and a pan of hearty stew.

"To keep up Lizzie's strength," she said handing the pan across the threshold to Lottie who, surprised by its weight, almost dropped it. A pram was donated by a local church group who had cleaned it up, repainted the chassis and the ladies from the church choir had knitted blankets. When Lizzie saw the gifts, she was overwhelmed at the extent of community spirit in this, her temporary home. She didn't dare to think what would happen when she had to leave.

Lizzie felt the happiest she had since before she lost Albert and Sidney. The only problem was her husband. She tried to overlook his misdemeanours, instead looking through it all to the man she thought she'd fallen in love with outside the tobacconist's shop. In vain, she searched for his redeeming features, but found none. William Casey was a bully, like his father. A drunkard who beat her, an adulterer who cared not whose lives he wrecked, a liar and if all that wasn't enough, he gambled, betting all his money on anything with four legs and a misleading track record. He left Lizzie penniless. He knew Edward could pay the rent without him having to hand any money over. He abused their kind nature to his own advantage. He barely looked at his daughter and inevitably, the time came when Lizzie was so embarrassed by his behaviour, she felt it time to move on and leave Lottie and Edward to rebuild their lives without the interference William Casey invoked on the household. Devastated by the news her friend intended to leave, Lottie tried to convince Lizzie, William's behaviour was only bothering them because of what it was doing to Lizzie. Unconvinced, Lizzie had made her mind up. She would keep an eye out for an opportunity and leave her friend to enjoy Edward and Molly Ann in peace.

Mary Alice thrived despite the lack of attention from her father or rather, because of it. Mary Alice needed nothing William Casey could give. He used the house only to return to when he needed to vent his anger and that was always at Lizzie, who otherwise enjoyed her life, her daughter being the new reason for her existence, her friend, the house, the neighbours and the spirit of togetherness which existed in the street. Except for William, her life was bountiful in many ways. She believed she'd escaped the horrors of the past and never, would she return to the confines of the buildings which still infused revulsion.

The announcement which prompted Lizzie to act arrived unexpectedly in late February 1900. Mary Alice was eighteen months old. William had not been home for almost six months and Lizzie had reverted to her maiden name. The reprieve the household had been given was a welcome one. Edward and Lottie had slept peacefully knowing Lizzie was safe and the two young children in the house were not subjected to William's behaviour. Harmony had been restored and although Lizzie felt a little conspicuous at times when she knew her two benefactors should have been alone, for the most part, it was a contented household. Molly Ann was besotted with little Mary Alice and when she came home from school in the late afternoons, she would seek her out and play with her. Laughter rang out in the house and a sense of well-being, aided not least by Lizzie's incredible hard work, reigned supreme. Not only was she Lottie's friend and confidante, but she had become in many ways indispensable in household affairs. Paying her way in other ways due to the lack of support from William, she felt responsible for helping Lottie out in any way she could. The arrangement worked well and although Lottie remained the lady of the house in every way, Lizzie expertly shared all the chores.

Contentment had been replaced with complacency. Lizzie had contemplated her options which were few, but the happy announcement of Lottie's pregnancy gave her a new incentive. Whilst she would be grievously affected by taking leave of her beloved family, she knew it was time. Whilst Edward was at work, she and Lottie discussed her intentions. Space would be needed in the house to accommodate the new baby and Lizzie felt compelled to allow Edward, Lottie and Molly Ann to begin a new life without having to consider her welfare. Her decision made, when Edward returned from work and whilst eating their evening meal. Lizzie broached the topic.

"I'm going to look for somewhere else to live," she blurted out. "It's time. You need time on your own and space for the new baby and a new life together as a family. You've been wonderful, both of you but I feel it's time for me to move on. You've put up with a lot, with William being the way he is and I'm sorry for his behaviour and for taking advantage of your hospitality. My mind is made up and there's no turning back. I just need to find a way. Perhaps somewhere to 'live in' where I can work to pay for my lodgings. I should be able to find something. I have housekeeping experience and a little nursing as well."

Edward and Lottie sat in relative silence listening to Lizzie's reasoning. Molly Ann had taken Mary Alice outside to play with a spinning top in the back yard.

Edward spoke first, realising his wife was choked and couldn't, although he suspected Lottie already knew of Lizzie's intentions.

"Lizzie, you must never think you have to leave. You're an inspiration. You've worked hard, we've loved having you around. The house wouldn't be the same without you. You've never been in the way. I can't believe that bastard husband of yours treats you the way he does. You're better off without him. We'd love you to stay and be happy here with us, but if that's your decision because you want to go, then I respect that decision."

Lottie burst into tears and ran upstairs.

"Thanks Edward," began Lizzie. "Yes, it is my decision. I need to do this. For me. It'll break my heart to leave you all, but I must find my own way in the world. You don't happen to know anyone who's looking for a housekeeper do you?" she said and smiled. They both laughed.

"I'll ask around," he replied. Patting Lizzie's hand, he added, "I'd better go up to her."

Edward went in search of his wife. Lizzie went through the tiny kitchen and stood at the back door watching the two girls playing and laughing together, her heart aching for the son she'd lost. The scene tugged at her heart strings.

'I have to go. William's not coming back. I can't stay here indefinitely with no money. I have no choice.'

Pulling a hanky out of her pinny pocket, she blew her nose, tied her hair back with a grey ribbon and shouted the children in for bed.

* * * * * *

CHAPTER THIRTY-FOUR

Treading the grounds of the ancient churchyard high up on the hill, gravestones lay strewn across graves, some almost sinking into the ground beneath where the remains of the townspeople rested. The grass had been recently mown and the pathway of ancient tombs beneath her feet were littered with mown down faded daffodils. It was a beautiful sunny April afternoon. Pink and white blossom trees surrounded the quiet church and muted rays of sunshine filtered through the windblown blossoms. The smell of new mown grass and the crisp breeze invoked thoughts of a time long past, when the resting parishioners would have walked the same pathway and felt the same sunshine.

Lizzie read the gravestones, some of them portraying their tragic family history with many loved ones, young and old, lying in one grave. She had come here to remember her sisters. She had wanted to be alone to grieve the devastating news of Mary-Ann's passing. News had arrived at the workhouse that Mary-Ann had succumbed to the ravages of her recently contracted disease. Contact had been made with Lottie, who went to the Workhouse to collect the letter from the matron. She sat with Lizzie while she read its contents and knew undoubtedly it was bad news. Lottie had offered to look after Mary Alice while Lizzie chose to be alone. Mary-Ann's remains had been buried in a pauper's grave near the London workhouse. Lizzie had neither the money nor the inclination to make the journey to London with Mary Alice, to stare down at a mass grave where the remnants of the sister she loved so dearly lay decaying. Instead, she preferred to visit an appropriate place which was beautiful, to walk with her memories of her beautiful sisters, one who had gone to meet her maker and the other torn away and shipped off to the unknown, and neither of whom she would see again.

A bench leaning up against the grey stone walls of the eastern side of the church provided a welcome place for her to vent her grief. She buried her head in her hands and wept bitter tears, not for Mary-Ann, who by now was safe and in the hands of her God, but for Katy, her cherished baby sister, taken away at such a tender age, torn away from her siblings and sent on a journey to a faraway land and never heard from again. The tears were also angry and frustrated ones. Looking back on her life and how it had dealt the cards, Lizzie wondered how it was, this God she was supposed to love had not turned the hand of fate in her favour. She reproached herself for these thoughts. 'I have Mary Alice. What more do I need?' Looking heavenward, she silently thanked whoever might be listening for the gift of her precious, healthy daughter.

Edward came home that night with some welcome news for Lizzie. A colleague had made some enquiries for him and his findings could prove beneficial for Lizzie. He was excited to impart the news but his excitement waned when he felt the sombre mood of the house. Lottie took him aside and told him Lizzie's devastating news about Mary-Ann. Edward took on a more serious approach than the light-hearted one he had planned and as they sat around the table, informed Lizzie of the events of the day.

Sitting up and paying attention, Lizzie felt a quiver of fear creep up inside her. This was it, the end of another era in her life and the beginning of a new one. Married but with no husband, no income and no savings, she and Mary

Alice would be embarking on an adventure she couldn't have dreamed of. Fear subsiding and giving way to anticipation, Lizzie asked her questions.

"Where is it? What is it? What job will I be doing? Is it far from here? Will I still be able to see you?"

Edward laughed. "Hey slow down! I'll tell you everything I know." He began.

"Right, it's a live-in housekeeping job. There's a place for you and Mary Alice. You'll both be given board and lodgings and a small allowance. You'll be living in a small cottage in a row of terraced cottages alongside the banks of a canal. I've been to have a look and I think you'll be happy there. It's only small, but plenty big enough for you and Mary Alice."

"And what will I be doing?" asked Lizzie, becoming more and more excited as Edward went on.

"There's a manor-house up the hill at the back of the cottages, overlooking the industrial works on the canal. The man who owns it, Mr Sutton, is also the owner of the factories, the chemical works, a cheese factory and the cottages. In fact, all you can see belongs to him. His housekeeper died a few weeks ago. He's been looking for a new one. He lives with his family and by all accounts he's a genuine fellow and looking for the same qualities in his new housekeeper."

"So, I'll be living in the cottage, but working in the manor-house?" asked Lizzie, now buzzing with excitement and added, "I'll be a sort of housekeeper?"

"Yes. He knows you have a child and you'll be allowed to take Mary Alice with you up to the house. There's a playroom but you'll have to keep your eye on her and work around her as best you can until she's old enough to go to school. He's more concerned with finding the right person and the long term benefits."

"Sounds pretty perfect to me," said Lizzie, a big grin widening, as excitement began flooding her senses, eradicating her earlier fears.

"My own little cottage, with my own daughter? Oh my goodness, what's the catch?"

Edward laughed.

"No catch Lizzie. Just found the right person at the right time. You lucky girl!"

They were all laughing jovially when the door burst open, banging back against the wall and William Casey staggered in. Everybody around the table jumped with fright. Lottie quickly ushered the children out into the yard.

"What's all this about then?" William roared with a drunken raucous laugh.

"What's the matter Lizzie? Not pleased to see me?"

William sniggered as he spoke, throwing himself onto the sofa. Lizzie felt sick to her stomach. She felt like shrinking into the distance and hoping he would go away of his own accord, but knew he wouldn't. Instead, she marched over to where he slouched on the sofa, his fat beer belly hanging over the top of his belt. Standing up straight and proud, she faced him and screamed at the top of her voice "Get out." And louder. "Get out of this house William Casey. You don't belong here with good decent people. Get out ......" She'd been about to add "and don't come back," but she didn't see it coming.

It happened so fast, she didn't have time to react. In half a second, William stood up and holding his right arm out at a perpendicular angle, he swung his arm as though it had a dumbbell on the end, hand outstretched. His hand wacked the side of Lizzie's head so hard, it knocked her flying to the other side of the room. Stunned and almost unconscious, she stumbled and fell against the sharp edge of the table, causing blood to gush from the ensuing wound. Lottie screamed and ran to Lizzie. Edward leapt over the two women and launched himself at William, who had crumpled back onto the sofa, having exerted himself too much in the attack on Lizzie. Edward pummelled William almost to a pulp and dragged him out into the street, kicking him several times in his fat belly, so severe was his anger at seeing Lizzie so brutally treated.

"Call the police someone", he yelled at the top of his voice. "Call the police."

Curtains twitched, front doors flew open and neighbours piled out onto the street to see the cause of the commotion. Edward need not have worried William might escape. He was comatose. Edward heard a whistle in the distance and two policemen came running down the street. They stopped at Edward's front door. One policeman dealt with William, while the other one came in with his pad and took notes from the family still in shock from the horrendous attack on Lizzie. The man taking the notes was a young man with a family of his own at home. He looked at the enormous welt and lesions on the side of Lizzie's head, the large bruise blooming and the wound, now dressed with a crude bandage, oozing blood. Lottie and Edward described the whole scene graphically, still in shock themselves of such a callous and unprecedented outburst.

"He needs locking up and the key throwing away," spat Edward at the policeman.

"He's in our hands now Sir. We'll deal with him. We'll need to come and see you again for some more details. I suggest you seek medical attention for the young lady. I think you should all have a cup of sweet tea. It's good for shock you know." He smiled and left the room to assist his sergeant who was still trying to establish if William was dead or alive.

Arrangements were made for Lizzie to see Mr Sutton the following week. Leaving Mary-Alice in Lottie's capable hands and dressed in her newly-pressed grey pinafore dress, she made her way to the station for the journey to Frodsham, a few miles away, where she would follow Edward's instructions and make her way up the hill on foot. She passed a row of old terraced cottages opposite an ancient-looking brick stable with heavy rotting wooden doors. Through the trees ahead, she caught glimpses of a large manor house, standing on the hilltop in affluent splendour. Turrets ran around the top, giving it the appearance of a castle. The cart track gave way to a small cobbled stone street along which ran another row of cottages, and although obviously occupied, their sandstone facades were crumbling. She passed an old red sandstone church, its original gothic style windows standing proud between the columns of crumbling masonry. A gateway warned visitors not to stand too near the gravestones lest they fell inwards. Lizzie shuddered at the thought and hurried on past. Looking back over her shoulder, she could see the railway viaduct over the industrial mills at the side of the canal. The water shimmered in the sunlight far down below.

Hurrying on, the end of her journey now in sight, she stood up straight and brushed down her dress, ran her fingers through her hair and took the path leading between the two brick pillars and up the drive towards the house. The nearer she became, the more imposing the house looked. There were two carriages at the end of the drive in front of the house. She walked behind them, up three steps and rang the oversized doorbell. Having a sense of déjà vu, she took a deep breath ready to announce herself. She had no need. Mr Sutton himself opened the door, taken somewhat aback by Lizzie's obvious recent wounds.

"Elizabeth Bradshaw, I presume?" he said in a teasing manner.

"Yes Sir. I'm Lizzie."

"Well, come on in then."

* * * * * *

CHAPTER THIRTY-FIVE

Lizzie found Mr Sutton a courteous gentleman and within minutes of arriving, felt totally at ease. She'd expected questions about her wounds, which she felt indisposed to answer, but hoped her general demeanour would display her integrity, leaving him, perhaps, with no reason to delve. His explanation of her duties left Lizzie in no doubt as to the extent of the work involved, but spurred on by the man's seemingly pleasant attitude, an arrangement was made for her to start, subject to viewing the cottage in which she and Mary Alice would reside.

As Lizzie was leaving Mr Sutton's office, she suffered a heart-stopping moment.

"How did you say you suffered your wounds?" asked Mr Sutton from behind.

She turned, looked him in the eye and said, "I fell, Sir."

* * * * * *

Mr Sutton, one of the maid servants and Lizzie settled into the comfy seats of a carriage and began the descent towards the mills. The countryside was in full bloom and Lizzie didn't think she'd ever seen anything so beautiful. The carriage turned onto the main road and proceeded straight for five minutes, before turning left into a narrow lane alongside the canal. The industrial units were on the opposite side. In front of her along the cobbled lane, she could see a row of brick-built cottages on the left hand side with white wooden front doors.

'Can't be here,' thought Lizzie, but took a sharp intake of breath when the carriage pulled up outside the second cottage.

"Here's the key. Go and have a look. Dora will go with you. Dora, Lizzie learned on the journey, was the temporary head housekeeper at the manor and responsible for making sure the tenanted cottages were kept in good order.

Lizzie felt strange as she turned the large key in the lock and opening the door wide, stepped down onto an uneven flagstone floor. The light poured in from the small window next to the door, illuminating what would be a dark room without sunlight. The furnishings were sparse, consisting of a wooden dresser beneath the window, a long settle with what she thought must be a straw mattress along the right hand wall and another on the left and opposite the door was a large inglenook open fireplace. To the left of the fireplace was a doorway. Lizzie tentatively looked around the room, drinking in the beauty of its practicality and simplicity and headed for the open doorway. Another step down took her down into a square room with a black range occupying one wall and a small table and two chairs on the other. A large black kettle dominated the open space of the range and two wooden shelves over the table housed a few old pans. A low pot sink and wooden drainer sat beneath the small window, a door at the side, Lizzie presumed, led outside. She asked Dora if she could open it and peek out. Dora informed her the tiny building facing them was the privy. A small tin bath hung on a nail outside the back door. Lizzie's findings saturated her with emotion. 'How could this be? How could she be so lucky?' She turned to Dora, but the words wouldn't come. She simply nodded her answer. Mr Sutton was delighted.

"Lizzie, can you start two weeks from today please?"

Lizzie's vocal chords were struck dumb. She nodded her head and managed, in a low whisper, "Thank you Sir."

"We'll sort out everything else when you come in two weeks. Don't worry about anything. All you need to worry about is working hard when you get here. No dilly-dallying. I don't tolerate laziness. Can you manage to find your way back?"

"Yes Sir, thank you Sir," was all Lizzie could say.

They left the house and Mr Sutton and Dora climbed back onto the carriage, waved to Lizzie and swiftly manoeuvred the horse and carriage around, to return the way they came. Lizzie stood waving and watched them turn right at the end of the road and they were gone.

Turning back round to face the cottage, a few tears of joy rolled down her cheeks. She smiled, turned and began her walk back to the station.

Edward and Lottie were at the dining table when she returned. She ran in and hugged them both, excitedly twirling round and round.

"You like it then?" quipped Edward, laughing at Lizzie's theatrical performance.

"I love it. I love it."

"Come on, sit down, your supper's ready. The children are in bed. Thought they both needed an early night. That little one of yours is going to be so excited when you tell her. When do you leave?"

"I start two weeks today."

* * * * * *

Lottie devoured every syllable as Lizzie rattled through everything. She was already planning to put together as many of the things Lizzie would need as possible. She had a few things spare and was happy for Lizzie to take them. She determined to do everything possible to make sure Lizzie wanted for nothing.

The two weeks passed quickly. Lizzie remained in a daze for most of it. Lottie wrote lists and crossed things off as they accumulated in a wooden box by the front door. Lizzie had peeked inside the sideboard at the cottage and been delighted to find some crockery in the cupboard and cutlery in one of the two drawers.

'Yes, everything's going to work out fine,' she thought. 'I'll concentrate on my work and develop a strategy for looking after Mary Alice. I'll bring her into each room with me and give her something to occupy her while I'm working.'

The thoughts of going home to the cottage each night with Mary-Alice filled her with a mixture of emotion. On the one hand, she was thrilled to have this wonderful opportunity, but on the other, she wondered if she would fear the walk down the hill with a child, especially in the winter months. She had never lived alone before either and the prospect was more than a little daunting. Nonetheless, Lizzie knew she had a strong constitution and would overcome whatever obstacles presented themselves.

'At least 'he' won't be able to find me,' she thought happily.

Moving day dawned. A drizzly, grey day at first, but by the time they were ready to go, the sun had broken through a little and the rain had stopped. Lizzie and Lottie were taking the children and the bare essentials and heading for the train. Edward and a friend who'd offered to help, would come with a horse and cart, bringing the bulkier items. The journey would take two or three hours but his friend's help was a godsend.

Lottie was to spend the night with Lizzie and the girls, helping her to get the place ready. Edward and his friend were staying in a local tavern and would collect Lottie and Molly Ann in the morning for their return journey. Lizzie would make the journey up the hill with Mary Alice and begin work the next day.

Excitement bounded all day and Lizzie, sad though she was to be leaving Lottie, knew she wouldn't lose her friend. She had to make a life for herself and Mary Alice and considered it a wonderful start on that journey.

* * * * * *

CHAPTER THIRTY-SIX

Lizzie and Lottie had worked late into the evening creatively converting the little cottage into a home. Edward had brought along some makeshift mattress materials so the girls could all have a bed for the night and when Lizzie and Lottie finally went to sleep that night, the transformation was complete.

On the morning of 30 April in the year 1900, Lizzie made her way up the hill to the manor house with Mary Alice, for the first time. Apprehension, excitement, a little fear but still with wonder in her heart, she set off early enough to arrive at least ten minutes before the appointed time.

Despite her apprehension, Lizzie was amazed at how much she already knew. Most of the work was similar to that of Maddingley Hall and the staff seemed pleasant enough to allay her fears of having Mary Alice with her. The arrangement worked well, although she felt she hadn't done much in the way of work the first day, as Mary Alice had taken centre stage. Lizzie believed she would be able to cope with whatever lay in store. Aware some interest was taken in the wounds to her face and head, she was grateful no-one questioned.

Lizzie and Mary Alice shared supper time with the staff, who had their evening meal before the Master and his family and guests were served. Lizzie had been exonerated from serving the evening meal upstairs in order to make her way back to the cottage. Although daunted by the prospect of both navigating the hill and entering the cottage alone, the daylight hours gave some consolation. Once inside, Lizzie flopped down on one of the settles to play with her daughter. Exhaustion forced her to prepare Mary Alice for bed and checking everywhere was safe, Lizzie lay on the makeshift bed, closed her eyes and slept.

Lizzie quickly developed a routine necessary to keep a healthy balance of work and family life and she saw Lottie as often as she could. As the months rolled by, falling leaves made the journey up and down the hill more gruelling. There was extra work to do both at the manor house and in the cottage, as the winter months brought considerable problems trying to keep warm. The cottage was draughty and there were fires to tend when she returned home, an extra burden she'd never had to deal with alone. Mary Alice was heavier to carry and at two years old couldn't always manage the often wet, mulchy and sometimes icy terrain. Lottie had knitted a hat, scarf and gloves for Lizzie and Mary Alice, a gift Lizzie treasured, the colder the winter became.

At the beginning of December 1900, on a cold, crisp winter's morning, Lizzie went up the hill as usual, Mary Alice clambering up as best she could, holding onto Lizzie's hand. There was a chill in Lizzie's heart, one she couldn't explain.

'Am I coming down with something?' she wondered. 'Am I being paranoid, and if so, what about?'

There was news waiting for her when she arrived, her bag full of the day's requirements for Mary Alice in one hand, and a puffed out two-year old hanging on to the other. Marjorie, the cook took the bag from Lizzie.

"I think Mr Sutton would like a word Lizzie."

Lizzie's heart froze. 'Could this be the foreboding feeling I had earlier?'

"Do you know what it's about?" she asked .

"I do." Marjorie responded, smiling and allaying Lizzie's fears.

Lizzie deposited Mary Alice in the playroom. Surprised to find other children she hadn't seen before, she wondered what was going on. Inspired by Lizzie's plight with Mary Alice, Mr Sutton had developed a strategy for employing much needed staff and opened a play/school room for the children of staff who otherwise wouldn't be able to work. He'd employed a nanny for staff's children and guests. Lizzie was delighted to learn Mary Alice would have other children to play with and was full of respect for her employer, who seemed to be more in touch with his staff's needs than anywhere else she'd worked.

Lizzie knocked and waited.

"Come in," she heard eventually. "Lizzie Bradshaw," her employer boomed out from behind his desk, making Lizzie jump. His face, previously having given no indication for her summons, burst into laughter.

"Don't worry Lizzie, I have a proposal I'd like you to consider."

Lizzie wavered a little, not knowing what was coming, and a little unnerved by Mr Sutton's apparent jovial manner. She waited for him to continue.

"I've decided to offer you a live-in position. You don't have to answer now. I'll give you time to think about it."

Lizzie was stunned. This had not been what she was expecting. Mr Sutton continued.

"You and Mary Alice would share a room here at the main house. Mary Alice would be cared for during your duty hours by our resident nanny. I think that'd be a sight better than you having to trudge up and down the hill with a child, particularly in view of the winter months. So long as your work continues in the present way, I'm offering you a long term position Lizzie. Should you wish to remain in the cottage, that's your choice. I need your decision by the end of the week."

Lizzie stared at Mr Sutton, wondering if he was going to say anything else. He didn't. His head was already back in his books.

"Thank you Sir," was all Lizzie could say. Mr Sutton looked up and gave a brief smile before burying his head back in his work. Lizzie turned and left the room. Utterly stunned by the significance of this revelation, there were only two things to consider. One. 'Do I want Mary Alice growing up thinking the manor is her home?' Two. 'Am I willing to give up my independence?'

Lizzie thought at first, she would make her mind up in a second, but as the week wore on, these two all important questions resounded in her head. She weighed up her options and attempted to quantify them in simplistic terms.

'Which is best for Mary Alice? What's best for me?'

By Thursday evening, she had her answer.

* * * * * *

The weather took a change for the worse. As she attempted the journey down the hill, the night had set in and the terrain was treacherous. Although she was sure-footed and knew the pathway blindfold, the icy conditions and falling snow prevented her treading the usual path. Both Lizzie and Mary Alice stumbled on more than one occasion. The arctic wind penetrated their thin clothing and Lizzie's mind was settled in the knowledge she'd made the right decision. She would inform Mr Sutton the next morning and accept his kind offer.

But, for Lizzie Bradshaw, life was never on an even keel.

* * * * * *

CHAPTER THIRTY-SEVEN

Something was wrong. She couldn't put her finger on it. She'd felt it all week. Something unnerving, frightening, scary.

'Is someone watching me?' she'd thought a number of times.

The thoughts of both going up the hill and coming back down, in the dark, were terrifying. There was no logic in her thoughts, she'd never felt like this before. Nonetheless, her intuition was based on a primitive fear of the unknown. Her fear had filtered down to Mary Alice, who was cranky and irritable.

Cold, frightened and clutching onto Mary Alice, Lizzie put the key in the lock. It didn't turn. In a heart-stopping moment, she turned the key the other way and tried the door again. It wouldn't open. She turned the key back again. The door opened. Fear gripped her in the knowledge the door was already open.

'Did I not lock up this morning?'

Uneasily, she pushed the door open. There was a strange smell, one not entirely alien to her. 'Beer,' she almost said aloud. In a split second, she knew.

'But where is he?' she panicked. 'Is he lying in wait for me, or is he so drunk, he's out cold?'

She quickly lit the nearest lantern and scanned the room. Finding it devoid of human habitation, she sat Mary Alice down on the settle and lighting a candle from the lantern, she moved towards the kitchen. He sat motionless, his legs sprawled out in front of him, his back against the chair, his face displaying a sardonic grimace. A vice clutched her heart and her legs turned to jelly.

Involuntarily, she blocked the doorway between her drunkard husband and her child.

"What do you want? There's nothing for you here."

"My wife," he retorted sarcastically, slurring his words

"I want you to leave."

William shuffled himself into an upright position. Lizzie couldn't gauge if he was capable of standing up, much less attacking her. She took a gamble he was too drunk to care and at the top of her voice yelled.

"GET OUT of my house."

She'd been wrong. William launched himself at Lizzie sending her crashing backwards onto the stone floor with his full weight on top of her. She struggled to get him off.

Lizzie heard crying from the doorway.

"It's all right sweetheart. Daddy and I are just playing, she tried to gasp plausibly. You go and play with dolly. I'll be there in a minute."

Screaming inside and with all her might, Lizzie fought William. Tearing at him, scratching and clawing, trying to avert the inevitable, by now fully realising his intentions.

'Oh God, no, not in front of Mary Alice.'

William inched his trousers down with one hand whilst pinning Lizzie with his broad arm, smashing it down across her face. Not wishing to scream out and alarm Mary Alice, Lizzie continued to thrash with every limb. Her back seared with a deadening pain which forced out an ear-piercing scream. At that moment, Edward appeared in the doorway. He took in the scene and with lightening reaction, attacked William with full force, sending William in an exposed state onto his back.

Edward's yell deafened everyone as he told William to leave.

Lottie summed the situation up and quickly scuttled Mary Alice and Molly Ann into a corner with a doll and a book. Edward and Lottie were visiting in the area and planned to give Lizzie a surprise visit before they went home. They saw Mary Alice's face at the window, in an unusually lit room. Having knocked and received no answer, Edward had tried the door and come in. Lizzie remained still on the floor, unable to move and crying with pain and anguish. Edward forcibly removed William from the house whilst screaming at him never to show his face again. Lottie was now on the floor beside Lizzie, who had received an almighty blow to her spine when William attacked her.

"We need help here," she shouted to Edward. "I think she's broken something."

"Don't try to move her," shouted Edward, already on his way out of the door. He added, "If that bastard comes back, kill him."

Lottie quickly retrieved one of the heavy iron skillets from the fireplace and placed it on the floor near Lizzie. She then dragged a cover from the bed and placed it over Lizzie who was cold and clammy and warmed some milk over the fire. Edward had locked the door behind him and taken the key so Lottie wasn't worried about William coming into the house, but every creak and groan she heard reminded her of the cruel twist of fate her friend had suffered at the hands of William Casey and she was glad she had the insurance offered by the iron skillet. She wouldn't hesitate to use it.

Lizzie was taken into hospital where she was to remain for six weeks, having suffered trauma to her back as well as a broken jaw, cuts and lesions to her throat and suffering from shock and hypothermia. Edward had informed the police of the attack on Lizzie, and given a description of William. Reassuring themselves they had done everything possible, Edward, Lottie and two girls asleep in the back of the carriage, set off for home.

The next morning, Edward didn't go to work. Instead, he went to speak with Mr Sutton at the manor to inform him of Lizzie's plight. Mr Sutton didn't agree to speak with him straightaway, still angry with Lizzie for not showing up for work when he desperately needed her answer, not to mention her skills for preparations for the weekend. After keeping Edward waiting an hour, he finally agreed to see him. Horror-struck after Edward told him, the anger subsided and gave way to sympathy. He handed Edward an envelope containing Lizzie's wages and asked if he would ensure its safe passage to her. He then dug deep into his trouser pocket and handed Edward three sovereigns.

"Please use this to get Lizzie anything she might need for her stay in hospital. Tell her I'm sorry to hear what's happened and I'll be in touch. I'll keep her position open until I hear from you."

"Thank you Sir," replied Edward. "I will. Thanks again."

His job done, he left the manor.

* * * * * *

CHAPTER THIRTY-EIGHT

During Lizzie's six week incarceration, as well as the intense pain in her back for which there was no effective treatment except bed rest, she suffered a sense of loss for all her loved ones. Her marriage to a man who beat her and tried to rape her in front of her child, was tearing her apart, but above all, she found the separation from her daughter intolerable. She missed her friends and couldn't dismiss the probability she may have lost her new live-in job. Edward had passed on her wages and informed her Mr Sutton was willing to hold the position open. Lizzie knew he couldn't do that indefinitely and thought, by now, the position would have been given to someone else. Flat on her back and barely able to move, she wondered what the future held. Striving to retain her upbeat attitude to life, despite everything, was as difficult as telling her body to heal.

The day for her discharge finally dawned. The doctors had instructed her not to go back to the cottage, or to work. She must be well cared for, for at least another couple of months. She must eat good, wholesome food, avoid domestic labour of any kind and have plenty of rest.

Lottie and Edward took her back home to Mary Alice. Lottie endeavoured to provide Lizzie with convalescence conducive to a full recovery in as short a time as possible.

Delighted to be out of hospital and living back 'at home' with Mary Alice, Lizzie's recovery began straight away. Each day she felt stronger, the pain lessening, happiness resuming and in less than six weeks, she was pottering around doing small chores. Lizzie wrote to Mr Sutton informing him she was fit for duty and was amazed, when his reply arrived, to find the position was still open.

"It's time for us to leave," said Lizzie one morning at breakfast.

"You can't possibly think about going back to work at the manor yet," said Lottie.

"Well, I can't stay here forever Lottie," Lizzie retorted. "And I'm not going back to the workhouse. Never ever."

"You don't have to go anywhere Lizzie. Just stay here with us."

"I can't. You need your own space and I need mine. You have your own family to think of. Kind as I know Edward is, he must be weary of having two more mouths to feed. No Lottie, it's time for me to go."

"Well, I can't force you to stay", answered Lottie, smiling at her friend. "I just hope you know what you're doing."

Two days before Lizzie and Mary Alice were leaving to go back to the cottage, which Mr Sutton had left empty awaiting her return, Edward and Lottie took the carriage, bought Lizzie some supplies from the corner shop and set off back to the cottage to ensure everything was safe. Edward found himself poised with anticipation when he turned the key in the lock. They hadn't been back since the fateful night Lizzie was taken into hospital. His quick reactions when he opened the door saved his life. He had a premonition and was primed. Quickly banging the door back against the wall with no prior warning, he knew any unwanted visitor would be taken off guard. The noise came to his ears as he entered, and he knew.

A fight broke out between the two men. Lottie ran hell for leather to the police station and begged an officer to come with her. William Casey was arrested and taken into custody for questioning. Mr Sutton was alerted he'd had an intruder living in the property and proposed to press charges. Edward was questioned and unconditionally released. William was locked up pending further investigation, his main and only concern, how he would procure some alcohol. When Lizzie heard the news, she broke down. Frustrated angry tears came. She couldn't stop them.

"Why did I have to get involved with him?" she asked out loud.

"Why? Why couldn't I have found a decent man, a decent father for Mary Alice?"

Lottie was lost for words and simply comforted Lizzie by wrapping her arms around her. "He's not worth drawing breath for. He's locked up for a while now. He can't hurt you any more."

"I know," responded Lizzie in rasping breaths while tears still flowed.

"But he won't be in there forever. I'll have to look over my shoulder all my life, wondering where he'll turn up. He knows where I live. I'll bet he knows where I work too. That'll be the next place he'll come looking. I can't go back there now. I can't."

"I have to say, I agree," chipped in Edward. "Lizzie's right. He's a bad lot, right enough. Be prepared. Whatever he wants, whenever he wants it, he'll come looking. I think Lizzie should consider an alternative."

"What are you suggesting?" snapped Lottie.

"I know Mr Sutton's agreed to let Lizzie move back into the cottage for a while until she's fully recovered and ready to return to work. I'm just saying I don't think it's a good idea for Lizzie to go back to the cottage or the manor just yet."

"So, what do you think I should do?" asked Lizzie, her tears drying up with the possibility of another solution.

"I think you should move altogether. Don't go back to the cottage or the manor. You have plenty of skills and experience. Shouldn't be too hard to find something else?" There was a lull. "Well, what do you think?"

Lizzie had listened intently. Edward was right. She needed a fresh start and despite her desire to retain the lifestyle she'd become accustomed to at the manor, she didn't like living alone and she feared for her life if ever William Casey showed up again.

'If he doesn't know where I am, he can't come, can he?' thought Lizzie.

Lottie spoke.

"I think he might be right Lizzie. I know it's not what you want to hear. But you have to think about Mary Alice. We know what he's capable of. I'd be terrified of you being over there all alone at night, knowing he knew where you were."

"Yes, but I wouldn't be at the cottage any more would I?" Lizzie said, hoping the manor might get a reprieve as a safer alternative than the cottage or the unknown.

"Why not?"

"Because I'd decided not to stay on at the cottage. Mr Sutton offered me a live-in job at the manor. The morning after the attack was the day I was going to tell him I'd accept his offer. So if the offer is still on the table, I would be living at the manor, not the cottage. I wouldn't have to make the journey up and down the hill every day."

Lizzie suddenly went cold. She remembered the disparaging feeling she'd had the week before the attack when she'd been going to and from work. Up and down the hill in the dark, icy and snowy conditions, feeling she was being watched.

"Oh my God," she said fearfully.

"What, what?" asked the others in unison.

"Did I tell you how I felt the week before? That somehow I was being watched?"

"No, you didn't," said Lottie.

"Well I did. I had the most awful foreboding feeling. Pretty much all week I thought I could sense someone watching me as I went up the hill and when I came back down again. It unnerved me, but I told myself I was being stupid. Then when I got back to the cottage, he was there." She burst into tears. This time, she cried for herself and her daughter and the sheer horror of the situation she'd really only just grasped.

"We'd probably both be dead by now if you hadn't come by," Lizzie said sobbing.

"You're not going back Lizzie. That's that. End. Full stop. We're looking for something else for you. Until we find it, you're staying right here with us. That's it. Done."

Lizzie looked across at her two friends.

"Where would I be without you?"

The following day, Edward went with Lizzie to the cottage to retrieve the few things she'd left behind and to see Mr Sutton for the last time. She felt sure he would see her and give her time to explain her situation, hoping he would understand and agree to a written resumé so she could seek alternative employment.

Mr Sutton was a sympathetic employer. He didn't suffer fools gladly, but in cases such as this, where he knew the consequences were not of the employee's own wrong-doing, he was quite distressed by her plight. To see a skilled worker with a happy disposition suffer under horrific circumstances, made him angry. He wrote Lizzie's resumé there and then, a glowing report of the talents and skills he'd encountered and heard by word of mouth while she was in his employ. When the meeting was over, he came round and shook her hand and without averting his gaze from her, pressed two coins into her palm, confusing her. She was holding the envelope with her resumé in the other hand. She looked at Mr Sutton inquisitively but his only response was his smile.

"Goodbye Lizzie. Good luck."

"Goodbye Mr Sutton. Thank you."

He turned and went back to his desk and Lizzie closed the door on Mr Sutton's office for the last time.

* * * * * *

CHAPTER THIRTY-NINE

Spring 1901 saw Lizzie fully recovered from her ordeal. With the knowledge William Casey would be locked up for a considerable length of time, happiness had returned and her strength regained. Thanks to the care of her friends, Mary Alice was thriving.

Lottie's time was looming and one of the bedrooms had been prepared for her confinement. Sadly, amongst all the traumas the family had encountered, they had lost the baby in early pregnancy but she'd become pregnant again almost straightaway and once again, excitement bounded in the Gallagher household. Lizzie had taken over all household duties, hoping to repay her friend, in some way for all the help she'd been given, but more so because she felt the weight of responsibility for the loss of their last baby. 'William Casey's fault again,' she reminded herself.

Lottie gave birth to a healthy baby boy, a welcome half-brother for Molly Ann and a source of constant amusement for Mary Alice, who never left the child's side. Lottie was a strong woman and following a short confinement, was up and about in no time. Normality reigned in the household and all was well. Lizzie continued her search for another housekeeping position but the one which caught her eye came right out of the blue.

The family and a few invited friends were celebrating baby Peter's christening ceremony at the local parish church. Lizzie had prepared a few sandwiches for their guests and opened some tinned fruit. Lottie had baked a sponge cake. Their guests offered small gifts for the baby and by mid afternoon, their guests had dispersed.

"I'm hungry," announced Edward at teatime. "I think we'll try the new fish and chip shop in Edmond Street. What do you say girls?"

Lizzie, quick as a flash, ran upstairs, dug her hand into her pinafore dress which hung on the back of the door and retrieved the coins Mr Sutton had given her.

Running back downstairs she announced, "I'll get these. What would everyone like?"

Laughing, she told Lottie and Edward about the money Mr Sutton had pushed into her hand the day she left. She'd stuffed it down inside her pinafore and forgotten about it.

"I want to go for these. It's a thank you for everything you've done for me, and my gift for Peter's christening."

Lottie and Edward both laughed and said "Okay. Thanks Lizzie."

Lizzie was glad to have a few minutes alone, to go outside and not worry 'he' would be waiting around the corner. She gathered her thoughts as she walked the two streets away to the homely shop selling fish and chips.

'What a treat for us all,' she thought.

She found her way easily enough and the heat hit her when she stepped inside. A couple of people stood at the counter, reading newspapers, whilst waiting for their orders. Lizzie placed her order and stood in the queue. She picked a newspaper off the top of the counter and leafed through to the classified section. She tensed as the advertisement caught her eye. It was written in a bold square and quite unmissable.

Live-in nursemaid wanted for sick lady and four young children. Please apply in writing to Mr Thomas Jackson at the address below.

Lizzie stared at the advertisement and re-read it half a dozen times. Her order was called. She looked up and saw the proprietor, head bent down, wrapping her order.. She quickly tore out the advert and stuffed it in her coat pocket, collected her order and ran back as fast as she could with the evening meal, trying to formulate the words she would write to make her application. She decided not to tell Lottie and Edward. She would apply for the position and tell them only if she was successful.

Supper was delicious. It had been a long time since they'd all eaten a proper hearty meal without having made it themselves. Having put Mary Alice and Molly Ann to bed, Lizzie announced a little earlier than usual, she was retiring to her room. She sat on the bed mulling over her plan. She would leave early in the morning and take the children for a walk. En route, she would take some of the change from Mr Sutton's coins and purchase a notepad, some envelopes and a stamp.

Writing her letter was not the ordeal she'd thought it might be. The words flowed easily enough and although she had to re-write it a couple of times, she was pleased with her effort. She wrote the address for the reply to be sent to, folded the piece of paper, as she'd seen Mr Sutton do and inserted it carefully into the envelope. She addressed the envelope to *Mr Thomas Jackson, 6 Lower Street, Etching*, licked it, sealed it and placed the stamp in the top right hand corner. Satisfied she'd done a good job, she shouted to Lottie.

"Just going for a walk to the shop. Do you need anything bringing in ?"

"No thanks, we're ok," shouted back Lottie.

The nearest post-box was in the same street as the fish and chip shop. Lizzie stood staring at both the shop and the post-box.

'Is this the beginning of another journey?' she mused, pushed her letter into the postbox and hurried home.

* * * * * *

CHAPTER FORTY

Lizzie hadn't used her married name at the foot of the letter, instead preferring the letter to be sent to Lizzie Bradshaw. She wished with all her heart she had retained her own surname on Mary Alice's birth certificate, instead, her monster of a husband's name was clearly written in scrawled writing by the registrar, Mary Alice Casey. She would have to deal with this problem when the time came for Mary Alice to go to school. Despite the lawful name written on the legal piece of paper, Lizzie referred to Mary Alice as Bradshaw. It was a letter addressed to Miss Bradshaw which, prompting great excitement, tinged with a little apprehension, dropped on the mat behind the front door less than a week later.

Dear Miss Bradshaw

I have noted the contents of your letter and thank you for your application. I have received twenty-two applications and am interviewing those on the short-list on Tuesday 28 May. Your appointment time is 10.30 am. I shall look forward to seeing you then.

Yours sincerely

Thomas Jackson

Lizzie stared at the letter in disbelief. She knew everyone downstairs was waiting with baited breath to hear the contents of the letter. She hadn't been going to tell anyone unless she was successful in securing the position. She couldn't help herself and did a little dance, she was so excited, and her laughter infectious. Together with Mary Alice they danced round in circles, laughing, before running downstairs to break the good news she had an interview.

* * * * * *

Having checked how long the journey would take a dozen times and leaving Mary Alice in Lottie's capable hands, Lizzie set out with hope in her heart. Something inside told her this was going to be alright. A premonition she believed had been heaven-sent. The town where Thomas Jackson lived was about an hour away, a train journey and a short walk. The weather had been kind to her and the sun was shining as she left her family waving on the doorstep. On the corner at the end of the street, she turned to wave one last time.

Lizzie saw farmers working their fields as she sat watching out of the train window. She saw wisps of smoke rising from a few isolated cottages and billowing smoke coming from the factories and mills. Her mind wandered to the future.

'What will I find? What will Thomas Jackson be like? Will I like him, will he like me? What illness does his wife suffer? Will I be able to nurse her? Will I be able to cope with five children? Did I tell Thomas Jackson in my letter I have a child?'

The train slowly chugged into Etching station. With butterflies in her stomach, Lizzie disembarked and after trying to see her reflection in the old tarnished mirror in the station's waiting room, she began the short walk to 6 Lower Street following Mr Jackson's explicit directions written on the back of his letter.

Entering Lower Street, Lizzie felt fear and apprehension. This was not what she was expecting. She knew this was not going to be a grand manor house, but she'd not expected to see the apparent poverty-ridden area she was walking through. Old rusty dustbins lined the street, with stacks of rubbish piled up against them. Grubby-looking children playing in the street made rude comments as she walked past. She ducked as one of them threw something at her. She noticed some of the curtains moving in the front windows and felt conspicuous and completely out of place. Holding her head high, she picked up her pace, arriving at number six a few minutes before her appointed time. Wishing to waste no time getting off the street, she knocked loudly. The front door opened immediately. An exceptionally tall man stood there.

"Sssssshhhhhhh," he said in a loud whisper. "Jane's asleep."

He left the door open and walked off down the hall leaving Lizzie to wonder should she enter or not. Closing the front door gently behind her, she went in the direction of the man she assumed to be Mr Thomas Jackson. Surprisingly, the inside of the house didn't reflect the ethos she'd encountered down the street. It smelt a little musty but seemed clean enough. Deceptively more spacious than its external appearance suggested, Lizzie went along the hall and through the door at the end where she presumed Mr Jackson would be waiting.

He was stood with his back to her when she entered the room.
"Lizzie Bradshaw?" he asked in a voice much louder than his 'shush' at the front door.

"Yes." Lizzie answered, becoming slightly more nervous.

"Right, let's have a look at you."

Thomas Jackson turned around. He was a huge man.

'Of giant proportions," thought Lizzie.

He had a mop of dark greying hair which hung thick around his head and slightly over the top of his large ears. He was a good deal older than the younger man Lizzie had been expecting. Beneath large bushy eyebrows sat twinkly dark eyes, a large flared nose, and a curled moustache extended from each side of his top lip, which hadn't yet broken into a smile. He wore a greyish colour shirt and tweed jacket over a pair of worsted trousers. His face was wrinkled and weather-beaten but there was something about him which put Lizzie at ease.

Thomas Jackson eyed Lizzie up and down, his face breaking into a wide grin. He stepped forward and held his hand out for Lizzie to shake. Nervously, Lizzie held out her hand. His grip was strong. She liked that. He pulled out two chairs from the kitchen table and asked Lizzie to be seated. Nervously, she sat down; Thomas Jackson took the chair opposite. He had a pile of papers in front of him she assumed were the letters of application. Lizzie's recognised hers on the top.

"I'm impressed with you Lizzie, your references are good and I can see you've had lots of experience which would suggest you could cope in the position offered here. Tell me about your nursing experience."

Lizzie began to relax a little as she portrayed a brief description of her working life. Thomas Jackson didn't interrupt, listening intently and making occasional notes.

"I'd like you to meet my wife, the lady you'll be nursing if you're selected. Come on, come with me."

Thomas Jackson headed for the staircase. For a split second, Lizzie was filled with apprehension. She hadn't seen any children, she didn't know this man at all, yet here she was in his house, following him up the staircase. It crossed her mind to open the front door in case she needed to make a run for it, but instead, meekly, she followed Thomas up the narrow staircase. He turned into the first doorway and she heard him speak to his wife, who was now awake.

"Jane, this is Lizzie."

As Lizzie walked into the room, she was shocked. The tiny frail, most ghostly-looking, person she'd ever seen in her life raised her left arm in acknowledgement. Eventually finding her voice, Lizzie, said, "Hello Mrs Jackson, I'm Lizzie. How are you today?" There followed an awkward silence. Thomas Jackson broke the silence, quietly whispering, "Jane doesn't speak very much Lizzie. I'll tell you all about it. Come on, I'll show you the room you'd have. I know you have a child. Three, is she?

"Well almost, she'll be three in August."

The room Lizzie would have as her own was quite probably the best room in the house. She wondered if it had been specially prepared for these interviews. There were two single beds side by side with a small table in the middle and one ancient looking sideboard with three drawers and cupboards beneath. On top of the sideboard sat a large lantern with a new candle and a smaller one at the side, 'for carrying,' Lizzie thought. There was a window overlooking the small yard area and beyond she could see rows of terraced houses in parallel streets as far as the eye could see.

'That'd do me nicely,' thought Lizzie.

"Come on, let's go back down. I'll be back up later," he added, addressing his wife. To Lizzie, he whispered, "You'll need to know what you're letting yourself in for."

Daunted by the whole experience, Lizzie wondered if she would accept, should she be offered the position. She didn't like the area, the house could easily be spruced up with a woman's touch and she loved the room which would be hers and Mary Alice's, but the rest left a lot to be desired. Looking clean and being clean were two completely different things. She wasn't sure about the lady she'd be nursing and she couldn't make her mind up about Thomas Jackson. 'Is he genuine?', she questioned herself a number of times. She decided to ask the question.

"Where's the children, Mr Jackson? What ages are they?"

Seemingly quite impressed by her question, Thomas Jackson answered, "Three at school, one down the pit."

"Oh! What are their names? How old are they?"

"Henry's twelve; he's learning the ropes down the pit. Clever lad our Henry but didn't like school. Then there's Dolly. She's eleven in a couple of weeks. Jack's nearly nine. And then there's little Rosa. She's five, just started school. It's a bit hectic here when they're all in. Well, what do you think Lizzie Bradshaw, do you think you could cope. It'd be hard work. You'd be looking after the entire family. Nursemaid, nanny and housekeeper, in that order. They're good kids, mind, but I'd expect you to be strict with them. No shannanigans. You wouldn't be taking no flack from them. Make 'em do 'n all."

Lizzie wanted to question further. Things like, what was wrong with Jane? Why couldn't she get out of bed, although remembering the sight of her when she walked in the room, Lizzie thought she'd been to heaven and come back again. She wanted to ask what Thomas Jackson did for a living. She wanted to ask which school the children went to and how far away from the house it was, so she could organise in her mind what time she would have to get up in a morning to get it all done. Then of course she had Mary Alice to attend to as well. Five children all under her care. But, the prospect of this challenge, although daunting in some ways, prompted a question. 'If I *don't* take the job (if I'm offered it), would I live to regret it, always wondering what life would have been like if I'd said yes.' Lizzie had her answer. Her mind was made up. If she was offered the position, she would say a resounding "Yes."

"Well?" asked Thomas Jackson.

"Yes Mr Jackson, if you decide to offer me the position, I'd love to come."

"Right. I have another lady coming at noon. She's the last one. Then I'll make me mind up and let you know by one week from today. Come on, I'll show you to the door. Thanks for coming Lizzie."

"Bye Mr Jackson. Thanks for seeing me."

Mr Jackson didn't linger at the door. As soon as Lizzie stepped outside she heard the door close behind her.

Lizzie's heart was a flutter. She knew it was an opportunity not to be missed. She would gain invaluable experience to further enhance her chances in the future. Again, she was lucky in that she would have board and lodgings for Mary Alice and herself, together with a small wage. She would be allowed a Sunday off. Mr Jackson would be at home that day to look after his family. Lizzie would be expected back for nine o'clock in the evening to make any last minute preparations for school and work the next morning. She may also be able to have Tuesday afternoons to herself, but that was to be an ad hoc arrangement each week.

'I wonder if he liked me? I think he did. He seemed impressed when I asked questions. I wonder what the other girls were like? Oh well Lizzie Bradshaw, you'll just have to wait and see.'

With that, she hurried back to the station, making one stop on the way. She'd seen a quaint old shop on the corner of one of the streets she passed and was curious to see what it sold. The bell on the door clanged as she went in, alerting the owner someone had entered. In the background Lizzie could smell bacon cooking, the aroma drifting in as a rather large lady came through the door from the back of the shop.

"Good morning," she said in a loud, jolly, Lancashire accent.

"Good morning. Can I have a look around please?"

"Course dear! Is there anything in particular you're looking for?"

"No. It's just I might be coming to live in the area and I wondered what sort of things you sell, so I know where to come."

"You have a good look round. I'm just going back to turn me bacon."

"Smells delicious," said Lizzie, as the lady disappeared back through the door.

Lizzie loved these sorts of shops. She could never really afford to buy anything from them, she just loved looking. There were bolts of material, lots of sewing aids, needles, thimbles, twine, cottons and some peculiar looking gadgets Lizzie had no idea about. There were large bins with wool, and knitting needles in boxes piled up on the long wooden counter. A flat glass cabinet on the counter displayed embroidered collars, handkerchieves and doilies. The floor was highly polished and Lizzie thought it had been done recently as she could still detect the delicious aroma of beeswax.

'Mmmmm, I like this shop,' thought Lizzie.

'Oh, I do so hope Mr Jackson gives me the job. I think I'd like it after all. I wonder what other little gems are hidden amongst the rows of houses.'

The shopkeeper came back through.
"Did you find anything?" she asked Lizzie.
"Oh, I love your shop," exclaimed Lizzie. "If I do come to live here, I'll call in again."
"I'll look forward to seeing you dear. Where will you be living?"
"I'm hoping to be a housekeeper for Mr and Mrs Jackson in Lower Street."
"Oh my!" answered the shopkeeper. "I know Mrs Jackson very well. She used to come in here a lot, she did. I heard she's very poorly."
"Yes," said Lizzie, "I'd be looking after her and the children, if I get the job. Is she a nice lady? I've only just met her this morning."
"Lovely family. She's been poorly for a long time. Used to be a stunning woman, not unlike yourself, if you don't mind my saying. Poor old Thomas Jackson's been looking after her his self, an' all the kids too. How did you find out he was looking for someone?"
"I saw an advert in a newspaper," answered Lizzie.
"He's a good man. Needs a bit of help, he does. Poor old Jane, never been a well woman really. He'll make

sure you don't want for nothing. Tragic story, that with his wife."

"What happened? Asked Lizzie, curious to know how the stunning lady finished up lying in a bed looking like a ghost.

"Got some kind of wasting disease she has. Doctors don't really know. Hasn't been out of her bed for two years now. Everyone feels sorry for Thomas Jackson. A good man like that and with all them children as well. He's managed to look after them his self all this time. Think it was getting too much for him. He has to work to support them all, but it meant Jane was on her own all day and he didn't want to leave her like that."

"Is there a cure for whatever she's got?" enquired Lizzie, more out of politeness than anything. "If the doctors don't know, how can they do anything?"

"Well, like I say, they don't know what it is. Thomas comes in here sometimes for bits for the kids, ribbons for the girls' hair and I always ask how his wife is, but he says she's going downhill fast. Sad, that's what it is, sad. But you seem like a nice girl. You look after them kids and Thomas, if you've got a mind. I hope everything works out for you lass."

"I will, if I get the job," replied Lizzie smiling.

The lady went through to the back of the shop. Lizzie opened the door, bell clanging, and stepped outside into the daylight. Hurrying to the station, she was filled with a surge of emotion she couldn't wait to share with Lottie.

* * * * * *

269

CHAPTER FORTY-ONE

Lizzie started her new life two weeks later. True to his word, Thomas Jackson sent the letter one week to the day of the interview. He wanted Lizzie to move in, in one week's time. He would give her the day to move in and she would begin her duties the next morning. Lizzie's excitement was tinged with sadness at the thoughts of leaving Lottie, Edward, Molly Ann and baby Peter. She wondered how Mary Alice would take the move.

'Will she settle in well? Will she get on with Thomas Jackson's children?'

It would be quite a change for all concerned and Lizzie hoped with all her heart she was doing the right thing. She notified Mr Jackson by letter immediately, accepting the position and informing him she would arrive with her belongings, the following Tuesday 4 June. She had one week, to gather her few belongings, pack Mary Alice's things and prepare herself mentally for a momentous change of lifestyle. Using a piece of paper from the notepad she'd purchased for her application, she wrote a heartfelt letter to Lottie and Edward.

'I'll give this to Lottie the day I'm leaving,' she thought tearfully.

Edward offered to take Lizzie and Mary Alice, together with their possessions, on his cart. He wanted to see her new home and hopefully meet her employer to satisfy himself and Lottie, Lizzie would be safe. Although Mary Alice didn't understand what was happening, Lizzie's excitement was contagious. Every time Lizzie packed a toy, Mary Alice pulled it out again. Lizzie would then chase her round the house, encouraging the child's laughter to ring out.

The girls held one another tightly, as Lizzie left on that early June morning. She'd said goodbye to Molly Ann and cradled the baby with fondness, and whilst she was looking forward to the challenge, it was with a heavy heart Lizzie sat in the carriage as it pulled away from Lottie's front door. Once again, they waved until the carriage turned the corner. Sniffling into a hanky, Lizzie pulled herself together, put her arm around Mary Alice and began preparing herself mentally for what lay ahead.

Edward and Lottie sat bewildered that evening. The house was unusually quiet, no laughter from Mary Alice or Lizzie. No-one to help with the chores and an empty bedroom upstairs which Lottie kept looking in, as if perhaps, Lizzie and Mary Alice might have miraculously materialised.

"How was she?" asked Lottie, crying again.

"She'll be fine. Seems like a nice enough bloke. Helped me in with all her things."

"What's her room like?"

"Neat, tidy, clean enough, two single beds, a small table and a large cupboard. A linoleum floor and fairly bright," answered Edward, thinking he'd given a fair description.

"How was Mary Alice? "

"Alright. The children weren't at home, so I didn't see them. She's coming to see us on Sunday with Mary Alice. That's her day off."

"I'll do us a nice dinner then on Sunday and we can sit round the table and listen to her tales."

"Yes," said Edward, "it all feels a bit strange. We're going to miss Lizzie."

Lizzie sat on her bed watching Mary Alice sleep. The notion came to her that all was going to be well here at 6 Lower Street. She had of course met all the children. The eldest, Henry, had been aloof but she hoped she could win him over. Dolly, Jack and Rosa seemed to take to her straightaway. She'd been in to see Jane, who looked more ghostly than ever. Thomas Jackson had been busy behind his pile of papers all day, letting Lizzie become acclimatised to her new surroundings. He had briefly shown here where everything was. There was a stew bubbling away on the stove for the supper, so she'd no need to prepare a meal for the evening, he'd said. Lizzie's duties would begin in earnest in the morning. For the children, there was a large bedroom with two double beds, one for the boys and one for the girls and their school clothes were laid out neatly on their beds. Her first duty, after taking Jane's drink, medication and breakfast of course, would be breakfast for the children and getting them to school. The breakfast things were to be prepared the night before. Porridge should be left to soak and bowls, spoons and mugs placed on the table. Henry would be leaving early and would sort himself out. Mr Jackson would leave with him. The rest was up to Lizzie. She was ready and hoped she could pull it all off.

'The children will help me,' she thought. 'They're old enough to know their routine. It's basic common sense really.'

Feeling positive, she undressed herself and prepared for bed. Lying there watching Mary Alice, mulling everything over, she wasn't aware when her eyes closed and sleep came.

* * * * * *

'Would I rather be at Maddingley Hall or Mr Sutton's manor house?' Lizzie asked herself the next morning when all hell let loose about whose socks were whose. It was bedlam, though Mary Alice, undeterred, weaved in and out of the others like she'd been doing it all her life. Laughing and giggling with the girls and tormenting the boys. Jane had her breakfast and could just about manage to eat it herself from the top of a hospital table pushed over the bed.

Lizzie rose at five o'clock and after getting herself ready for the day, lit the fire and put a large pot of porridge on for breakfast. The kettle was steaming merrily and the children were still fast asleep. She looked around the kitchen, evaluating the jobs which needed doing. The wooden draining board needed a scrub. She delved into a cupboard containing cleaning items and located an old scrubbing brush and carbolic soap, which she knew was also used for bathing. She rubbed the soap all over the draining board and scrubbed. She found what she supposed was a 'dishcloth', poured a little water from the boiling kettle into the stone sink and rinsed the wood as best she could. Pleased with the result, she had a look round for anything else glaringly obvious. It was going to take time.

'A small job here and there in between other household chores will soon have the house looking spick and span,' she thought.

Like a mother duck with four trailing ducklings, Lizzie managed to get Dolly, Jack and Rosa round to school on time. Pleased with her first morning's work, she headed for the little shop she'd found, with Mary Alice excitedly running along beside her. There were a couple of items which caught her eye a fortnight ago and she wanted to purchase them. Taking a few coins from her purse, leaving the money Lottie and Edward had given her as a leaving gift, she clanged the bell on the shop door and entered. There were a couple of other ladies talking to the shopkeeper, who recognized Lizzie instantly and waved from behind the counter. Lizzie headed straight for the cupboard in the corner where she'd seen a few books. The one which had caught her eye was still there. She snatched it up and had a look for a price, hoping with all her might she had enough to buy it. Wanting so much to please her employer, she'd thought this book, with all its tips, recipes and housekeeping notes would be the ideal thing to read in the evenings when her chores were finished and she retired to her room with Mary Alice. Lizzie didn't know if it was self-preservation pushing her to purchase this book, or was it to impress Thomas Jackson. Either way, she decided, it would be a useful tool to have, to enhance her housekeeping skills.

When the shopkeeper, whose name Lizzie learned was Charlotte, finished serving, she turned her attention to Lizzie.

"Nice to see you again so soon. Did you come to live round here then?'

"Yes," answered Lizzie, "I got the job."

"Oh my!" said Charlotte, holding the sides of her cheeks with her fingers.

Puzzled, Lizzie enquired, "Is that in a good way or not?" and looking quizzically at Charlotte, she searched her facial expression.

"You're the lucky lady then. Lots of the girls around here applied for that job, I heard. You'll not be very popular with them, I'm afraid," she said and laughed.

Lizzie laughed as well, understanding Charlotte was pleased she had the job.

"I saw this book last time I was in. I'd like to buy it please. How much does it cost?" Lizzie placed the book down on the old wooden counter. Charlotte looked at it and laughed. "You can have it ..... for nothing!"

Lizzie gasped. "For nothing? Why?"

"'Cos it's not for sale. I was throwing it out. Don't need it any more. I just forgot I'd left it there. Must have had it in me hand when I came through to open up. Take it love, it's yours now. There's some good tips in there. Sounds to me like you're going to do him proud. What's your name?"

"Lizzie. Lizzie Bradshaw, and this is Mary Alice, she said patting Mary Alice on top of her curls.

"Well, good luck Lizzie. I'll see you soon," and with that, Charlotte dashed through into the back.

'Probably to rescue more bacon,' Lizzie thought and smiled.

She shouted after Charlotte, "Thank you. See you soon."

She doubted whether Charlotte heard her, but clutching the book, once again she left her favourite shop in the world, looking forward immensely to bed time so she could devour every syllable of her precious acquisition.

* * * * * *

CHAPTER FORTY-TWO

Thomas Jackson had never experienced a Christmas like it. He'd known before he took Lizzie on, he'd made the right choice. There was something about this young woman. She had guts, strength of character, a willingness to give, and her gentility and charismatic smile warmed the house, not to mention the wonderful smell of baking bread when he came home from work. There was always something for him to eat. He gave her a housekeeping allowance out of which she'd to buy food and other household provisions needed to keep the home running smoothly. Jane's needs were catered for under a separate account. The mood of the house was undeniably happier than before Lizzie came. The children were thriving. Even Henry had warmed to Lizzie. She spent lots of time with the children. She helped them cook and bake, teaching them new skills wherever and whenever she could. She read with them. He wondered about that.

'How has she become so eloquent? What's her real background?'

He knew about Maddingley Hall and Mr Sutton at the Manor House, but what about before that? 'Where has she come from, this beautiful, warm-hearted, skilful lady who reminds me so much of Jane, twenty years ago.'

He vowed to ask her one day.

'Perhaps she'd like to sit with me one evening instead of retiring to her room? No, that's presumptuous,' he thought. 'Perhaps I can talk to her one afternoon before she collects the children from school?'

Although his thoughts were purely platonic, Thomas Jackson had feelings about this woman, although he hadn't categorised them yet.

'She's just a damn good housekeeper and I'm glad I chose her out of the five girls I'd short-listed. Good choice man.'

Thomas Jackson was a good twenty-five years or more older than Lizzie. He'd worked down the pit himself from an early age. His parents had been devout Catholics and he'd grown up with fourteen brothers and sisters. Many of his siblings had gone on to bigger and better things, sending his parents extra money for the upkeep of a large family. Thomas's wages then had been negligible and he'd had to give very little for his keep. He was a frugal man and had saved all his life. He'd had a relatively good life with Jane. There had been no children at first and there had been talk down the street there was 'something wrong.' The gossip became unbearable and eventually they'd moved. Thomas became a pit manager at the local coal-mine and a promotion increased his salary and their savings soon built up. This ultimately allowed him to rent a larger property. When Jane became sick, he was comfortable enough to be able to reduce his hours to care for her. The doctors had been blunt with Thomas. Something was besieging her immune system and letting in the disease she now suffered and whatever the cause, Thomas Jackson was under no illusion, Jane would not recover. It was just a matter of time. Over the last two years, he had cared for her as best he could, ensured she had everything she needed and more, whilst also being attentive to his four children and holding down a suitable position at the pit.

Thomas Jackson's acceptance of Lizzie and Mary Alice left Lizzie in no doubt Thomas was a good man. She watched him with his children and wished William

Casey had shown a fraction of the interest in Mary Alice. The two men were so different in their approach to life, to work, to their wives and to their children. Lizzie found herself wishing she'd found someone like Thomas Jackson instead of the wretch who now languished in a prison cell somewhere.

'But at least he doesn't know where I am,' thought Lizzie.

Her first year in the Jackson household reigned in Lizzie's mind as one of the most difficult to master. Compelled to do well, to care for Jane in a friendly and sympathetic manner, to inspire all the children to accomplish and to make Thomas Jackson proud of his decision to take her on, was a daunting task. Lizzie's feelings for his children were as though they were her own. In many ways, towards the end of her first year, it almost felt they were. She knew all their foibles, all their needs, wants and desires, she tended their small wounds, she kept housekeeping to a minimum expense whilst providing good wholesome food for all the family. Tending Jane's personal needs became a fulfilling commitment, talking to her, reading to her, sharing snippets of conversation even though she knew Jane wasn't coherent enough sometimes, to understand. She became, in all ways except one, the lady of the house.

Thomas Jackson noticed. He knew she worked her finger to the bone for him, his wife and his family. He watched her subtle decorum, her ability to create something from nothing, to weave a happy family from a disjointed one, to care for each of them as individuals, yet to take little for herself. He began to notice more. Lizzie went to visit Lottie most Sundays and he felt bereft. Her absence left a hollow somewhere deep within him. Although their paths seldom crossed because of his long working hours, the contentment in the house since Lizzie came was undeniable. Jane was less irritable, his children were thriving, there was always plenty to eat and his house was kept in good order. Proud of his ability to select such an employee, he wished to keep the equilibrium of his household and any feelings he harboured for Lizzie were kept tightly under wraps.

* * * * * *

CHAPTER FORTY-THREE

During the late summer of 1902, Jane's health began to deteriorate further. Slowly at first, becoming more rapid. When the other children were at school, most of Lizzie's days were spent with Mary Alice in Jane's bedroom. Mary Alice would take a book, a game or a toy and play or sometimes she would sit on Lizzie's knee and listen intently to the stories Lizzie read out loud to Jane.

Thomas Jackson came home early one day. Finding no-one downstairs, he climbed the stairs to sit with his wife a while. He hesitated before opening the door. He could hear Lizzie's gentle voice, clearly reading from the pages of a book. Not normally a demonstrative man, nor possessing the freedom to be so, he wished at that moment, he could take Lizzie in his arms and thank her for all she had done and was doing for Jane.

He opened the door ever so slightly and stole a look at the scene, before sneaking back down the stairs and setting the kettle on the fire to make both the women in his life a warm drink. Sitting there by the late afternoon firelight, smelling the delicious aroma of the stew beginning to bubble in the pot, he pondered the future. He'd never really thought too much about the aftermath of the inevitable. He knew the time was approaching when he would have to consider his options. The house was quiet, his children not yet home from school. He remembered Lizzie saying another child's mother was taking them to the park to play and then bringing them home in time for tea. He continued to sit in the fireside chair, the long hours beginning to catch up.

When Lizzie and Mary Alice came back downstairs, they found him sleeping. Lizzie ushered Mary Alice to the other side of the room to play and stood watching Thomas. He was still a handsome man, rugged, with the ravages of time etched deep into his face. She felt the urge to brush his hair back from his face with her hands but restrained herself as he opened his eyes and caught her watching him. He straightened himself up in the chair and they both laughed. In that moment, there existed an electricity in the space between them. Lizzie brushed her skirt down with her hands, turned and busied herself preparing the evening meal. The door burst open and three rowdy, happy, giggly children ran into their father's arms.

Jane Alison Jackson departed the world in a tempest of agony. In the gruelling month preceding her death, Thomas never left her side. She hadn't recognised her husband for over two years but he sat holding her hand and talking with her. The doctor had done all he could to ease her pain. They didn't take her into hospital, as her wish had been to pass away at home. Momentously savage for those living in the house and hearing her cries, Thomas had been prompted to seek alternative accommodation for the children. A relative of Jane's with an already overcrowded house offered to take them in. Lizzie's role still included taking the children to school and back to their new temporary abode, whilst the rest of the time was spent tending Jane's needs. It was a time of anguish, of heartfelt emotion and Lizzie sobbed frequently to see the sadness of a man suffer whilst watching his wife die.

The funeral was a simple service at the graveside. Only Henry had been allowed to attend and stood beside his father. They watched as Jane's body was gently lowered into the ground before father and son both turned and walked away, their facial expressions leaving Lizzie in no doubt of their grief. Her duty now, to collect the younger children and return home to the sombre household. Lizzie prayed for bedtime to be alone with her thoughts.

* * * * * *

CHAPTER FORTY-FOUR

It had been later than usual when Thomas came home that late October evening. Nelly, the old lady at number 24 had given Lizzie some extra blankets for the children, claiming it was to be a bad winter. The children were all asleep upstairs, snuggled beneath their benefactor's cuddly woollen blankets. It was a particularly cold night and Lizzie had stoked up the fire and set aside a pan of potato soup on the hearth for Thomas coming home, before she retired. She had been busying herself scrubbing the wooden table with a new bar of carbolic and time had run away. The lanterns were lit and flickering like the flames licking up the chimney. A cold waft of air almost blew them out, as the door opened. There was quite a wind getting up and Thomas tried hard not to let the door bang back and waken the sleeping children. He closed the door gently behind him. The scene in front of him warmed his heart. The smell of the potato soup, the warmth of the fire, the flickering lanterns, the knowledge his children were all safe and the beautiful woman responsible for his happiness, bustling about his kitchen making good the house for the master coming home. Lizzie hadn't heard Thomas enter, so engrossed was she, making sure everything was in order.

"By the heck, it's cold out there," Thomas said in a low voice, startling Lizzie.

"Ooh, you made me jump. I didn't hear you come in," she said laughing.

All Thomas could do was stare. He set down his bag and drew in everything before him. He looked at Lizzie, the light from the lantern casting a golden glow around her, her long, cascading dark curls shimmering in the lamplight. He knew in that moment. Deep in the pit of his being, he knew this night was the one he'd ashamedly been waiting for.

Lizzie bent down to retrieve the pan from the hearth and wait on him. He crossed the room, intoxicated by her beauty and touched her elbow, staying her hand from picking up the heavy pan. Gently he brought her up to a standing position.

"I can get my own supper. You should have been in bed long ago."

"I was just making sure everything was in order before I went," answered Lizzie, feeling the change. Her heart began to beat a little faster. Thomas, his whole body pulsating wildly, standing so close, frightened the feeling wasn't reciprocated. For a brief moment, it seemed like the magic had vanished. But then involuntarily, their hands brushed together and the spark ignited.

Thomas turned Lizzie round gently. Face to face, they looked into one another's eyes. He put his hands either side of Lizzie's beautiful head and pulled her into him. She didn't resist. She buried her face on his chest, listening to the intense beating of his heart. She could feel the surge of adrenalin pumping through him, a feeling matched by the rhythm of her own body. They stood locked in the moment until Thomas lifted her face up to his. Feeling the softness of her newly-washed hair between his fingers, he tentatively moved forward and brushed her lips with his own. Lizzie was responsive, accepting his gestures with pleasure. He broke the magic only to move them both towards the sofa. Removing the blanket from the back of the sofa, he moved them both back towards the fireplace. He released her and quickly threw the blanket on the floor in front of the still raging fire. Turning back to face her again, he whispered, "Will you lie with me Lizzie Bradshaw?"

In reply, Lizzie took his face in her hands and drew his mouth to hers.

* * * * * *

James Bradshaw was born towards the end of July 1903. Lizzie's labour had been intense and for the most part lonely. The 'midwife' had been fighting to save the life of a mother at number nine, across the road, and dashed in just as Lizzie was about to give birth. A healthy baby boy, the midwife, tired from the gruelling afternoon, cleaned James up and within minutes he was snuggled up to Lizzie, already trying to suckle. Auntie Edie, the lady who'd been helping out with the children, had taken it upon herself to collect all the children from number six. Crossing the road with her were Henry (reluctantly), Dolly, Jack, Rosa and Mary Alice following behind squealing with laughter as 'Auntie Edie' sang funny songs as they made their way towards the house they'd lived in whilst Lizzie tended Jane in her final days.

Thomas had been sent for and, much sooner than expected, appeared in the doorway with a grin from ear to ear. In his right hand he carried a bunch of lemon roses while his left hand waved across the room to Lizzie and his newborn son.

"Come see him," prompted Lizzie, holding a swaddled James outwards towards his father.

Thomas came forward and laid the flowers on the dresser at the side of Lizzie's bed. Taking his son in his arms, he bent down and kissed the top of Lizzie's head.

"Well done. He's a fine boy Lizzie."

Lizzie thought she detected a quiver in his voice. She wondered if perhaps he was thinking about his wife and older children's births. Perhaps he was a little ashamed, but Lizzie was much too happy to sadden herself with thoughts of people's opinion of their indiscretion. Not today anyway. She looked back on that first occasion with an open joy.

* * * * * *

CHAPTER FORTY-FIVE

Lizzie had become accustomed to the jibes from some of the local residents. For many months before Jane's death, she'd felt the unfounded suspicion, seen it in the eyes of passers-by and by the time her pregnancy was obvious, she felt completely ostracised by all but the stalwart few, whom she trusted and who'd taken the time to welcome her into their fold. Surprisingly for Lizzie, one of her supporters was the lady in the shop, Charlotte, who happened to think Lizzie's arrival had been the best thing that had happened for Thomas. With the support of those few, Lizzie felt confident enough to blatantly flaunt her pregnancy. Only she and Thomas needed to know the circumstances of that night and she held her head high and conducted herself, as always, in a dignified and graceful manner. Once the initial shock tremors had died down, her indiscretion with Thomas Jackson became yesterday's news. New scandals appeared fuelling the gossips with fresh material to discuss and Lizzie once again became a much-loved member of the community. When word spread of James's baptism, the kindnesses were overwhelming. Bestowed with gifts from almost every resident of the street, Lizzie felt elated that finally, she had come home.

* * * * * *

When Thomas heard the thrilling news at the end of October 1905, he was to become a father again, he

287

swept Lizzie up and swung her round, placing her down on the floor and kissing her so hard, it took her breath away.

"This is the spur I needed," he said, obviously excited.

"For what?" questioned a puzzled Lizzie.

"We need to move. I've been thinking about it for a while but now, I have the incentive to make that move."

"Where will we move to?" asked Lizzie, a little disappointed she might have to leave her friends.

"There's an end terrace in Albert Street, a much larger house with three bedrooms and I've been thinking about whether or not we should move into there."

"How much more will it cost?" questioned Lizzie, alarmed they'd be stretching their budget.

"Well, not too much more I don't think. I know the man who owns it and I know the man who lives there is leaving next week. There was a contagious lilt in Thomas's voice and Lizzie found herself excited at the prospect of having more space for their ever growing family.

"It needs a bit of work doing but I can do most of it. I know you've got the knack for sprucing it up. Why don't you come with me and have a look?"

"Alright. When can we go?"

Thomas smiled at her. "Tomorrow!"

Lizzie had a sense Thomas had already made his mind up and made a mental note to arrange for someone to look after the children.

* * * * * *

Thomas Jackson and Lizzie Bradshaw moved into their new house on Albert Street two weeks later. Lizzie hadn't been able to contain her excitement following the visit to the new house. She had the ability to visualise what it might look like when the two of them had completed the necessary work and the landlord had agreed to do a couple of jobs before they moved in.

Lizzie swung between total elation and an overwhelming melancholy her two sisters would never share her joy as she spent the two weeks packing up the house in preparation for their move. She had, of course, told Thomas she was a married woman at her interview and the fact she'd been married hadn't surprised him. He was au fait enough to realise a stunning woman like Lizzie must have had previous lovers. Shocked to hear her husband was in prison, he'd been happy to accept things the way they were but Lizzie hadn't dismissed the knowledge she was behaving immorally.

'I'm still a married woman. My husband is in prison and I'm living with a man twice my age, sharing his life, his house, his bed. I can never remarry. What am I doing?'

As quickly as the thoughts entered her head, so too did the savage brutality of William Casey and the life she would have endured had she not left. The feelings of remorse didn't linger long and happy with their decision to leave 6 Lower Street, she busied herself with the task in hand.

The house in Albert Street bore no resemblance to the one they'd just left. Happy it was not too far away, Lizzie contented herself she could keep in touch with her old neighbours and make new acquaintances. The children attended the same school, she shopped in the same establishments, although they were a little further away and despite their being much work to do, Lizzie felt fortunate her life had taken her down this path. A lifetime away from her poverty-stricken beginnings, the traumas of her past slowly began to dissipate as she tended her family, brought her new home up to scratch and made new friends.

Thomas Jackson was a good man, working hard to allow them to live well. Both pulled their weight in equal measure and good strong family relationships existed in the household. Lizzie bore Thomas two more children, Kate born in the spring of 1906, named after her beloved sister and Eleanor in the early April of 1909. Following the birth of Eleanor, Lizzie was confined for much longer than expected. At thirty-nine years of age, bringing Eleanor into the world had taken its toll and exhausted from an extensive labour and loss of blood, she remained bed-ridden for almost a month. Auntie Edie helped out where she could and friends and neighbours rallied to help whenever time allowed.

Thomas and Henry continued at the pit and Jack was now of an age to work. There was a little extra money coming in. Lizzie's days were hard going in the months following her confinement but despite a brave face and her usual air of grace and dignity, Lizzie was worrying about something else. At first she hadn't been able to identify the cause of her worry, but as the months wore on, Thomas's behaviour became more noticeable and Lizzie found herself becoming increasingly concerned. At sixty-three, the ageing process was rapidly bearing down and a lifetime at the pit beginning to cause health problems. A household full of boisterous youngsters, failing health and the added exertions of extra household chores weighed significantly on Thomas's demeanour. Lizzie finally managed to persuade him to seek medical attention. Following the doctor's advice, Thomas was declared unfit for work for a period of eight weeks. During this time, the dawn of a new era came to rest at the front door of the house in Albert Street.

Eleanor was approaching her first birthday in the spring of 1910. Lizzie found it a gruelling year both with her own health and looking after Thomas, who was more demanding following his eight weeks off work. The mood in the household had changed dramatically. Eight weeks loss of income put an enormous strain on Lizzie, who had continued to run the household with as much normality as possible. All her previous experience had been brought into play and with the help of her closest friends, she'd managed admirably, but Thomas's mood resonated throughout the household.

On one of Lizzie's visits to see Lottie, she poured out her heart to her closest friend who listened intently. Sadness was etched on Lizzie's face, and Lottie knew in a moment all was not well.

"I don't think he'll be able to work much longer," Lizzie confided to Lottie. "Henry and Jack are bringing a little money in from the pit, but that won't keep ten of us. I'm going to look for a job, it's the only way I'll be able to make ends meet."

"But you can't go out to work. You've still got the little ones to look after."

"Well I could try for a part time position. It's only Kate and Ellie who aren't yet at school. A couple of the neighbours have helped me out a little. They might be willing to have them while I do a few hours, maybe a couple of times a week."

"What are you thinking of looking for?"

"I thought of going back into service, but of course they would want me to live in, so I think a factory of some sort. They sometimes offer part time for people with young families."

"Do you have somewhere in mind?"

Lizzie laughed. "Yes, actually I do. Just can't decide to actually do it until the two little ones are at school."

"Why don't you take in some laundry work? Get people to bring it to you. There's a lady down the road here who takes in bags of ironing. Gets a good few bob every week too."

Lizzie jumped up and hugged Lottie. "You're wonderful Lottie. I've been so wrapped up in self-pity, it never occurred to me to do something like that. That's exactly what I'm going to do until Katy and Ellie are at school and if I can manage to put an odd few pennies away each week, that'll help towards looking after us when Thomas retires. He can't continue working for ever."

"Let me know how you get on. Get one of the children to come and let me know if you need help with anything."

"Thanks Lottie, I will."

Lizzie left Lottie's that morning with a spring in her step, a new focus and a refreshed vigour she hadn't felt for a while.

Yes,' she thought. 'I can do this. I can bring some money in. Maybe that's what Thomas is worrying about. The fact it's getting harder for him to go down the pit, but knowing he can't do it forever. I'm going to put a notice in the shop, and one in our front window.'

She almost skipped home, Katy and Ellie either side of her, also sensing the change in their mother's mood.

Before the end of the week, Lizzie had three customers, the best paying one being the lady who'd seen the advert in the shop. She'd been in for buttons and asked the shopkeeper if she knew who'd posted the advert and did she know anything about her. Of course, the shopkeeper had praised Lizzie to the heavens and so began her relationship with Mrs Livesley who lived in a large smallholding on the outskirts of town.

Lizzie had gone home following her visit to Lottie and as Thomas had returned to work, she spring-cleaned the entire house. She washed and ironed all the bedding, brushed carpets, dusted down the ceilings and walls, polished, scrubbed the kitchen table, blacked the range and prepared a hearty stew for her family coming home.

When Thomas and the children returned, they found the house back to normal. Lizzie's mood had lifted and normality reigned. Thomas seemed in good spirits and the few extra shillings per month was helping to aid the family's recovery.

* * * * * *

CHAPTER FORTY-SIX

Three days before Christmas 1911, a bombshell dropped on the mat in Albert Street. It was a Friday afternoon and Thomas had returned from his early shift. There was an animated air in the house and the children were excited beyond belief. Lizzie had asserted her efforts to create a magical wonderland for the Christmas festivities. A beautiful Christmas tree stood in the front parlour. Garlands of holly and ivy were strung up across the top of the range, the house was scrubbed and clean and the family were all looking forward to spending the next few days together.

The letter had arrived earlier that morning. Lizzie had been finishing off her laundry work. Three large piles sat on the dining table waiting to be collected later that day. She had looked at the envelope, believing it to be a Christmas greeting. It was addressed to Thomas Jackson and so she hadn't opened it. She presented Thomas with a happy homecoming. The children flocked around him, excited to shout out what they were hoping Father Christmas would bring. Lizzie had made a plate of sandwiches and a pot of tea. An apple pie made from the fruit from Lottie's garden also sat on the table on a tin plate. A couple of other envelopes had also arrived that morning and Lizzie scuttled the children away from Thomas so he could look at his mail. The Christmassy ambience of the house entirely belied the weather conditions. A thick fog was descending upon an already dark afternoon and the lamps were lit earlier than usual.

Thomas took a sip of his tea and placed the cup on the hearth, in front of the roaring fire. Picking up his mail he opened the envelopes one by one. There were a couple of greetings cards from neighbours, to string up with the others. Lizzie was busying herself lifting crockery down from the dresser. The children were washing their hands ready for tea. Lizzie came through with some coal and almost dropped it as she saw Thomas, his face as white as a ghost, the contents of the envelope on the floor.

"Thomas, are you alright? What's the matter?"

He pointed to the letter. Lizzie bent down and picked it up. Reading its contents, her world crashed around her.

* * * * * *

CHAPTER FORTY-SEVEN

Remembering another New Year's Eve when she embarked on a new existence, Lizzie spent the next week in a total daze. They tried, in vain, to maintain the equilibrium of the Christmas spirit for the children's sake, but the contents of the letter made that almost impossible. The landlord had served them ten day's notice. The house had been sold and the new owner would move in on the first day of January 1912.

Thomas, after his initial shock, became angry and confronted the landlord who lied and informed him he'd had an offer he couldn't refuse.

"Offer came right out of the blue Tom. I had no intention of selling. You've been good tenants. You've looked after the property. I'm as shocked as you but the offer was too good to pass up."

"Who's bought it?" asked Thomas. "Do you think the new owner will let us carry on renting?"

"No lad. He's a cash buyer. Not from these parts and wants to move in straightaway."

Thomas felt there was no point questioning further. There was nothing to be done. They'd have to find somewhere else and move out.

* * * * * *

Lizzie spent Christmas attentive to the children. Their happiness depended on it, she told Thomas.

"We won't tell them until after Christmas," she said.

For the most part, she'd held her own counsel and the initial shock was shelved and had it not been for the cloud of doom hanging over them, Christmas would have been one of the happiest yet. On the morning of the twenty-seventh of December 1911, Lizzie and Thomas gathered their offspring and broke the news as gently as they could. The girls broke into tears, even Ellie, who being the youngest, was probably copying the others. The boys took it like men, matter of fact. They were all given the job of packing up their own things, even the younger ones, while Thomas went back to the pit with Henry and Jack, and Lizzie continued to gather their belongings, in between her laundry duties and trying to run the household as normal.

Three days before their eviction, Mrs Livesley came to collect her laundry.

"Are you alright Lizzie?" she enquired. Lizzie looked drawn and tired.

The house looked chaotic, leading Mrs Livesley to believe all was not well.

"Not really," Lizzie replied.

"Do you want to talk about it?" asked the older woman in a gentle manner.

Lizzie broke into loud rasping sobs. "We've got to move out of here on New Year's Eve. The landlord has served us notice."

"Do you know why?"

"Yes. Someone has bought the house. They're moving in on New Year's Day."

Mrs Livesley looked as stunned as Lizzie felt. "Have you somewhere else to go?"

"No, not yet. Thomas is going to see some people today to see if there's anything suitable, but we're not going to get anything like this for what we can afford."

"Do you know who's bought it?"

"No. Landlord said it's someone from out of town. A cash buyer."

"Something will turn up Lizzie. It will."

"It'll have to be quick or we'll be out on the street." She'd been going to add 'again', but stopped herself.

Mrs Livesley collected her pile of laundry and carried it out to the carriage waiting outside. Lizzie stood at the door to wave her off. Closing the door behind her, she sat down at the kitchen table and cried. Katy tugged at her skirts to come and look at what she'd packed and Ellie wanted food. Lizzie dried her eyes and tended her children's needs.

Thomas wanted to know who'd bought the house he and Lizzie had strived so hard to maintain under trying circumstances. He'd caught the landlord earlier in the day and questioned him again but received no further information.

'There's something fishy going on here,' he thought.

'No-one's been to see the house. How can someone buy a house when they haven't seen it and why would they do that?'

He didn't have to wait long for his answer.

On twenty-eighth of December, another letter dropped on the mat. It wasn't addressed to Thomas or Lizzie. Lizzie's body froze as she stared at the envelope.

"What the hell is this?" she cried out loud, a deep nauseas feeling creeping up from the pit of her stomach.

She dropped it as though it had burnt her. The letter was addressed:

Mr William Casey
124 Albert Street

Her heart pounded as she stared down at the envelope lying face up on the floor, William Casey's name burning her eyes as she looked at it in disbelief.

'Is this some kind of sick joke?' she asked herself. 'How can it possibly be? Why is it addressed to him? He's in jail. Why's it come here, to Thomas's house?'

She scooped the letter up as if it were something dirty and without opening the envelope, stuffed it into her cloth bag, grabbed Katy and Ellie and ran with the children to tell Lottie.

Lottie's alarm bells began to ring when whoever was knocking on her door was clearly visiting on an urgent matter. She opened the door to a totally unexpected Lizzie who was obviously distressed. Lizzie nearly fell in the door as Lottie ushered her into the kitchen and promptly made her a cup of tea. She settled the kids in a corner with some toys and sat opposite Lizzie with her own drink.

"What on earth's the matter? What's happened?"

Lizzie took the unopened letter out of her bag and placed it on the table in front of Lottie, who simply stared at it, hardly comprehending the implications.

"When did it arrive?" she asked softly.

"Just this morning. It's like a horrible monster from the past has reared its head to haunt me," answered Lizzie. "Why has a letter with his name on, come to our house?"

In the moment she asked that question, she realised.

"Oh my God. No. It's him isn't it. He's the cash buyer. It's him who's bought the house. He's found out somehow, where I'm living. But where's he got that kind of money from? Oh Lottie, I can't stand it. I just can't stand this. How? How's he done this?"

Lizzie was hysterical and it took all Lottie's expertise to calm her down. The harsh reality and all its complications struck them both.

"You'll have to move away Lizzie. It would be more than your soul could bear to have him around, living in *your* home, seeing him, never knowing when he would strike. You have to move away if you can."

"But why should I? This is Thomas's home, our children's home. My home. How can he do this? We can't move away. Thomas's job, the children's school, my laundry work. He can't do this. He can't."

Hysteria caught hold of Lizzie again, prompting the children to come to their mother to see what was wrong. She hugged them both and asked them to continue playing, saying they'd be going soon.

"Well, it's looking like he's done it. He's obviously out of prison and seeking revenge because you left. Not to mention he'll know you're living with another man and have more children. We have to be sensible and realise that's exactly why he's done it. Lizzie, you're not safe here. You have to leave."

"I'm scared Lottie. I'm scared for my children. If he's capable of doing this, he's capable of doing anything. You're right. I have to go, whether Thomas comes with me or not. This is going to kill him. He won't want to leave the area, his job and everything. His whole life has been around these parts. It's not fair to ask him to leave and anyway, where could we go? I'm scared Lottie." Lizzie began sobbing again.

"Right Lizzie. Come on. Pull yourself together. We have to figure a way around this. Crying isn't going to help. I'll put the kettle back on and we'll have another cup of tea while we sort this out."

She handed Lizzie a rag pulled from her pinafore pocket.

"Here, dry your eyes. We'll sort something out. One way or another."

* * * * * *

CHAPTER FORTY-EIGHT

Lottie sent word with Molly Ann, that she'd made enquiries up and down her street and there was a property available but they wouldn't be able to move in until the end of the first week in January. Lottie had offered to accommodate some of them for the interim period, if Lizzie could make arrangements for the others to stay elsewhere. The house Lottie found was smaller than the one they were in at present, but it would tide them over for a while.

Lizzie went straight to Lottie to hear all about the new house. When she went home later that day, the biting wind tore at her face and the icy conditions beneath her feet bore up through her body. The children were huddled underneath woollen scarves and hats, their coats wrapped tightly around them. Lizzie had forgotten her own coat, so keen was she to hear Lottie's news. Lottie had lent her a wrap which she was unable to hold around her as she had tight hold of the children's hands as they made their way back to deliver the news to Thomas. The older children would be home from school soon and she reproached herself the house wasn't ready to receive them, nor was there anything on the stove for them to eat. Lizzie was inspired by Lottie's suggestions, and having pulled herself together for the sake of her family, determination prevailed.

'Yes William Casey, you can try, but you won't grind me down. You will not.'

With only two days left before their notice of eviction expired, the house was fairly well organised for the move. It hadn't taken Lizzie long to bake a cheese pie for tea and while Thomas digested the latest disastrous news, there was a knock on the door. Surprised anyone would come calling at this late hour in the day, Lizzie's heart wrenched. She asked Thomas to see who it was. He came back in the room with Mrs Livesley. Lizzie looked up in surprise.

'Oh no,' she thought. 'I haven't got time to do another load of ironing. We're moving in two days.'

Mrs Livesley wasn't here to give Lizzie more laundry. She had come with an offer. It was the second one of the day and by far the best.

Mrs Livesley's offer way surpassed anything Lizzie had dreamed of. She handed Mrs Livesley a steaming cup of cocoa and they sat around the table.

"Would you like to eat with us Mrs Livesley?" asked Lizzie, nervously.

"No thank you Lizzie. I'll get straight to the point."

Thomas sat beside Lizzie while Mrs Livesley spoke clearly and decisively.

"The farm is too big for me now. Since my husband passed on, I'm finding it more and more difficult to keep it up. I need someone, a family like yourselves perhaps," she said, smiling, "to look after it for me. I wonder if you would consider taking the job on? There would be enough room for you all. It's not in such a bad state. I'd expect a fair rent, of course, but there are some chores on the farm which would mean you'd get it a bit cheaper. What do you think?"

Lizzie and Thomas just stared. Unable to speak, they turned and looked at one another. They both turned back to face Mrs Livesley and replied in unison.

"Yes please."

"That's settled then," answered Mrs Livesley. "You can move in whenever you like. I'm leaving all the furniture and everything in the house." She added, "If that's alright with you?"

Lizzie and Thomas just nodded. Mrs Livesley continued.

"I'm going to live with my sister up in Scotland, so I'm leaving you in sole charge of the farm. We'll finalise the details before I leave on New Year's Day. You can move in whenever you like before that. I'll arrange for a cart to come for your belongings. I'm sure you'll want to bring some of your things with you and there's plenty of room for some of your furniture if you want to bring that too."

Mrs Livesley left Lizzie and Thomas in a whirl of emotion. They hugged one another for the first time in months. Thomas admitted to Lizzie later he was a little sceptical about how it would all pan out. He would have to continue working down the pit, so arrangements would have to be made for him getting to and from work.

"Perhaps a bicycle," he suggested. "Would take me about half an hour each way."

Lizzie was concentrating on how she would get the children to school and home again. The older ones would have to look after the younger ones and make the journey together. There was another village half a mile away from the farm in the opposite direction. Lizzie decided she would do her shopping there, rather than risk bumping into William, and the two youngest, when it came time for them to go to school, could go to the school in the new village. Their decision made and the house all packed up, Thomas, Lizzie and their eight children would be ready to move into "Homestead Farm" on New Year's Eve, the day before their notice of eviction expired.

Mrs Livesley, true to her word, had sent a cart to collect their furniture. Some of it Thomas had sold to work colleagues. Lottie had taken a few pieces to keep for Lizzie until she'd found the room to take them. She had been more than delighted when Lizzie had made a quick visit to deliver her news. The children, excited at their new venture, skipped round happily as they entered the grounds of Homestead Farm for the first time. There were squeals of delight to find chickens running around. Mrs Livesley took the children to show them where to collect eggs.

"That'll be your job," she said to them all.

She took Thomas and showed him the ropes, with the help of one of the farm hands, who would be staying on to manage the place. He lived in a small cottage further down the hill and would continue his duties as normal. A single man living alone, he was agile and it seemed to Thomas, he would have been well able to run the farm single-handedly. It was only then Thomas realised, Mrs Livesley had truly offered them an opportunity too good to be missed.

Happier than ever before, Lizzie and Thomas began to enjoy their surroundings. Mrs Livesley had taken into account the few jobs they would be doing around the place, plus the money Lizzie would lose on the laundry and had adjusted the rent accordingly. She had wanted someone to take over whom she knew would look after the farm as their own. She had been planning to execute her decision the moment she met Lizzie, whom she'd come to realise was a hard-working individual, who kept house well, turned-out perfectly groomed children and kept herself looking well.

'A fine young woman,' she'd said to herself. 'Exactly the sort of family I'd be looking for to look after the farm if I decide to leave.'

The news of Lizzie's eviction was the perfect chance for her to make that decision and now it was done.

They all enjoyed an evening meal together in the huge farmhouse kitchen. Lizzie had been overwhelmed and burst into tears when she entered the kitchen and saw the sheer size and facilities it offered. A huge range dominated the room with an array of cooking pots and oven pans. A large wooden dresser, similar to the ones she remembered in the workhouse, sat proudly on the other side of the room, packed with beautifully patterned crockery, four drawers filled with cutlery from teaspoons to fish knives and forks. Sitting in the centre of the room on the flagstone floor was the huge wooden farmhouse table with a dozen chairs scattered around it crowning the room to perfection. Lizzie couldn't believe it. A pretty picture window above the stone sink and wooden drainer, looked out over a garden she could only have dreamed of. A vegetable garden beyond an archway would yield enough to feed her family. Of course, she would have to learn how to tend it, but she looked forward to that with anticipation. A happier family could not be found anywhere.

When Mrs Livesley retired to her room for the last time in her farmhouse, the children went upstairs to their allocated bedrooms, Thomas and Lizzie sat around the fire in the large kitchen and laughed till they cried. The sheer emotion of the past ten days had finally caught up with them. They gazed around the room, they wandered around the other downstairs rooms trying to take it all in. Lizzie began sorting through some of their belongings and putting them away. The furniture they'd brought with them had integrated well with the existing pieces. It wasn't going to take them long to make this place their own. Lizzie, looked forward to it immensely and silently thanked William.

* * * * * *

CHAPTER FORTY-NINE

Having served his time with no remission, William Casey left the Carlston Prison, angry and vengeful. Having nowhere else to go, he sought his parents' whereabouts and having no remorse for his previous behaviour or misdemeanours, continued defying the law whilst keeping a low profile. His attempts to locate Lizzie failed, only serving to fuel his anger further. His deranged mind hell bent on finding her and causing disruption to whatever kind of life she'd found. He didn't intend to kill her. No, he didn't want to go through the hell of prison life again. What he wanted was to make her pay, in some way, for the grief and misery she'd caused him. Crossing four counties in his search for her, he had come into further bad company, a gambling syndicate, setting up major sessions across the North West. It was at one such meeting, his good fortune dropped into his lap. An unknown had wormed his way into one of the sessions. Losing badly, and having relinquished all his cash assets, the foolish gambler put up his property as collateral.

William had been having an unusually good game and couldn't believe his luck when he won. Unfortunately for Thomas and Lizzie, the outsider had been their landlord. Of course, William, who was still searching for his wife, had no idea of the extent of his luck that day. His first visit to Etching was bizarre. He had the address of the house in his hands. The man whose property he now owned, had omitted to inform him there were tenants living in the house, having given William a date in January when he could access the property. William had used some of his previous ill-gotten gains to secure a room at a tavern on the outskirts of Etching.

The day he first saw Lizzie, he thought he was seeing a ghost. With two young children running alongside her, squealing and laughing, he almost allowed himself to be seen, before coming to his senses and ducking behind the wall of the corner house as she dashed past. He could hear her laughter.

'Is that Mary Alice? No. Can't be. She'll be older than that now,' he thought.

His anger fuelled further, he carefully followed her making sure he kept well out of sight. Disbelieving his eyes, yet knowing there could not be another with identical beauty, he watched as she unlocked the door of a house. Never having been to this town before, he'd no idea where Albert Street was, and almost choked on his cigarette when he passed the name of the road. He stopped behind a billboard poster and took out the piece of paper with the address he'd been looking for.   '124', he mouthed, and waited until Lizzie had closed the door behind her. Cautiously and with his cap pulled down over his head, he moved slowly down Albert Street on the opposite side of the road. Keeping the collar of his jacket pulled up and his head down, he passed the houses, glancing over at the numbers on the gate posts. One hundred and eighteen, one hundred and twenty.

'No, it can't be.'

He held his breath as he drew level with the house across the road where the person resembling Lizzie had entered. One hundred and twenty-four, right at the end of the street. He turned around and quickly started walking back towards the other end of the street.

'It can't be.'

He wanted to laugh out loud. Loud raucous laughter echoed inside him.

'I have to make sure.'

He ran towards the end of the street, turned left and ran up the street, turning left again. Running like the wind down the length of the next street, turning left again at the end and then cautiously slowing down and inching his way along towards the corner where number one hundred and twenty four stood.

'This can't be happening.'

He wanted to pinch himself to make sure he wasn't dreaming. The house on the corner of Albert Street, when approached from that street had a high brick wall running the depth of the building. There didn't appear to be any windows in the gable and he couldn't be seen over the top of the brick wall. As he gingerly scurried past, he could hear voices. Children's voices. Then he heard someone calling them.

"Dolly, Rosa, Mary Alice, Katy, Ellie. Come on, tea's ready!"

Without a doubt, he knew his wife's voice.

'Mary Alice. That's my daughter. Who are all the other brats with her. If she's with another man, I'll kill her. It's one thing finding her and tormenting her life, but it's completely a different set of rules if she's bedding with another man.' He re-iterated to himself, 'I'll kill her.'

Lizzie's perception of danger hadn't let her down that afternoon. She'd been calling the children in for their tea and heard the terrier next door barking. The small back-yard which backed onto their own was home to the dog who only barked when a stranger passed by. It was as if he knew the footsteps of everyone who walked past and barked only when it was an unknown. Lizzie couldn't have known that just on the other side of the brick wall, passed the husband she believed to be a million light years from the life she now lived. But William Casey was just a few inches away and planning to destroy her. In the dead of night, William Casey returned to one hundred and twenty four Albert Street and after writing his name and Lizzie's address on an envelope, he sealed it with no contents and pushed it through the letter box.

* * * * * *

CHAPTER FIFTY

Lottie had spoken wisely to Lizzie the day she'd taken the envelope bearing William Casey's name on it to show her. She advised her to contact the police and explain. Not knowing the contents of the envelope at that time, Lizzie had followed Lottie's advice, having first discussed it with Thomas, who was incapable of coherent speech, such was his anger. He'd eventually reluctantly agreed it was a precaution well worth taking. The policeman Lizzie spoke to scribbled down a description of William and the address and said they'd keep an eye out for any suspicious behaviour. Marginally relieved, Lizzie felt she'd countered William's blatant attempt at his frightening technique. Following their move to the farm, making sure they weren't followed, she felt fairly safe. John, the farmhand would be on hand to ward off any unwanted visitors at the times Thomas wasn't at home and she was convinced she'd be far too busy to dwell on her criminal husband's pursuits.

On the day of the move, Lizzie had asked Lottie and Edward if they'd make themselves available as look-outs for William Casey. They reported they hadn't seen him. Relieved, Lizzie put William's intrusion to the back of her mind, safe in the knowledge he didn't know where she was.

William had been furious.. The day before he was due to move into Albert Street, he'd assumed Lizzie would be moving out and he'd intended to be around to find out where to.

'I'm moving in tomorrow. She'll have to be out and I'll be there to find out where she goes.'

But William had been so elated and flushed with success and enough money to get drunk at the tavern, that's exactly what he did. By the time he came to, in the late afternoon, he hurried across town, feeling like death warmed up, only to find the house looking empty. "Damn!' he cried out loud. "Damn them to hell. I'll find her. I'll bloody find her and kill her."

* * * * * *

A situation arose in the spring of 1912 which although grave for most people, gave rise to a sense of happiness and well-being at the farm. A nationwide miner's strike prevented Thomas from going down the pit. Being an overseer, he had to put an appearance in most days, but his long shifts had, for the time being, come to an end. This meant he was able to spend more time at home with Lizzie and the children. At almost sixty-four years of age, this came as a welcome break for Thomas. He loved his life at the farm, and had grown to love Lizzie with an unquenchable passion. They had fixed up the farm to the best of their ability and were filled with a sense of pride. Apart from the usual daily routine hiccups of everyday life, Lizzie and Thomas began to feel they'd finally settled. With thoughts of William, safely tucked away at the back of her mind, Lizzie began to enjoy her life as never before. Lottie and Edward visited frequently and a couple of Lizzie's old neighbours wandered up from time to time. Lizzie still felt too intimidated to venture into town, just in case, but was quite happy to entertain her guests as often as they wished to come. She was able to go with Thomas to get their provisions, using the facilities of the village on the other side of the farm. One of the local farmers provided her with milk from his herd. Their own chickens, provided enough eggs and John occasionally brought a chicken for the table. Vegetables grew in profusion in the garden and Lizzie baked her own bread. Life had never been so good. Henry and Jack were at home to help with chores and young Jack became skilled at woodwork, collecting old bits of wood thrown out in timber yards to create unique pieces of furniture.

There was much amusement down the ranks when Henry brought home a daughter of one of the local farmers whom he'd met whilst he and Jack were procuring wood for one of Jack's projects. Jack, too, had met someone and although he hadn't told Lizzie himself, Henry had spilled the beans at dinner one night, amidst great amusement from the older girls.

Lizzie learnt the art of vegetable growing, taught by the farmhand, John, without whose knowledge and expertise, they might have perished, particularly in the winter months up there on the hill, where the weather conditions seemed much worse than down in the towns and villages. The wind howled alarmingly through the farmhouse. Keeping the fires lit and the place warm was an art form, but Lizzie and Thomas thrived. Scarcely able to believe they'd been fortunate enough to meet Mrs Livesley, they were strangely grateful to William for pursuing his gambling habits, which they eventually found out from their ex-landlord, is how William acquired the property and unwittingly put his wife out of her home.

Life went on, daily routines developed until they managed their tasks around the farm like veterans. Mrs Livesley visited and was seriously impressed by what she saw. Thomas Jackson had returned to work following the strike but on reduced hours due to his age. Lizzie began to take in laundry again, brought up to the farm by John who collected it three times a week.

The Christmas of 1913 was a relatively peaceful one, with the family together. Weather conditions had not been excessive and the momentum in the household generally one to treasure. Lizzie prided herself on her culinary expertise, conjuring up delectable meals over the festivities and enjoying life to the full. Lottie and Edward had been up a few times, bringing supplies which Lizzie couldn't get in the village, so the house was well stocked with store cupboard goods in case the weather should turn bad during the first quarter of 1914. Lizzie and Thomas were proud of their family and nurtured the love growing between them. Life on the farm during the first half of the year was a peaceful existence.

Their temporary euphoria was shattered, when World War I, triggered by the assassination of Franz Ferdinand, was announced in August of that year when Britain declared war on Germany. The world became a fusion of tempest most people could barely comprehend. Nations and entire generations were traumatised. News of unspeakable atrocities reached the ears of those who listened and conditions worldwide took a dramatic downturn, forcing most families to endure unspeakable hardships, whilst embracing an unrivalled sense of camaraderie. Lizzie was amongst the lucky ones. Thomas was deemed too old to fight.

* * * * * *

CHAPTER FIFTY-ONE

Lottie's husband, Edward succumbed to conscription in December 1914, and was killed in the trenches of the Somme during the spring of 1915. Lizzie's unrequited love for her friend forced her to leave the safety of the farm and visit. Lottie, Molly Ann and Peter accompanied Lizzie back to the farm, following some pressure from her friend to come and live with them for a while. It was on the journey back home one Saturday afternoon Lizzie witnessed a wedding party coming out of the local parish church. She stopped dead in her tracks as she saw William emerge from the church doorway with a young bride on her arm. Lottie steadied her, unsure at first what had caused Lizzie's near collapse. She looked in the direction Lizzie was staring but they were still quite a way from the church. Lizzie urged her friend to dive for cover round the corner of a nearby building. Lottie's heart lurched, as she thought Lizzie had seen enemy aircraft, or something else sinister causing her to react this way.

She finally saw the cause of Lizzie's trauma. She too, could see, with absolute clarity Lizzie's husband walking down the path, the church behind him, his bride linking his arm and a number of guests, none of whom either Lizzie or Lottie recognised.

'Friends and family of the bride,' they both thought simultaneously. Lizzie felt sick. If discovered, his unlawful behaviour would put him back in prison and her natural instinct was to shout the word across the street and alert those gathered for the ceremony William Casey was not free to marry. She didn't shout out. She thought of her own circumstances. Although not on paper, she too, had been defying the word of God and living with another man, bedding with him and bearing his children. Despite the fact she could justify her own actions, she couldn't bring herself to confront her demons. Perhaps he would leave her alone now. Perhaps she was safer in the knowledge his attentions would be directed, good or bad, to his new bride, whether legally bound or not. She decided discretion was the better part of valour and Lizzie and Lottie, together with the children, who had been quite happy watching the wedding across the road, left the scene undetected. The physical and emotional shock which she initially believed would have had long-lasting psychological effects, soon wore off and Lizzie concentrated on the more painful task of helping Lottie through her bereavement.

Lottie stayed at the farm far longer than she'd intended. She made a couple of trips back to her small house to collect some personal items and to sort out affairs following her husband's death. She therefore witnessed Thomas Jackson's quick demise. Thomas became sick in the weeks following Lottie's arrival at the farm. At first, they thought it was a fever which had attacked him.
'Perhaps the flu,' they thought.
He was sent to bed and they tended him as they would any patient but Thomas didn't improve. Lizzie's financial status had taken another step back as her growing family needed more food, Thomas had no income as he was unfit for work and she wouldn't take the little money Lottie offered her. Propping one another up, the two women fought on, Lottie coming to terms with Edward's shocking death and Lizzie fighting to keep Thomas focused on getting well. He had developed a boil on the back of his neck. Lizzie had seen this phenomenon before but never as prominent or painful and he wasn't getting any better. Henry was sent to fetch a doctor.

Thomas was transported to the infirmary at the local workhouse, an institution Lizzie thought she would never have the misfortune of entering again. Initially he was admitted for treatment, but his fever persisted, the boil became a carbuncle and ultimately turned to blood poisoning. The medication administered was no match for the extreme pain Thomas suffered and after a week of agonising waiting for the treatment to work, Thomas died a painful death as the poison infiltrated his entire body. Lizzie was with him when he died. Through the tears, she held onto him as she watched his life slowly ebb away. Lottie was waiting for her in the anti-room and knew without doubt the outcome as Lizzie fell into her arms without speaking.

The same day, there was an explosion at the mine. Henry and Jack had been working their shift. A fire had started from one of the miner's candles. A scuffle had taken place to put out the fire. One of the men who'd been supporting the roof momentarily panicked and left his post to put out the fire. According to one of the survivors, this action caused the roof to cave in, trapping Henry, Jack and another worker beneath an avalanche of rubble. They initially thought the rubble had crushed them, but one of the men heard someone calling out. The men scrambled to get help. When the bodies were removed from the pit, the coroner returned a verdict of carbon monoxide poisoning and suffocation.

Thomas Jackson and his two sons were buried in the graveyard behind the church where Lizzie had seen William Casey. She cared not whether he saw her. She was inconsolable and she'd no intention of hiding the pain drawn across her face. Her agony during the service was heartbreaking for everyone present, including the minister, who'd rarely seen grief of this magnitude. Lizzie was utterly unable to contain her intense sorrow. There wasn't a dry eye as the bodies of three members of her family were lowered into the grave, sharing their destiny forever.

* * * * * *

CHAPTER FIFTY-TWO

The air-raid sirens sounded, loud and foreboding. Lizzie, Lottie and their children scuttled into the bunker John had prepared for them as the war continued to rape the towns and cities of the United Kingdom. They had provisions down there, enough to last for the duration of a raid. Lizzie wouldn't take any food. Her body was frail and lifeless, her face pale and wasted. She'd no appetite and wouldn't listen to the cries of her family begging her to pull herself together.

Mrs Livesley visited to convey her condolences. A major decision must now be made. She'd deliberated over it since she heard the news. Her own sister had passed away and there was no need for Mrs Livesley to continue living in Scotland. Her sister's estate had been divided up between her family. Mrs Livesley had received a portion of the estate but she needed the money from the sale of the farm to survive herself, yet how could she deliver this news to this beautiful lady who was torturing herself from the deaths of three loved ones. She didn't want to intrude into family affairs, nor did she wish to burden herself on these people who were suffering. She made the decision to do nothing. She had enough money to get by for a while. She would hold out as long as she could but ultimately she would have to deliver the news to Lizzie, the farm would have to be sold.

* * * * * *

The war became intolerable for millions of people all over the world. Tragedies and suffering on an

320

unimaginable scale worldwide was passed by word of mouth and lingered on everyone's lips. Lizzie's own depressed state wasn't helping other members of the household. In 1916, Mary Alice announced she was getting engaged. Dolly and Rosa had already moved out, one to join the women's royal navy and the other into service in a large manor house in the south west of England. Lottie's daughter Molly Ann had joined the forces and rarely came home.

Mary Alice's random announcement caused Lizzie to rally in shock. She hadn't noticed Mary Alice's movements during the last few months. Ashamed of her behaviour, she took Mary Alice aside one evening after supper and begged her forgiveness. Mary Alice opened her arms to her mother for the first time in months and the two women sobbed together, pouring out their hearts about the events, feelings and emotions of the last few years. This was the jolt Lizzie needed to put her life back on track. In those few moments with her daughter, it came home to her. She had suffered the tragic losses, but so had her children. She had shut them out, something she would never forgive herself for. She vowed to spend the rest of her life making that up to them and began immediately by asking Mary Alice to bring her fiancé-to-be to the farm. Mary Alice wept tears of joy and left immediately to go and tell Archie all would be well and invite him to the farm.

Lizzie brought the tin bath in that night. She filled it with water as hot as she could stand and there in front of the blazing fire, she washed away the sorrow. She washed her hair until it gleamed, she cried into the water for the souls of all her lost loved ones, she laughed at the joy of rejoining her family and she positively and decisively began planning her future.

Following her soul and body cleansing, she called the family together round the kitchen table. She hugged each one of them. They laughed until they too cried for joy. There was no need for words. Her general demeanour informed everyone Lizzie Bradshaw was back.

* * * * * *

CHAPTER FIFTY-THREE

With unprecedented surety Lizzie took hold of her life. She wrote a letter to Mrs Livesley informing her she could no longer remain at the farm. Of a perceptive nature, Lizzie knew Mrs Livesley had refrained from selling, to avoid further hardship to Lizzie and her family and she thanked her for that.

Lottie's house lay empty. The two women had made the conscious decision to leave the farm with the remaining youngsters. They would return to Lottie's house in Etching and share the childcare, whilst enlisting in one of the factories supporting the war effort. Together with the sale of Lizzie's furniture and some artefacts which belonged to Thomas, they'd amassed a small amount of money. With Lottie's war pension, they thought they'd be able to manage.

Within a few days, Mrs Livesley had replied. This time, with Lottie's help, Lizzie spruced up the farmhouse till it gleamed. Mrs Livesley was pleased as punch to inform them she'd sold the farm to a wealthy landowner, who due to family circumstances prevailing due to the war, wanted to purchase up north. If it all went through, he'd be taking over the farm within the next few weeks. She was delighted to hear Lizzie had somewhere to go. John was staying on to help for a few months. His new employer would decide whether to keep him or not. Lizzie doubted there would be any question of that. In her opinion, John was worth his weight in gold.

James followed in his father's footsteps and was working full time down the pit, one of the vacancies provided by the deaths of Henry and Jack. Lizzie had been worried sick when James had applied, but at least it would provide him with some income and, Lizzie reasoned, a young man needed independence. Shelving her fears, apprehensions and sorrow, Lizzie held her head high as she marched down the hill into Etching in the early autumn of 1916.

'Do I care if William Casey sees me? No I do not.'

As dignified as any lady could be, she was totally in control of her destiny, knew what she was going to do, how she was going to do it and cared not what other people saw, felt or thought.

The new owner of Homestead Farm offered to purchase some of Lizzie and Thomas's furniture. A couple of locals bought the rest and some she gave to people who'd shown her kindness during her tough times down in Etching. A few of her favourite things they were taking with them.

'I won't be destitute again and I won't be going into that loathed place, no matter how I have to prevent it. I'll sell my soul to the devil first. I'll never enter those portals again.'

Mrs Livesley provided her with another surprise, this time in the form of money. The older lady had seen fit to have her property valued before Lizzie and Thomas moved in, mainly in order to assess what rent to charge. She'd arranged to have it valued again before she sold it to the farmer. The increase had been astounding and she knew it was in no small measure to the way Lizzie and Thomas had worked on it.

'I want to give you some money Lizzie. A small sum from the equity you all helped to procure.'

The envelope she handed to Lizzie contained twenty pounds and a small note of thanks. She asked Lizzie not to open it till later. Lizzie simply sat and stared at the contents when Mrs Livesley had gone. She was alone when she opened the envelope. No-one else knew about it and Lizzie decided to keep it that way, secreting the envelope and its contents into a small pouch which she hid in one of Thomas's old socks, stuffed right down to the bottom of her cloth bag.

'For my family when I've gone,' she thought.

From now on, she would earn her own keep and pay her way, depending on no-one for help. Lizzie and Lottie agreed they would halve their living costs. This would be achievable by working and that was Lizzie's next step. She had to find a job.

She decided against going back into service because of the implications for the children. She and Lottie had decided factory work would be the best avenue to pursue. She'd heard a number of the local factories had changed their production in favour of the war effort, one of them an old glass factory.

'I'll try them first,' she thought.

Lizzie was welcomed onto the work force with an immediate start. Following a hectic couple of days organising the sleeping accommodation in Lottie's small house, Lizzie began work for Archibald's Glass Works. It was heavy work and hard labour. She completed three eight-hour shifts each week and was amazed at the number of items required for the war effort. She found the work interesting, highly motivational and felt proud to be supporting the British Armed Forces with every second of her working day.

Lottie too, was successful in her quest for work. They worked split shifts at the same factory. Between them, they managed to secure a decent enough income to keep their heads above water. Lizzie continued to take in laundry on her off-duty days and James was helping out with income from the pit.

Lizzie continued to astound everyone with her zest for life and good humour and they soon discovered, despite everything, she was a force to be reckoned with. The family thrived, helping other families out where they could. The women in the street looked to Lizzie and Lottie to help out with childcare from time to time. So used were they to having a house full of children, it made no matter whether there were five children in the house or fifteen. There was always enough time to spend with them and enough food for them all to eat.

During the summer of 1918, preparations were steaming ahead for the wedding of Mary Alice to Archie. James announced he was applying for a job in service in the seaside resort of Blackpool. Lizzie sat down with him to question his reasoning. She wished she hadn't. She wished she'd guessed for herself the reasons why he no longer wanted to go down the pit. Proud of his resolve, she helped him to write out the letter of application which he sent to one of the large houses along the promenade requiring domestic servants. He hoped to attain a better life by working above ground with people, than ever he would down the deep dark pit where his stepbrothers perished. Lizzie heaved a sigh of relief, her son would not die in the mine.

James received his letter one week later, gave two day's notice at the pit, packed his bags and left for his new home, promising to write to Lizzie at least once a month to keep her informed of progress. Giving him a hug and pressing a few shillings into his hands, Lizzie felt the old nausea sweep over her, as she said goodbye to the first of her own children to leave home. Mary Alice would be next. The wedding was in two months and James had promised to be back.

It was a small ceremony in the local registry office, followed by a buffet in Lottie's front parlour. Lizzie excelled, providing her eldest daughter with what she termed 'a good send-off'. The couple were going to honeymoon in a small bed and breakfast in South Wales, a wedding present from Archie's family. It was a beautiful day, enjoyed by all. Mary Alice looked as stunning as any bride, in a white gown and veil, although Lizzie suspected perhaps she wasn't as innocent as the white gown suggested. She smiled, thinking of her own early days. The memory promoted yearnings she'd long forgotten, though she doubted those yearnings would ever be fulfilled again. She'd no husband, no man and little inclination beyond gentle flirtation. 'Those days are over,' she sighed.

Lizzie stood with the others on the front pavement waving Mary Alice and Archie off in their carriage, tin cans clanking along the road while the horse picked up a canter to take them back to Archie's house. Lizzie turned and went inside. One of Archie's relatives was playing the old piano in Lottie's front room. An excellent musician, it wasn't long before everyone was singing along. Lizzie took a flagon of beer and joined in. The party went on until midnight, when Lizzie flopped down onto her bed, exhausted but somehow liberated.

'Yes, I'm going to enjoy what I have left of my life,' she thought, the effects of the beer forcing her eyes to close.

CHAPTER FIFTY-FOUR

Summer quickly turned to autumn. The leaves fell rapidly from their splendour atop the trees, yellow, gold, bronze and red, floating to the ground, defeated at last, lying there to be scrunched underfoot and mulched into the pavement sidings when the rains destroyed their last vestige of colour.

Lizzie noticed Lottie's sudden reluctance to rise early, her lack of enthusiasm for doing anything with the children and her lethargic movement. She urged her to seek a doctor's advice. With strong resistance, Lottie conceded, following which she was bedridden for two months. She'd picked up a virus and the doctor prescribed complete bed rest. Molly Ann had been granted leave and came to stay for a week, despite her mother's request not to. Lottie began to improve towards the end of the year and was up and about again in time for the Christmas festivities.

Lizzie wasn't convinced Lottie was as well as she insisted. There was something wrong, something which worried her. After Christmas, she begged Lottie to go back to the doctor.

"Just to make sure," she told her. The doctor told Lottie his suspicions.

"Could be a month or could be five years," he'd said.

That night, Lizzie and Lottie sat either side of the fire in Lottie's small kitchen and reflected on their lives. The good times, the bad and the downright miserable.

"I think, overall, I've had a pretty good life, all things considered," said Lottie sensing Lizzie's sadness. "I have Molly Ann and Peter. Meeting you and Edward make me one of the luckiest people. I have all the memories of our times together."

Lizzie had a lump in her throat and couldn't get the words out. Lottie continued. "I know you're upset Lizzie, but you shouldn't be. We've had a friendship most people long for. Look at everything we've come through together. And I've got to die of something."

Lizzie heartened to hear Lottie's blasé attitude towards the disease ripping through her body.

Swallowing down the lump, she crossed the floor to Lottie's chair and gave her a hug.

"I'll always be here for you Lottie, just as you have for me."

Two months later, Lottie caught the flu, a normally expected curse during the winter months. Only this time it was the pandemic flu sweeping across the world killing millions. Lottie was dying. Lizzie took precautions and procured some masks from work, openly telling Lottie she and the children would wear them to avoid the contagion. Lottie understood. The infirmary at the workhouse wasn't taking patients with flu, in order to preserve the lives already there and to avoid many more perishing. As Lottie's illness progressed, Lizzie sent the children to a house further along the street which hadn't yet been infected. Lizzie made a mental note Molly Ann and Peter would have to be informed, both of them now serving in the forces out of the country.

Lizzie knocked on the house next door and asked for someone to send for a doctor, who was so heavily involved with other cases in the street, he didn't arrive in time to help Lottie. Lizzie suspected even if he had, there would have been nothing he could do to save her. In the early hours of a cold damp February morning in 1920, Lizzie lost her nearest and dearest friend, agonising, powerless to help her, just to be at her side, holding her hand and watching her die.

Sure in the knowledge the children were safe, Lizzie lay on the sofa, exhausted, and sobbed herself to sleep, her grief once again tearing her apart.

'One by one, they're all leaving me,' she said over and over in her mind, before finally drifting into a fitful sleep to awake in a few hours to find herself completely alone, without the friend who'd brought her through so much.

Her troubled sleep was short, disturbed by a knock on the door. Half asleep, half awake, she staggered to the door and opened it. The gust of cold air which attacked her was nothing compared to the shock of seeing William Casey in a drunken stupor. She let out a terrified scream and with all the strength she could muster, she slammed the door shut, trapping two of his fingers between the door and the jamb, severing them. Listening to his agonised screams from the other side of the door, she held her skirt up and leapt the stairs three at a time. She opened the window in her bedroom and climbed out onto the roof of Lottie's outhouse, shimmied down the drain pipe on the other side of the wall and hammered on the back door of the house next door, yelling at the top of her voice for someone to open the door quickly. Her neighbour opened the top window and peered out.

Breathlessly, Lizzie screamed out the words, "Let me in. He's trying to kill me. Let me in quickly. Please."

The neighbour, understanding the urgency, flew down the stairs, opened the door and a bedraggled, sobbing Lizzie fell inside.

'I've chopped his fingers off,' she yelped, hardly able to get her words out. They could hear William's screams as he tried to break the door down with his other arm.

The neighbour screamed for her husband's help.

"We need the police. Get out of bed and go for the police. Hurry. Now."

Her husband shot out of bed. Still in his pyjamas and using the back alleys, he ran to the police station bringing back with him a burly policeman, who gave chase to William, still screaming, blood pouring from his hand and tackled William to the ground. His uniform covered in blood, the policeman recognised the man who'd given him a run for his money a number of times. Clinking the handcuffs on, he wrapped the bloody hand in his handkerchief and dragged the screaming William all the way back to the police station. William almost passed out on him twice, but the officer pushed him forward. A police wagon rushed him to the workhouse infirmary to have his hand attended to before he was locked up. The sergeant doubted William would see the light of day for many years.

Lizzie was comforted by the neighbour while her husband climbed in through the bedroom window next door, retrieved the fingers, wrapping them in an old tea-towel, opened the door and cleaned up the mess before Lizzie was allowed to go home. Her nerves completely jagged, and hardly bearing to enter the house again, her neighbour went with her, made her a cup of tea and tucked her up in bed. A few of the neighbours who'd heard the commotion knocked on Lizzie's door but Lizzie was fast asleep. Her neighbour asked the lady who was looking after the girls if she could keep them a day or two longer and told her what had happened, about Lottie and about William Casey.

Lizzie slept for twelve hours but when she awoke, she was coughing and sneezing, barely able to get to the privy. Her neighbour had the good sense to check on her and sent for the doctor.

"You're strong Lizzie, you have the flu, but I think you'll make it. Rest up, stay in bed, take plenty of fluids and you'll be alright. I'll come back and see you tomorrow."

* * * * * *

CHAPTER FIFTY-FIVE

Lizzie did survive the flu which killed millions, but it left her weak. The trauma of the events that night took their toll and some said it was the beginning of the end for Lizzie Bradshaw. In the summer of 1921 Molly Ann came home after being demobbed and Lizzie went to live with Mary Alice and Archie who had their own small terraced house near the sea front in Blackpool. James came to see her every day.

Lizzie never fully recovered from the events of that night, her strength and resolve crumbling. Looking back on her life, trying to piece together the years, she was saddened by the memory of those who had left her. She had remained positive throughout her trials and although she never recovered fully from any of them, the final test came when she lost her last and dearest friend.

Lizzie lived with Mary Alice and Archie for four years. She was a good house guest and took her share of the household chores. She tried not to be an encumbrance and enjoyed spending time with her grandchildren. But for Lizzie Bradshaw, the joy of life was over. No longer did she want to sit in front of a roaring fire, proud of her day's achievements, proud to have been the mother of all her children, to have cared for them the best way she knew how, proud to have given the men in her life the best of herself, and played the cards life had dealt with acceptance and dignity. All Lizzie wanted now was to leave her beautiful family in peace and reacquaint herself with those whom she'd loved and lost.

The Lord left her wanting until the autumn of 1925, when Lizzie was granted her wish. She left behind a grief-stricken family but Lizzie's heart and soul lived on in each of them. From beyond the grave, she supported them all. Her legacy to her children, her grandchildren and all those who would follow was strength of spirit, helping them to overcome their own painful experiences, willing them on to great things and never, ever forgetting Lizzie Bradshaw.

The End

Coming Soon:

DRAGONFLY ODYSSEY

Sequel to SPANGLES

by Samantha McKeating